SLOW VISION

BOOKS BY MAXWELL BODENHEIM

Minna and Myself, poetry (1918)

Advice: a book of poems, poetry (1920)

Introducing Irony, poetry (1922)

Against This Age, poetry (1923)

Blackguard, novel (1923)

The Sardonic Arm, poetry (1923)

Crazy Man, novel (1924)

Cutie: A Warm Mamma, short story (with Ben Hecht, 1924)

Replenishing Jessica, novel (1925)

Ninth Avenue, novel (1926)

Returning to Emotion, poetry (1927)

Georgie May, novel (1928)

The King of Spain, poetry (1928)

Sixty Seconds, novel, (1929)

Bringing Jazz!, poetry (1930)

Naked on Roller Skates, novel (1930)

A Virtuous Girl, novel (1930)

Duke Herring, novel (1931)

Run, Sheep, Run, novel (1932)

Six A.M., novel (1932)

New York Madness, novel (1933)

Slow Vision, novel (1933)

Lights in the Valley, poetry (1942)

Selected Poems, poetry (1946)

SLOW VISION

Maxwell Bodenheim

Introduction by Paul Maher, Jr.

Tough Poets Press
Arlington, Massachusetts

Introduction

BODENHEIM THE RADICAL

In 1933, the brutal sway that the Great Depression held over the United States was insufferable. The country had lost half of its entire gross national product. There were 13,000,000 souls unemployed, and the stock market was one-tenth of its peak from 1929. Book firms failed left and right, including poet and novelist Maxwell Bodenheim's former publishing house, Liveright Inc., which eventually succumbed to bankruptcy. In September 1933, Bodenheim's greatest advocate, Horace Liveright, who was broke and sick of pneumonia in his New York City apartment, would die at 49 years of age.

Liveright, one of America's most important publishing house founders and editors had made possible the publication of fourteen of Bodenheim's books. Under Liveright, the publishing firms of Simon & Schuster and Random House were founded in New York City and together they made a singular impact on 20th-century American literature.

Like Bodenheim, Liveright was a foolhardy man who gambled excessively against the business proceeds of his firms and generous to a fault. He advanced to his authors far more money than he could ever make, even during the best of years. He was a hopeless alcoholic. This generosity and foolish squandering of his money and of his health eventually cost him his life.

During the spring of that year, Bodenheim's wife, Minna, and their son, Solbert, were packed off to Provincetown, Massachusetts, to await another windfall by way of one of Liveright's advances and promised by Bodenheim. Bodenheim, then staying at Woodstock,

New York at a writer's retreat, wrote her: "I am writing nothing but excellent proletarian poetry and postponing the resumption of my next novel." Bodenheim was in the process of moving the scope of his poetry from Imagism to address proletariat matters. He chose not to lean to the right as a conservative or to even adopt a militant tone, but instead by maintaining his defense of the embattled victims of society, that of the indigent and marginalized. In one poem, "To a Revolutionary Girl," he addresses one woman's loss of the call of motherhood for the cold, arduous chore of revolution:

> "You are a girl,
> A revolutionist, a worker
> Sworn to give the last, undaunted jerk
> Of your body and every atom
> Of your mind and heart
> To every other worker
> In the slow, hard fight
> That leads to barricade, to victory
> Against the ruling swine.
> Yet, the softer regions of your heart,
> The shut-off, personal, illogical
> Disturbance of your mind,
> You long for crumpled 'kerchiefs, notes
> Of nonsense understood
> Only by a lover."

Bodenheim, with his new girlfriend, Lillian (an acquaintance of Minna) continued their involvement with communist activity in Woodstock, both feverishly engaged in the demands of the movement. Bodenheim's intentions were pure. He intended to aid those who were affected by the insurgence of Nazism in Germany. Earlier that year, a news item appeared in the *Brooklyn Eagle* on January 23, 1933:

"Maxwell Bodenheim will act as master of ceremonies, and Hall Johnson will be among those present at the benefit show to aid Nazi victims being held at the Village Grove Nut Club this night."

For the time being, Woodstock served as a bucolic retreat from the realities of the Great Depression. When Bodenheim returned to New York City in the fall of 1933, he saw that the Depression was eating away at the city. Soup kitchens and bread lines sprung up on every block serving over 100,000 people a day. For most, it was their only meal of the day. Entire families slept in the streets in cardboard boxes and contrived lean-tos. Collectives of wooden shanty towns, dubbed "Hooverville" by the media, became a necessary tolerance. People wrapped themselves in newspapers called "Hoover blankets." Every animal that crossed a hungry man's path became an instant meal: rabbits, rats, gophers, and sometimes dogs (called "Hoover hogs"). The situation became so deplorable, that policemen even assisted in this new brand of citizen survival. To this necessary extremity of street survival, many patriotic citizens sided with labor organizations, socialists and communists to march and protest against a government that had collapsed and left their working citizenry to languish in the gutter. Part of this desolation was that of the country's artists, musicians, writers and intelligentsia stranded by the loss of cultural interests in lieu of economic survival. Just writers alone accounted for over 2,000 unemployed in New York City.

Bodenheim's friends, author and editor Samuel Putnam and novelist Edward Dahlberg, invited Bodenheim to join an organization to plead with the federal government for aid in instituting writers' projects. They called themselves the "Unemployed Writers' Association," and were backed by the Poetry Society of America. Along with Putnam and Dahlberg, the committee also included writers and editors, Theodore Dreiser, Sherwood Anderson, Floyd Dell, Ida Tarbell and now Maxwell Bodenheim.

It wasn't his only outfit. Bodenheim, in a desperate attempt to remain solvent, had joined the John Reed Club in support of Marxist-Communist leanings for labor. These were formed by staff members and contributors of *New Masses* magazine earlier in October 1929. All of these efforts became the foundation of what would eventually become the "Federal Writers Project," implemented by President Franklin D. Roosevelt in 1935.

Bodenheim began attending Communist Party meetings in the fall and winter of 1933 in Greenwich Village. Meetings were conducted every Tuesday at locations scattered around lower Manhattan. Later, the Works Projects Agency (W.P.A.) and the Federal Bureau of Investigation would amass conflicting reports of Bodenheim's involvement in communism. Bodenheim told the W.P.A. investigators that he formally joined the Communist Party in March 1934 and that he also joined Communist units in Chicago and Los Angeles, as well as New York. He maintained a Communist Party dues card for five years until January of 1940. Far earlier than that, 22 years prior, Bodenheim made the rolls of subversive activity in November of 1918, when he was listed with anarchic political activist and writer Emma Goldman at a war protest in Boston. The FBI note reads:

> "Maxwell Bodenheim — Alleged Anarchist, War
> Matter, Boston, 1918 Nov."

SLOW VISION

With Bodenheim's previous novel (*New York Madness*, 1933) behind him, he began a new one in the autumn of 1933. This time he chose to depict a young couple, a pair of average Americans swept up in labor struggles and reduced to painful subsistence. The story serves as a continuation of *New York Madness* by lieu of the protagonists' gradual understanding of labor unions and those psychological/philosophical/political trials that led toward sympathetic affiliations in Socialism and Communism. Thus initiates their "slow vision," a simmering understanding of the manifestations of Leftist movements and of especial relevance to the climate of the first two decades of the 21st century.

Bodenheim utilizes his own personal background to form the characterization of Raymond Bailey, who comes from lower-middle class Chicago before completing a year at the University of Chicago, and then moving to New York City. Bailey is conservative in his beliefs. He is patriotic and never questions his allegiance toward the United States. He is optimistic of the country's ability to right itself back to recovery. As the grip of the Depression continues to tighten, Bailey scours the city for work to no avail. One day a black man sits next to him in a park. He is reading a communist newspaper as he rails against the country:

> "The whole, damn system heah is wrong, get me, *wrong*." said the black man. "Theah'll nevah be no change to amount to anythin' unless you teah the whole thing to pieces—bust it wide open, see? Othawise, you ain' got a chance, man. Not a chance. . . . Don' tell me—ah *knows*."

Bailey concurs, but also shares that he devoutly believes in his country. He believes in democracy: "If we get more sense in our heads and elect better men to office . . . start a drive against those bastardly gangsters, and back up the Unions more . . . but no dirty Bolshevism for us! If the Russians want it, O.K., but its got no place over here. Get that and get it straight."

The man with the newspaper responds: "Ef we Reds is dirty, then there's no name fitten to describe some uh them bastards down in Wall Street—that's all ah's got to say."

Bailey's girlfriend, Allene Baum, the daughter of his landlady, does not agree with Bailey's opinions of America. When they are caught one day in Ray's room, he is ordered to leave. Allene, who is very fond of Ray and too proud to let him go, decides to leave her mother's house and go with him. Though Ray is miserable because he is jobless and resents his poverty, he finally lands a job as a busboy in a cafeteria. He is over-worked, under-paid and abused by his employer. Through the constant talk of unions, Bailey realizes that a union could prevent this brand of employer exploitation. After a fellow worker argues with Ray that labor unions were now the enemy, he comes to believe that the only way to remedy this kind of corruption was through a Communist-based union (Food Workers Industrial Union).

This solution still rang as too radical for Bailey. He begins to sense that outside influences also have a hand in controlling business. Everywhere strikes and social unrest were the dominating tone of everyday America. Workers could not earn enough money to subsist. Ray and Allene, now part of the proletariat and among millions of struggling, working class people, are unable to make ends meet. Ray still maintains hope that President Roosevelt can revive the country, but he detects other forces still at work. There was a polarity where those at the top and the underclass were constantly fighting for control. Subsequently, the working class became caught in the crossfire. Wall Street was holding on to the money by not issuing loans. Businesses could not work efficiently because they were undercapitalized, and living wages could not be paid because gangsters were extorting money from the bottom.

Bailey, reduced to borrowing change from fellow workers just to eat, is the very picture of penury (much like Bodenheim at this time). His clothes are in tatters. His measly paycheck is squandered on trying to pay rent which seems to be constantly in arrears. By the time he can chip away at his debts, he is broke again. Bailey is caught in a vicious whirlpool of destitution and now was in fear of drowning.

Allene's defection from an unreasonable office job causes her to accept another secretary position for a magazine company in Boston. This job, though, turns out to be a scam. She is only offered door-to-door sales. Ray is lucky enough to find a job as an elevator operator at a Boston hotel where he is again treated poorly. His pay remains inadequate. Talk of labor unions prevail:

> "A gang of stinking Reds were lurking around the hotel, trying to poison the men and lure them into joining up . . . and that every effort must be made to warn the employees against them. . . . They're paid by another country to stir up trouble over here, the whole, crappy outfit of them. . . . They tell you that decent, respectable men are no good, just because these men don't want you to smash up the windows and ask for forty a week, right off the bat. We'll have a union here sooner or later, sure, but it's going to be a decent, law-abiding crowd, when we do put it over."

Bodenheim's remarkable foresight for the year of 1934 rings an alarm for the advent of "un-American activities." As with all of his novels, economics, society, and personal pressures always undermine and complicate relationships. *Slow Vision* methodically illustrates the difficulties of maintaining a relationship during arduous financial times. Under such strained conditions, the pair continues to love each other despite all that continues to work against them, particularly in a climate where many Americans chose to stay with each other under these conditions because of economic fear. Divorce rates were then at a historic low despite domestic life remaining severely strained.

* * * * * * *

On May 1, 1934, Bodenheim signed a contract with Macaulay Company to publish *Slow Vision*. The conditions were the same as

New York Madness. He would receive $650.00 upon signing (both Minna and Max were there to sign the contract)

Slow Vision is a lost novel of American proletariat writing. It remains effective in comprehending and even sympathizing with the plight of depressed and desperate workers. It is not a memoir, but an authentic book written in the trenches of the Great Depression in 1934. It successfully examines the presence of the Communist party in everyday labor, and the conflicts and reactions by its workers. *Slow Vision* maintains that to join the Communist Party, or Communist-affiliated unions, was not against the law. Nor was it un-American. It was not radical or subversive. It endured as part of the system. Workers fully understood that government actions led to the Stock Market crash. Labor leaders and workers were becoming increasingly maligned, ridiculed, and beaten in picket lines by a force that put them there. It was the old "bait and switch" game, to divert guilt by blaming and punishing those who were not at fault.

The Detroit Free Press offered a lukewarm review of *Slow Vision* on September 30, 1934:

> "Maxwell Bodenheim's latest novel, "Slow Vision," can hardly be given literary credit. Although it is competently written and frequently hits its target, there is a kind of adolescence prevalent throughout. Bodenheim has apparently become extremely bitter toward all humanity. His story describes the struggle of the workers, white collar slaves, more particularly. It is neither unbiased nor objectively told. Ray Bailey and Allene Baum are the two central figures in this sordid tale. About them and their almost futile effort to get along, the author has woven an unpleasant tale of struggle and defeat. Workers may be pleased with the general thesis, but the literary contribution is hardly worth while."

The New York Herald-Tribune gave a more positive take:

"While there has always been a burden hidden behind the writing of Maxwell Bodenheim—hidden for those who were either too lazy or too unwilling to see it—he has never touched, in a novel, upon the raw sores of humanity as powerfully as he has done in this volume. He is noted for being a good story-teller, and he loses nothing of his ability in *Slow Vision*."

After *Slow Vision*'s publication, Bodenheim was considering a trip to California in a desperate effort to sell one or two of his books to motion picture studios. He was also hoping to obtain help from his old friend, screenwriter Ben Hecht. Bodenheim wrote fellow Marxist and book critic, Louis Untermeyer, asking for money:

"I have written eight books of verse, many of which you have praised, so perhaps that will induce you to pardon the audacity of this letter. After many years of making a fair living with my novels—eleven of which have been published—I find myself destitute and on the rocks. Now after a nightmarish summer, in which I was compelled to work as a dishwasher, waiter, etc., I find myself at the end of my rope. I'm trying to raise the fare and expenses, to go to Hollywood, Cal. They have flirted with my works of fiction before, but some hitch always seemed to spoil negations. This is my only chance to escape, as I am forty-five now and have been supporting for years a wife, with whom I do not reside, and a child, now twelve. If you can possibly give me any sum of money that will help me, I'll appreciate it, and if not, I'll understand."

Untermeyer responded immediately with a check. Bodenheim wrote back that he was deeply grateful, and that his "friendly note cheered more than any stereotype phrases of thanks I would be able to convey to you." During the spring of 1934, Bodenheim lectured at the John Reed Club and tried, in vain, to recover funds lost by his ill-fated trip. The studios showed no interest toward his books, and so, by late June, he was out of money and out of work. He returned to the east coast a destitute and desperate man. There were reports that he was hitchhiking around California, penniless and despondent.

He returned to New York.

Though he continued to write verse through the remainder of the decade, Bodenheim had methodically burned all of his bridges. In January 1935, he attacked media mogul William Randolph Hearst for the *Daily Worker*. He writes:

> "And what is the answer of Hearst? Distortions, venom, the shriek of generalists, and foul vaporings, aimless inciting to hatred, to cover up the miserable lack of anything remotely resembling a constructive program to free the American workers, the plundered American middle-class, from the suavely veiled viciousness of Wall Street and its cold-blooded attacks on life, liberty and the pursuit of happiness.

> "This man, William Randolph Hearst, sitting in the hacienda of his vast ranch in California, sleekly entrenched, remote from the tortured needs of millions in factories, mines, mills, farms and offices, pretends to be a staunch defender of American men and women—the very man who opposed the right of his own reporters to join a union advancing their interests, the man who spits sex-scandals and triv-

ial divorce-cases into printed headlines throughout the land, the man who blazons the news of prize-fights and society-revels on his front pages and tucks the distorted report of a workers' strike on page twenty-seven, bottom corner."

This levied attack caused Bodenheim to be blacklisted in all of the newspapers controlled by Hearst which shut down much of the meager income he relied upon, mainly reprints of his verse and the occasional commissioned article. Bodenheim was railed by tabloids (as he always was) and the promotion and critical assessment of *Slow Vision* was killed off, to which the novel did not survive its first and only print run.

By late winter 1935, Bodenheim was a sight to behold. When he walked into the Home Relief Agency, he was hatless, his hair was mussed, his face darkened by stubble and his clothing wrinkled and soiled. He filed a claim that six weeks before, he applied for bread money and was assured that his case would be investigated. The decision was made in fifteen minutes. A receptionist informed him that there was "no card for Mr. Bodenheim."

"All I want," Bodenheim said, "is enough for three meals a day and a cheap room. I ask no wine." Desperately, he led a band of writers back into the relief headquarters, where he was then promised $15 a month for rent and $3.19 a week for food."

He was given a check for $2.50.

Bodenheim's troubles continued to compound. There were no royalties for *Slow Vision*. It sank without a trace. He was an alcoholic and his lifelong bout with tuberculosis had reared its head once again. Hew returned to Woodstock to cure himself of drink and sickness. Accompanied by a beautiful Village model who posed for painters, Ena Douglas, he was drunk once again when he stepped into a kettle of boiling water. In a desperate plea for money, he sold off all of his signed copies of his books to auction (and bought by Hecht's wife) at the Vagabon Club in New York City.

By August 1935, he was lying on a cot in Bellevue Hospital. At his feet was a sheet of paper on which was written the word: "Alcoholism." He wrote his estranged wife:

"My head still pains me. I slipped ascending a street stairway and struck myself unconscious. I'm trying to get back on Home Relief. My novel is temporarily halted, since I'm still without an abode. It's slightly, though pleasantly difficult, trying to keep alive, finish a novel, seek some sort of bed for the night, without resources. My many friends are poor people, too, tho' not at my extreme. It's a bit tantalizing, with the novel almost done, in pencil, and the completion and typing of it, so near and yet remote. There is a tendency on the part of a few people to become unconsciously smug. One can slip occasionally on a tight-rope. I once heard a tiger insist that workers should not be immoral—the triviality either way. When the revolution arrives, there will still be a thousand minor brands of narrow-mindedness to be overcome. Those in the same common grip of exploitation and misery should not search one another with a fine comb, peering for flaws. I am always a hopeful person."

Bodenheim begged solicitude, of which little was forthcoming from Minna or anybody. By January 1940, Bodenheim resigned from the Communist Party. He would spend the remainder of the decade unable to escape its clutches, and the stigma thereof made him a marked man for the rest of his life. He continued an ever-spiraling downward decline of health and welfare. By February 1954, reduced to taking up quarters with a deranged dishwasher, Bodenheim and his third wife, Ruth Fagan, were brutally murdered in a Bowery flophouse. News of the doomed poet's death sparked a signal of the death, not only of the poet, but that of Greenwich Village. He was seen as a mere relic of the Jazz Age, the "Last Bohemian" and once he was forgotten, so was his work.

Most of his books, thirteen novels and nine volumes of verse, were out of print. Some were resurrected as cheap pulp paperbacks after Bodenheim had lost rights to his own work. *Slow Vision* was not one of them. Presumably, nobody wanted to be reminded of the Great Depression. *Slow Vision* would be Bodenheim's last published novel and to that, literary history has forgotten it. The book is a hard find, even for the most dedicated of Bodenheim collectors, of which there are few. Copies without a dust jacket seldom surface in the marketplace, and those with the original artwork, are downright impossible to find. This courageous new edition of *Slow Vision* from Tough Poets Press hopefully signals a rebirth of all of the abandoned works of this sadly-neglected and much-maligned writer. He dedicated his life solely to his craft and perhaps deserves nothing less than our reevaluation.

Paul Maher, Jr.

Part One

❖

THE AUGUST day in Union Square was hot—the sticky, rising hotness so much like wave on wave of barely moving grief, no longer caring. The large-windowed buildings in almost colorless grey or blackish brownstone—or sallowly coated brick—stood in precise huddles straight-lined down the side streets. They were slavepens moderate in height and almost undurating except for small, pyramidal sky-lights and round water-tanks above levelly uneven roofs, or columns and traceries flanking the entrance-exits. The structures held tiers of garment shops: wholesalers and jobbers in dress-goods, notions, and leather-ware: and offices where leeches in agencies, loan-firms, mortgage-companies, law offices, real-estate concerns, speculative banks, and other forms of indirect connivance and politely veiled extortion drew blood from the body of the public. In a medley of signs and lying superlatives, the buildings sheltered the acme of abject prose, joined only by close walls and the common desire to wring by exploitation and secretly unscrupulous competition an increasing profit from human flesh.

Many of the windows displayed the dark blue eagles upon National Recovery Act placards and banners over the words: "We do our part."—A Washington Administration, fearing the riots which result from a lasting depression, and anxious to avoid strikes with forced arbitrations, had brewed a patent-medicine concession in the form of "shorter hours and raised wages." The near-sighted masters of Union Square, among others, were pretending to swallow this medicine but nullifying its "after-effects" with a host of ingenious tricks, such as doubling the prices of their commodities, or discharging and re-hiring their workers at minimum wages, or appointing clerks to fictitious, executive positions. These masters were eager to dim the presence of unemployed millions, some of whom held embattled mass-meetings only a few feet away from the police-girded business-interests of the Square.

Street-cars, trucks, and pleasure-machines congested the sides of the Square—and emitted an arrogant shrieking and rumbling. Contrasted with the hopelessness and exhaustion of the poor was the cruel interest, or equally cruel indifference of well-dressed men and women sitting in sensual indolence against the upholsteries, or behind the wheels, of shiny automobiles and staring out with indulgent, cruel, or sightless eyes. The shred of a breeze, a roving fugitive, found nothing to ruffle except the sparse leaves on the puny saplings stuck on the elevated, stone rimmed park-enclosure. The name of a retail concern was flung over the Square—a place where gowns and coats were sold at low prices to swarms of women indifferent to the employment conditions under which the fabrics were made or forced to ignore them by the necessity of stretching out their meager dollars. Fronting the Square, on the south, a first-story window-corner revealed three girls circling a carpet for an hour at a time and showing fur coats, jackets, and stoles. The girls had been selected for their tall and trimly rounded proportions, and their well-groomed appearance served to attract many customers to the palatial establishment of their employers. Their faces, adorned with cosmetics, seemed petulant, self-sly, unaware of more than the surfaces of a struggling world around them; and yet their faces were warm, and a little trouble was deep in their heads, their hearts—ignorance, hope, the urge to happiness, taught to be submissive, scheming, and mincing, by a mercenary environment.

The gong of a clock on the top of a nearby tower struck the hour of three. A peevish weight, not quite misery, was in the heart of Raymond Bailey. His mind was discomfited, scattered, jarring against invisible blind-alleys and trying to retrace its steps with some pretence of unconcern. The day bothered him and the slow pressure of heat made him feel less hopeful and yet more outwardly cocksure, to counteract the change. His thirty years had muddled him and now, in this soul-splitting period, still vigorously and yet insecurely between the middle and wane of youth, he was coddling his bruises, inflating an idea of past successes, to vindicate and ignore the dying and mistreated desires in his life.

His dark suit was clean, but worn and mended—a winter outfit too heavy on his legs and hips—with the wide trouser-cuffs and snug coat affected by city blades. He had slung the coat over his bench and loosened the collar of his white shirt beneath which a polka-dot tie hung. Approaching tallness, his well-muscled body, slightly bowlegged and uneven in the shoulders, slumped down upon the bench. His bravado, like tin-foil, was now peeling off under the heat. Beneath the chestnut hair, his face was a study in apathy and self-importance—the suggestion of two wrestlers collapsing together and sometimes drowsily stirring in their vain efforts to rise. The long, straight nose, the widely slit mouth, and a dent in the chin, ruled by blue eyes seeing everything and nothing—they expressed an intelligence hampering to itself, capable of sudden insights, but generally unwilling to delve into the actualities of life.

The young Negro in a spotted grey ruin of a suit, sitting on the same bench of cement and wood, looked at Raymond with a discreet touch of friendliness uncertain on his coffee-colored, huge lipped face.

"Wanna read this, comrade?"—he extended a copy of a newspaper known as "The Daily Worker."

Scarcely looking at the other man, Raymond accepted the paper and scanned the front page.

"Oh, the Red sheet, huh? No, I guess not, buddy." He tossed the paper back to the Negro and they examined one another. Ray could be brutal, but only surfacely, to bring back the big-boy dream to his consciousness, so often checkmated and dwarfed by existence in large cities. He was not innately snobbish although he had been willing to ape this trait, on occasion, in the hope of financial gain. He was a salvaged mixture of honesties and dishonesties scarcely pausing to stare one another in the face. Now he regarded the young

Negro with aversion and curiosity, barely lifted above the casual, by his desire to escape from the boredom of this hot afternoon. 'Dirty-looking and homely, but still, what the hell, he was a human being, wasn't he? Yes, but here they sat, two human beings a million miles apart, nothing joining them except the same general physical features, the return to food and sleep and something of the same urge to squeeze a woman's flesh. Why wasn't there one human race. What in the devil had split them up in hundreds of nations, races, languages?—damn interesting when a fellow got to thinking, but if there was any answer, he had never discovered it. The history-books at school told what happened but never why. What was really behind all this splitting and splitting? A man would have to be a magician to find it out. Maybe it was God, if there was a God. He was on the fence about that. When a fellow was afraid, he believed in God, and when he wasn't, he didn't think much about it one way or the other.

'This spotty-looking chocolate drop was one of those Reds, too—wonder what made him hook up with the windy soreheads from Moscow?' . . . . The Negro's eyes were steady but uncertain, unable to decipher whether Ray's stare was friendly, or hostile, and his face showed a gradual resentment dotted with attempted smiles. 'Hard to tell about these white men. When they was not class-conscious they had little use for a colored man except to rob him in some way, or turn their noses up, or go after his women, or softsoap him to get his votes. This boy here looked like he was a worker, too, but he didn't know that his bosses were always getting the workers sore at each other, to stuff the bosses' pockets—pushing the white worker on to hate his Negro brother, and the Catholic worker to hate the Jewish one, and the Wop worker to hate the boys of his own flesh and blood, if they wouldn't stick a black shirt on their backs. Hate, hate—they couldn't keep their system running one day without it, but some day their hate-stuff was going to trip them up, when the workers started hating their bosses and hating those reformer-kids, out to reform everything except the cause of the whole damn game itself—wringing dollars out of the workers' sweat. Take himself now—he still liked to booze around, bring a nice, colored baby up to his room, and he still told lies sometimes because he had got into the habit years ago, and he had a weakness to strut around with a nice suit on, instead of what he was wearing, but something had happened to him just the same—something big. He was wise to himself now. No more hanging out with the shady colored boys, figgering how they could shake down somebody else up on Lenox—preying on their own race, the damn fools. No more letting the gang jolly him along for the next round in a Seventh A. speak'. No more going out on a tear and then busting some other guy in the nose, for no good reason. Fight, if you was being imposed on, sure, but not just because you was all ginned-up. Yow . . . sah, no more of that. . . . Better talk to this white fellow here. If this white man kept on staring like that, he was due to collect a nice clip on the jaw.'

"Say, what's eating you, comrade? What you pasting you eyes on me for . . . huh?"

Ray knew that he had been rude: felt that he was in for a scrap: held a sluggish, unprobing contempt for the Negro because 'the shine was against his own country': disliked the day and the heat: thought that a hit of an argument would relieve the tedium of the day: and wished that he were a thousand miles away from the bench, in the half-unseeing muddle which is emotion in certain people.

"Well, you're looking back at me, aren't you?"

"Yup, 'cause *you* started it."

"Alright, alright, let's forget about it."

"Suits me fine."

In the ensuing pause, their eyes sparred with one another—the Negro more openly—and then Ray spoke again.

"Say, are you one of those Reds, kid?"

"Shuah 'nough. That's what ah am."

"What for?"

"What for? 'Cause ah got wise to what's goin' on. Ah want to see the workers on top, 'stead of down at the bottom."

"Well, join a Union then."

"Yeah, an' get clubbed down ef you strike. The whole bunch of us struck in a big cafeteria uptown—ah was a bus-boy theah—and what did they do, what? They goes an' hires a pack uh lousy scabs an' then they arrests our pickets 'cause the place signed up undah that doggone N.R.A. joke. Don't tell *me*."

"Well, didn't you get better wages and better hours under the N.R.A.?"

"We did like hell. The wages went up three bucks and they lopped off a coupla hours a day, shuah, but what did the boss do? Boy, he did plenty! He docked us ef we come in two minutes late. He sped us up an' *sped* us up, till we nevah had time to catch ouah breath. He smacked us two hits ev'y time we broke a plate. He made us pay for laundryin' up the aprons an' the coats. He . . . boy, boy, what *did'n* he do . . . mm, boy."

The cynicism, the painfully acquired knowledge of practical conditions, in Ray's heart and mind, tried to patch up a truce with his larger allegiances to the institutions and the government of his country. He spoke more sharply now.

"Yeah, I know there's a thousand rackets going on all over New York, sure, but that doesn't mean you've got to be against your own government and your own flag. This country isn't perfect by a damn sight, but you can fight for better working-conditions without hooking up with a few, damn lice paid by Moscow—paid to stir up trouble here!"

Ray had driven himself into an anger which beautifully swept away his sense of obscurity on this hot afternoon, rescued his own irritation at being out of a job, with almost no money, and brought a sweet militancy to every qualm and fear within him. The Negro had a wide smile on his face and he thought that this white man was full of dope, a cock-eyed liar, and the same old hot-air merchant a Red ran into everywhere; but nevertheless, he had a twinge of respect for the sincerity within what he considered to be the dumbness of the other man.

"Fight for nothin'! Lissen, man . . . the whole, damn system heah is wrong, get me, *wrong*. Theah'll nevah be no change to amount to anythin' unless you teah the whole thing to pieces—bust it wide open, see? Othahwise, you ain' got a chance, man. Not a chance. They kids you along on one side and then they robs you an' they manhandles you on the othah. Don' tell me—ah *knows*."

"Alright, sure . . . I know what goes on. . . . I'm no fool . . . but I believe in my country and I believe in democracy just the same. We're improving slowly, all the time, and we'll keep on improving, too, if we get more sense in our heads and elect better men to office, and, uh, start a drive against some of those bastardly gangsters, and back up the Unions more. Things like that, sure, but no dirty Bolshevism for us! If the Russians want it, O.K., but it's got no place over here. Get that and get it straight."

In the Negro's estimation, Ray was "sniffin' the same ol' pinch uh snow" to let him forget that he and others like him were always back-slapped, jollied along, and then squeezed out to swell the pockets of a few men, who deserved to be put against a wall and shot. In Ray's opinion, the Negro was a funny-looking monkey who had fled to Communism and swallowed a few agitators'-slogans because he was gullible and had the usual envy toward men brainy enough to amass large sums of money. They looked one another over on the bench—two humans, leagues separated, hugging different angers: atoms in the complicated tension of a huge city; and unable to wring the slightest benefit from the accident of their meeting. The Negro rose and delivered a last shot.

"Ef we Reds is dirty, then there's no name fitten to describe some uh them bastards down in Wall Street—that's all ah's got to say."

"Go on, you're just green in the face because you haven't got brains enough to pile it up yourself."

They drove a last scowl into each other's faces. The Negro walked away and Ray was left to his sweating, inflated isolation. He rubbed his forehead with a partly soiled handkerchief. Slowly, he receded from the mechanical though sincere indignation of "the larger out-look on life" and became a personal, involved human being, with his feet sore from having walked over three hours in the vain search for a job, and his heart a medley of discontents, vanities, sexual desires, and hopes. His head cleared of the rousing phrases, was now emptier, and humbler. What he had said was darn right, certainly, but what did that make him—a prince? Quince, yeah. Three weeks behind in the rent. . . . Allene's folks ready to toss him out on his ear, if they ever discovered that he was close to her, and her mother dunning him every time he slid back to the rooming-house!

A blank, just resisting the heat and taking in the buildings, the dusty, paper-strewn platters of grass, the disc of crimson rhododendrons at one end of the Square, with eyes tired almost to blindness. He rose, stepped slowly down the broad cement walk. Knots and sprinkles of men stood and argued intensely, and as he lingered for seconds on the fringe of them, he heard snatches of sentences—"I tell you, every American's life is safe in Cuba, if he doesn't butt into the fight between the workers and the Grau San. . . ." "Get out, there were only 600,000 Jews and over 5,000,000 Reds in Germany, and if you can't draw your own con." . . . "Yeah, in addition to Gabriel they ought to bring the whole choir of angels down to the White." . . . "Go on, you're a damn counter-revolutionary, and what's more." . . . Alien phrases, to Ray. He smiled, cynically—'aaa, poor saps, the minute they got a roll in their pockets, or a good chance to get one, they'll forget all about it. The ones who didn't have it were always shooting their mouths off about the ones who did.'

He passed a stone colonnade and portico—a shady retreat with a "Keep-Off" sign hanging from a chain—and departed from the Square. His dollar-watch pointed to six. People were trickling, darting, from the angular, flat-faced bulk of buildings along the narrow lane of Lower Broadway and the walks became packed with the jostle, buzz, and heel-click of men and women pacing, trotting, too straightly, or with too much of a flourish, and lifting their noses too high, in the effort to conceal the exhaustion, the rip of nerves, the secretions of unimportance, which their day of toil had stored within them. The external sameness was everywhere—the oval-box straw hats with bright bands, or the floppy ones indented on the top, and the creased cylinders of trousers, and the women's hats with a brim slanting through the middle, to give a saucy, semi-derby effect above the prinked-up, long, vari-colored dresses, the high heels, the leg-snug, sheer stockings . . . the pathetic dash of a gaudy scarf below a beaten-down, rouge-stiff face . . . plucked, shaved eye-brows over kitten-tame eyes . . . the thickest smear of scarlet on soft lips too tired to close . . . a hook-nosed Jewish girl with fat cheeks, sniffing, bridling, at passing, male stares, to forget that her back and arms were aching from nine hours beside a hemstitching machine . . . a cloak-model with a white fur fluffed around her shoulders—gleaming absurdly in the heat of the evening—and a curious, scheming fortitude on her pretty face as she tripped beside the paunchy, amorous buyer, whom she was accompanying to supper and theater on the orders of her boss . . . a young needle-worker with straight black hair and grimly brown face, hurrying to her tenement house to wash and swallow a bite before attending the Union meeting at which a strike would probably be ratified . . . an old Jew in a dented, black derby, with militant eyes above the greyish-brown bush on his chin and cheeks and a radical button in his lapel . . . a man with a face like a hopeful curse . . . another one on the verge of falling asleep, the eyes remaining open through intense will-power . . . another man with a face jowled, tiny-eyed, unkindled—a foreman saving his money to "get a partnership in the firm" . . . a Negro porter in tan hand-me-downs, with an anger dodging around the whites of his big eyes and barely suppressed, and a newspaper, bearing the toned-down account of the latest Southern lynching, tucked in a coat-pocket . . . a boy in a grey cap, with his shoulders bent from carrying heavy bundles all over town, and a surly, planning alertness eating into the callow eyes and mouth.

Surging, knocking elbows, in this narrow artery, these people were similar in their garments, external traits, and helplessly dispersed in their ideas, their mutual suspicions, and in the prejudices cunningly injected by the masters, who employed these men and women for financial gain and strove in every way to keep them deluded and separated. Many of the faces, forever sliding onward, were plundered, misled, cocained, hardened, but others among them were utterly different—thoughtful and alert, proud but not overbearing, with chins down and shoulders high, below a straightness in their eyes.

To Ray, however, these faces held an opposite aspect. The women had no significance, to him, outside of sex—or a friendship allied to the hope for sex—and he measured their bodies from the corners of his eyes, or threw flirtatious glances into some of their faces. He was in love with Allene Baum, his landlady's daughter, but the love was in a budding stage, plagued by his poverty and the imminent enmity of her parents, and so, shamefacedly, and partly through the lunge of habit, he looked at the passing women with a clash of lust in his eyes and simultaneously in his mind apologized to Allene. The men on the street—striding along with a hard-eyed confidence, to forget the slavery of their recent hours—were subjects of envy, to Ray, if they wore good clothes, or had the arm of a pretty girl, or showed him faces which were handsome, in his grudging estimation. Others among these men aroused his envy when they whizzed away in polished sedans. Beyond these attentions, his attitude toward the men shifted, unconsciously, between comradeship and hostility. Each man was out for his own selfish ends, in Ray's opinion, and was to be watched distrustfully, beyond the tacitly accepted fusion against women and the taken-for-granted obedience to the basic institutions and laws of a country.

Ray strode past the Flatiron Building—the now small, greyish, glass-eyed relic of a more leisurely materialism—and, as he swung down 23rd Street, his feet were heavy and aching inside of the re-soled oxfords. He thought that money was a side-show freak with one part a bearded tyrant and the other a sweet coquette. 'Never mind—he'd show them yet! Just give him a break, that's all. Remember that time in Chicago he won a cool thousand on the Kentucky Derby? And the job behind the desk at The Palmor—fellows slipping him tens to keep mum about their sneaking some pretty girl up to their suites. And the crap-game for real jack, where he rolled ten naturals, one after the other, without blinking an eyelash. Just give him a break. Just ... give ... him ... aw, it was too hot to think.'

Allene Baum's face shot from the back of his head and became real before his eyes. The skin was pink, a pink suggestive of the first, ineffably placid second of dawn above the horizon, and the low forehead was surrounded by flaxen hair, like a handful of sunlight caught and curled from a white floor, and the eyes were grey and wide, with a bit of silver in them, like the moon on dusty roads, and the nose was long, with thin nostrils and the mouth thick and large, drooping at the corners, and so, with a mind at the opposite extreme from poetic imagery, Ray said, to himself, that 'she was a beaut' of a blonde and he sure skipped a beat, or something, when he looked into those big, warm eyes of hers, and her nose spoiled her face a little but not too much, and her mouth didn't look pretty at all but when he kissed it, it *felt* pretty, alright. He reached the three-storey rooming-house on one of the side-streets near 23rd, between Ninth and Tenth Avenues. The front was brick painted dull red with oblong windows showing dark green shades and the froth of starched, white curtains vaguely resembling lace, and a flight of chipped, brown-stone steps, bordered by iron railings flicked with rust, led from the sidewalk to the main door, with a semi-basement below the steps. The house was squeezed in a row of others varying only in an additional storey, or dirty yellows, browns, and creams on the bricks, and tin headgears, and the impression was cheerless, prostrate—a proclamation that the life within these structures, for the most part, was continuing to function with the liner edge, the soul, wrenched out of it.

Standing on the open porch before the door, Ray hesitated. Mmm, his esteemed landlady, Mrs. Fanny Baum. That dame seemed to have an instinct for the exact time in which he arrived—

scarcely ever failed to catch him, even if it was only at the top of the first flight. Oh well, what the hell. . . . He entered the house and had begun to ascend the stairs, slightly, when he heard the familiar, high-pitched, nasal voice—"Mr. Bai-lee . . . Mr. Bai-lee . . . just a minute." He checked himself, weariness and anger colliding, and turned, clutching the oak banister to brace himself for the inevitable tirade.

"Mr. Bailey, can't you pay me something on the rent money tonight?"

"No, I'm sorry, but I can't. I hiked all over New York today and couldn't locate anything."

Fanny Baum surveyed him for a moment with racial aversion, weak sympathy, and righteous greed working on her face and with all of these qualities schooled to sustain one another under a minimum of thought. Her face was fat and round, rough and raw-salmon under a shock of kinky red hair sprinkled with grey. Below the out-curving nose, the heavy lips were clamped and the eyes piggish, sorrowful, defrauded, in the throes of a minor brutality and a begrudging generosity driven together beyond any trace of mutual recognition. Standing at the foot of the stairs, with the bulges of her body wrapped in a pink cotton house-dress, she was menacing and humorous.

"You didn't find no work? So what? I'm not running a charity bureau—it's a rooming-house. You understand? A *rooming*-house."

Ray felt unutterably small, blue. Words had to be spoken but if he had had a choice he would have plunged his hand into fire, to avoid them.

"Yes, I know, but I'll get a job in the next two or three days and start to pay you, if you'll only be a little patient with me."

"Patience you want—patience. I've been hearing the same story from you for three weeks now—three weeks, and—"

"But I'm doing the best I can. I can't do any more."

"That's alright, but the landlord comes around the first of every month, on . . . the . . . dot, and he asks me for the money on the house. How can I pay him with people like you standing me up week after week?"

Staring down at her peevish face, Ray could have strangled her, for a moment. Day in, day out, he had listened to this berating, with only slight variations in the phrasing, and the situation had become galling to his pride. 'In a way she was right, of course—she had to pay her own bills—but what was the good of all this raving and slamming? She seemed to take a relish in it, damn her. It was ridiculous—why didn't she lock his door and shove him out, or shut up and give him more time?'

"Well, alright then, you can boost me out, if you want to, but what good will it do you? If you give me more time I'll pay up in full after I land a job. Otherwise you'll get nothing, that's all."

Fanny had an indecisive squint in her eyes. He had voiced the main reason for her failure to eject him up to the present evening, though in the past, as now, she had felt a self-denied twinge of sympathy for him. The independence running through his pleadings appealed to her a little, against her will. 'He had a backbone alright, even if he was a *Goi*, but he was a schemer too. All the *Goiyim* were schemers, she knew. Well, give him a couple days more. He had very few belongings and he could easy sneak his two suitcases out, say about two in the morning—she couldn't move her bed up to the front door—Morris might object'—a dying sex-grin with once more the mercenary and, unwillingly, a little sympathetic . . . 'a nice-built boy with a good chin on him, but . . . but on *his* looks she couldn't live.'

"So well, I'll give it you two days to pay me a little something, even if it's only three or four dollars. Two days you get, and *absolutely* no more. You understand me, Mr. Bailey?"

Ray almost smiled. This talking window-pane down there wanted to know whether he understood her.

"Yes, of course. I know how you're fixed and I'm really very grateful to you for letting me stay here as long as this. I'll try my darnedest—I can't say anything else."

He trudged up the stairs and Fanny, in the loose, brown slippers worn at night by her husband, shuffled back to the semi-basement where the family lived, and felt certain that some day her foolish generosity would ruin her, although she censured herself and patted herself on the back at one and the same time. Ray occupied a small room in the rear of the top floor. The furnishings were ill-assorted, worn, and gloomy—a wicker arm-chair painted a dull orange, with a dirty cushion, once grey and dull green, on the seat, and a white-enamelled, iron bed-frame with the paint peeling off, and a frail, varnished pine-table beside a chest of drawers with a scratched mirror over them—one of the previous roomers had struck safety-matches on it. The only window showed an array of irregularly rising, reddish brown, brick walls: wired, tin chimneys over roofs of pebbles on tar: cement-bottomed courtyards, or yards of beaten earth, with bits of grass and a few stunted elliptic-leaved trees looking artificial and overwhelmed amid the hard dirty masses. Clothes, mostly in white or washed-out pinks and blues, dangled from upper lines drawn in and out on pulleys between the half-open windows, some of which had white and tan curtains gathered by brighter ribbons near the middle and remindful of girls whose heads could not be seen, and drably busy sparrows were in the air. Voices darted from the buildings and the yards where tired men and women sometimes sprawled on canvas-backed chairs—laughter once in a while, but more often the high-keyed quarrel and repartee of people frazzled and knifed by the poorly compensated tension of an ebbing city day. The entire effect of the scene was not precisely dreary but doomed and devitalized, with life seeking intensely to be happy despite the oppressive grooves through which it was being forced.

Removing his coat, shirt, and shoes, Ray pitched himself on the bed and slept almost instantly. . . . When he roused himself, the room was in a twilight which made it seem attractively virginal in a soft cohesion of shadowed slants, angles, and diagonal patches interspersed with unevenly curved patterns of waning light, but the escape from realities lasted only a few seconds, as Ray rubbed the sleep from his eyes. The heat in the room was terrific, delving into every pore of his body, and yet the air was like an invisible hypnosis. Flies circled below the raised window-frame and buzzed, perched on his face and chest. He was grumpy, misty-minded, still tired, for he had been partly awakened by the strength of the heat. He switched on the unshaded electric light and then became panicky—'had to meet Allene at a quarter-to-nine—must be that, or more, right now, and he wasn't even washed, much less fully dressed.' He stepped to the top of the drawer-chest where he had placed his watch . . . 'owwow, sixteen to nine, and this tin ticker was always three or four minutes slow, too.'

A gentle rapping sped from the door—'Allene's knock, thank heaven.' He opened the door and she tiptoed into the room. He locked the door behind her, instantly. She was short and her head barely rose above the level of his shoulders. She wore a light grey moire with the balloon sleeves of the nineties, which were "coming back," and a touch of pink around the high neck, and the semi-bob of her flaxen hair was parted in the middle and flatly twisted in the rear. Her face sagged a bit, tired from concentrating on titles, bills of sale, and rent-accounts throughout a hot afternoon in a neighboring realtor's office where she clicked keys and took dictation. She had a body full within narrow confines, despite the well-defined hips, and her feet were a little too large, and the body signalled that it was young and though beginning to be shoved down by life it was still eager to dance and drink, and steep itself in the tingling antidotes of sex.

She was sitting on the edge of the bed with Ray and exchanging whispers and long kisses.

"I've got to hurry, dear. I brought Mrs. Pivat's iron back and mom'll start nosing upstairs, if I stay too long."

"Mom! That old raspy-tongued—"

"Ray, I *don't* want you to speak that way about my own mother. Please."

"Oh, alright, alright."

"But I *mean* it."

"Christ, there's no time to argue about it now. Let's make it the corner of 18th and 9th this time—the one with the Coffee Pot. We're taking too much of a chance meeting on 23rd. Either your father or that old—"

"Ray, I *told* you."

"I'm sorry, but 18th and 9th, d'you hear?"

"Uh-huh. Alright, dear. . . . I'm so glad I came up here. I had a hunch you'd over-sleep, you poor kid. And listen, I'll watch when you go out and then I'll start, well, I'll start about ten minutes later."

"That means I'll be on the corner waiting for you around nine-twenty."

"Oke, Ray dear. . . . Gee, stop kissing me. I hear somebody in the hall down-stairs. Hurry dear, please."

They slid to the door and she slipped out of the room. After he had washed and was changing to the only other suit he possessed—a brown crash beginning to be dirty but still just wearable—he felt puffed-up over nothing which he could immediately discern, the rebound of an ego refusing to be routed by sordid facts, the absence of money, the disregard of others, much as a fighter rises at the count of nine, smiling in his haze and making optimistic passes in the air—an easy target for the next uppercut. The optimism, questioning itself a little, found the need to invent pretexts. 'He had a swell girl and they were nuts about each other. She was still new and sweet to him every next time he was with her, which was the only test of love a fellow could produce. Land some kind of a job tomorrow, go back to being a counterman, if he *had* to, and this time keep his temper tied like the other men did, so he wouldn't get canned, then, save up his money, get a front, locate a nice salesman's job, like he had had times before. After all, he was educated—a whole year at college—and he could roll his tongue and kid them into buying—he wouldn't be where he was now, if he hadn't lost his four hundred in the damn stud game at the '14th Democratic'—well, he'd win it back again—smaller games and not so damn reckless whenever he had high threes and the other fellow, after drawing four cards, began to raise like a house on fire . . . sure, get a job, save his money, gamble a *little*. You know, he'd always had a hankering to open a small night-club. After cashiering in that Chi' joint, The Blue Swan, for six months, what he didn't know about that racket wasn't worth mentioning. Plant a few wise good-looking girls around the tables—those who had wits enough to act refined, even when they didn't feel that way—and protect them with proper introductions, of course. Then, pay some slick rounders to bring a few of their society acquaintances down—the particular members of the smart sets, who prided themselves on being wonderfully fast and gracious—and have the publicity-man spread the fact of their attendance, in the entertainment-columns of the papers. Then grease the right gorillas and their shadowy higher-ups, and hire a quick-stepping floorshow—'girls with lovely shapes daringly exposed'—and a master of ceremonies with a razor-like tongue, but a respectful grin turned on the 'celebrities' at the ring-side seats. Lots of the main performers were willing to take fifty per as long as it was advertised that they were receiving hundreds—funny, wasn't it? And let's see—a pair of doll-faces in the check-room, fluttering over the important patrons and just barely nice to the others—and take care that the columnists and reporters were always royally treated. The ins and outs were certainly numerous, but he knew most of them. . . . Oh well, a job, no matter how hard it was, and then . . . marry his sweets, Allene. And after all, even now, a walk through Central Park, and a cool breeze or two, and a lot of cuddling with Allene on a shady bench, they didn't make such a bad prospect, all in all.'

Ray left the house, whistling "Was That A Human Thing To Do?" about a fellow whose girl had mistreated him and made him sadly complaining because he still loved her—a catchy, flitting tune in the mass of love, sweetness, mild, sexual innuendos, and 'Dixie-Land homesickness' and frolics, from Tin Pan Alley. He walked into The Shamrock Grill and ordered a five-cent glass of beer, scarcely more than two small gulps. The place had an N.R.A. sign, the provisions of which it was violating through the customary tricks—giving the bartenders and the porter a twenty minute "lunch-hour," and even less on the rushed night-shifts, and paying them higher wages out of which the workers were compelled to contribute a 'kick-back'— money for an employees' protective-association secretly controlled by the grill-owners themselves. The establishment sold hard liquor to trusted customers and resembled an old-time saloon with its face lifted and primped—brass bowls of flowers at each end of the bar; green and gold bunting interspersed with large shamrocks around and upon the long mirror behind the bar: a fancy tile floor in green and white; and round tables with blue-and-green checked cloths, where the women and their escorts could sit and drink.

Ray conversed with two acquaintances, Max Bessler and Gene Sullivan. Sullivan had a hatchet-edged jaw nicked on the left side, and coal-chip eyes—a young furniture-mover who believed that God and Tammany Hall were old friends—while Bessler was a middle-aged shopkeeper with a nose like a crocus-bulb, fat cheeks, and a mien forever talkatively conciliatory.

"They're putting up La Guardia on a Fusion Ticket. He ain't got a snow-flake's chance in hell."

"Well, I don't know—we need a clean-up in my opinion. That pack of grafters down at City Hall are getting too damn fresh, believe me"—Ray experienced a fine thrill of civic indignation as he uttered the words, and it lifted his position in life and gave him the argumentative zest of an important citizen and voter, despite the fact that his feet were stiff and he had only twenty cents in his pocket. Sullivan's anger was a practical one—'why in hell shouldn't the Wigwam go after it? The boys were a damn sight better than the Republican stuffed shirts and high-collar snobs, and the jokes calling themselves socialists, and the boys were always handing out favors and dough to the poor people of their districts, weren't they?' He dished out the stock contentions, in a rasping voice, but Ray, swung along by his day of futile tramping and the need to counteract it, refused to retreat.

"I hope La Guardia does get in. I've been out of work for three weeks now and I can't find a job to save my life. Take my word for it, conditions have got to improve and they will, too, the minute we get an honest city-government into office. Roosevelt's a fine leader, through and through, and he's certainly doing a lot for the country, I'll admit, but he can't dig his fingers into all of the rotten spots in little, old Manhattan—he hasn't got the time."

"Oh, what's the use of arguing about politics? What's the sense of it? Everybody has his own beliefs and that's all there is to it. We're all pulling for better times, certainly we are, but we'll have to be patient about it because we're fighting our way out of one of the worst depressions this country's ever had"—Bessler, who ran a small clothing-store, swung his palms, squirmed between the tasks of placating a local bully and another man, who might be a possible customer after he found the next job. Sullivan still frowned as he ordered a fresh glass of beer.

"Alright, alright, I'm not laying down the law, but I stick to what I said. Any guy who doesn't string along with Tammany ought to have his nut examined. We're raising millions of bucks for home-relief and we're trying to help the regular people right down on the street, see? And what's more, the whole bunch of those reformers are nothing but pieces of tripe, if you ask me. All they want is to get their hands on some of the easy dough lying around, that's all they're after."

Ray stayed good-natured because the tilt was not deeply serious to him, at this juncture, and Sullivan was a taller and broader man.

"That sounds great, Sullivan—you can tell that to the big shots down at Washington now. They're democrats too, but they haven't got much use for Tammany, believe me, and they're not making any bones about it either."

Sullivan, with an uncertain look, mumbled "aa, who cares about them?," and he was trapped between his immediate allegiances and the awe in which he held the highest officials of his country. The bar was crowding up and Conroy, one of the bartenders, with a conical, battered face and black hair pasted on the half bald skull, eyed Ray with covert disfavor—how long was that mug going to stand there for his nickel, huh? Ray finally detected the looks and walked out of the place. He'd never patronize that joint again—It was poor business to be unfriendly to a man out of work. He might come up in the world again darn soon, for all they knew.

After he had met Allene, she slipped a dime into his hand for the subway-fares and he felt embarrassed, robbed of the indulgent superiority of treating his girl, which went with his manhood, in his belief. They spoke about it as they waited for a local train.

"Gee, but I hate to take coin from you, 'Lene, even a dime. It makes me feel cheap, honest it does, but what in the devil can I do ?"

She looked at him with a silly, protective smile.

"Oh, never mind . . . dear. *I'm* not objecting, am I?"

"No, but that isn't the point."

A silence.

"Well, you can add it all up and pay it back whenever you get a job . . . foolish."

"That's exactly what I'm doing. Together with this dime it makes four-sixty up-to-date . . . and you're going to have every cent of it back with interest, believe you me."

Allene was tender and the least bit skeptical—'men had such a scratchy pride, didn't they?—and they did so ache to be the social masters, especially in money things, and as a few rotten experiences had shown her, some men made dozens of promises and then never lived up to them, but . . . she loved this fool boy . . . guess she did anyway . . . not absolutely certain but pretty much so. Why? Oh well, he was hot-headed, and independent . . . and as far as he seemed . . . a nice, honest boy, and he told fibs to save his vanity, like when he tripped up in the story of some great success in his past and then piled it on even heavier, to cover the slip, but then all men did that, if only occasionally . . . and what was the difference between not being really handsome and yet being not bad to look at either?

A person knew whether she did, or she didn't, but she couldn't *ever* know really why.'

They had reached Columbus Circle and were entering Central Park. Around the electric lights on top of tall iron poles, small clouds of insects circularly hovered, and the darkness was swarming with cries, scuffles, spoonings, mosquitos, lollings on benches, the purr and cough of speeding machines. As a special dispensation on particularly hot nights, people were allowed to occupy the expanses of grass stretching everywhere, and when the temperature receded a few degrees the grass was once more preserved as an object for admiration, with policemen, indomitable esthetes, on the alert to guard its beauty. On the present night, thousands of men and women were squatting on the wide lawns—fagged-out workers, the footsore unemployed, women, and families diving into lunchboxes. Except for the minority of children and extreme adolescents, these humans showed little animation. They rested, for the most part, flat on their backs—like stricken, robbed, over-humble ones sleeping, or brushing insects off, snipping grass, looking vacantly up at the stars, grateful for the feel of springy turf, the cool slap of a shred of breeze. The wide drives were thick with racing cars— people hurrying to pleasure, or at least to fairly comfortable homes, and sometimes the grass-squatters along the drives threw surly glances at the whizzing machines and edged away from the gasoline fumes.

Policemen, in dark blue with nickel buttons and shields, dangled their clubs from leather thongs and paced down the walks and through the ranks of the resters, and while some of them had genially alert faces, the majority revealed varying degrees of dull-minded hardness, officiousness, over-eager suspicion, and the desire to inflate themselves at the expense of small offenders. The lagoons were dotted with short-hulled boats in which young beaux rowed their girls—often at the cost of last, precious coins—or tried to pick up the girls in other boats, by "accidentally" bumping into them. Hang-dog, seedy men and women, usually old, stood at the intersections of the walks and sold peanuts, candies, bottled soft-drinks. The trees and bushes in groups and sprinkles upon the hilly rises, the levels, and around the jutting rocks, were greenish black creatures slightly stirring and utterly at peace in a world far removed from the injustices, delusions, and sodden rest among the people scattered beside them, and the sky displayed its timeless, wide-flung confusion of pointed, uncomprehending stares. It was the curiously formalized meeting and isolation of country and city effects touching one another on the surface, leagues separate under-neath, and dwarfed a bit by the massed, unevenly aligned, tall shafts of light-blinking buildings hemming the park on all of its straight sides. The human atmosphere was a monotonous inter-play of iner-tias, love-makings, horseplays, cruelty and kindness deadlocked, with always the grim class-disparity of the gleaming automobiles versus the prone turf-sleepers, the well-dressed strollers versus the host of shabby men, who shuffled up and begged for nickels, or dimes.

Allene and Ray talked as they walked down the cement paths and looked for a shady, unoccupied bench.

"That mother of yours is a bad pain to me."

"Ray, you stop it this minute. I know her faults better than you do, and I've quit her and father twice and went to live on my lonely, but . . . if anybody's going to knock her, it's going to be me. She hasn't had any bed of roses, I'll tell you, and she's had plenty to make *her* sour."

"Well, it's done the trick alright. She *is*."

"Oh, be quiet."

"Are you sore?"

"Just a little."

"Oh forget it, sweet."

"Then don't be always pounding on it, Ray."

A pause.

"Say, 'Lene, are you still seeing Al McCormick?"

Another pause.

"Are you?"

"Yes, I am"—Allene felt justified, a bit deceitful, and self-hating, all in a jumble.

Ray was jealous and woebegone.

"What for? Why can't you stick to me, Allene?"

Again a pause.

"D'you know, sometimes I think you don't really love me, 'Lene."

"I'm not absolutely sure, Ray, but . . . almost. Before I give up everyone else, Ray, I want to be positive, see?"

"Alright, make up a hundred affidavits to yourself and then look me up, when I've got grey hairs, kid."

"Oh Ray, don't be so mad at me. I've got to have a little fun sometimes, and that eighteen a week I get doesn't stretch very far either."

"Yeah, I know, he can take you out to shows, and dances, and—"

"But Ray, I see you at least four times a week." A pause. "Whenever I'm really sure I love you, I'll run away and live with you, and you've got to be patient, dear. I won't be so very long."

Ray battled it out within himself—'it was natural for a girl to want a good time once in a while instead of always sitting on park benches, or sneaking up to a fellow's room on rainy nights, or sitting downstairs with her mother jawing her head off, but if a girl loved a man she ought to be strictly loyal to him when he was down and out, and not just loyal most of the time, and besides, that McCormick chap got into his hair—cocky and close-fisted, and not much in his head,' and then Ray was honest enough to admit that he wouldn't be panning McCormick so much if the other man had not been chasing Allene, and he ended in a sputter of "aars" and "aas," and squeezed Allene's hand to forget them. 'Christ, it's all because I haven't got a job. If I don't scoop in some money soon, I'll go off my nut, honest.'

Allene became much less selfish, to herself, to drive out her recognition that the charges of disloyalty held a measure of truth and to escape from the fact that she was mentally inadequate to cope with the problem of her present relations with Ray.

"I'm not going to quit you just because you're broke . . . never. Don't you ever worry about that, Ray."

She returned the pressure of his hand while mournful and hopeful feelings, indeterminately permeated, made his breathing uneven. Unable to locate a shady retreat without a couple, they compromised by taking a bench barely overlapped by bushes at one end and standing near one of the oval-bowled electric lights over a driveway crossing.

II

AL McCORMICK and Art Nelson loitered on the sidewalk near the Baum rooming-house, in which McCormick lived. Al worked as a truck-loader and chauffeur in the delivery-service of a huge department-store and Nelson was a clerk in a chain grocery-store and occupied a room near the end of the block. The men were tired, shifting from one foot to another and yet straightening their shoulders, clapping their hands and pivotting in beginnings of fox-trot steps, in the always half-starved need for recreation, and physical importance. McCormick's face had a pugnacity, calmly restrained to a minimum and yet easily identified, and ready to lash out whenever it felt justified. Nelson, two inches shorter than McCormick's five-eleven, was more amiable and inwardly wrapped in a nervously glancing way, which was not precisely fearful but always willing to placate, in a first attempt to ward off any impending encounter. Born in the neighborhood, Nelson was the product of many a street-fight, in most of which he had been whipped by older, or stronger, boys. Fist-fights were tacitly encouraged by the rulers of the locality— political heelers, the larger businessmen, and the gang-sergeants taking their orders from a headquarters on Broadway—as a proof of manhood and an effective way of settling grievances, and through the planting and acceptance of this spirit, with policemen ignoring brawls unless they led to a hospital, or to murder, the workers in this Chelsea region had been induced to turn their general resentment to smaller angers directed against one another, and to forget other matters such as the meagerness of their pay and the material discriminations within their lives.

Under the cocked, imitation Panama with a round, green feather peeping from the black band, Nelson's carrot nose and stringy lips jerked in a malicious smile.

"There he goes, Al?"

"Who?"

"Bailey, walking down the other side. See him?"

McCormick turned and squinted down the street.

"Yeah, I see him, but what's the idea pointing *him* out? I've got nothing against him, but he's no partic'lar friend of mine."

Nelson had the look of one who was intent upon kidding but not certain of how far he could venture.

"Well, if you stick around a while you'll see another person going down the walk in the same direction. You know who I mean."

McCormick scowled, smiled reluctantly, scowled again, this time more half-heartedly, and wound up with a look of belligerent fortitude.

"Mind your own business, Art."

"Aw, take a joke, can't you?"

McCormick needed the relief of utterance more than the pride, which, suddenly, was loading him "for no good reason."

"Damn it, Allene and me, we were getting along swell, perfectly swell, before he butted in. I took her out twice a week, sometimes three, and believe me, we used to do some necking out in the hallway after I brought her back."

"Ever get her up to your room, Al?"

McCormick glared and clenched one hand, with the secretive gallantry which can be a mere sheen for narrow-mindedness but which is sometimes relatively selfless nevertheless.

"One more crack like that out of you—"

"Aw, stop being so touchy, will you? You've told me plenty about other girls."

"Well, they were tarts and they didn't mean anything to me, but Allene does, see?"

"I'm sorry, Al. How was I to know?"

McCormick relaxed.

"I'd like to find out what she sees in that guy, honest I would."

"Maybe it's his line of gab, or the way he makes love to her, or—Christ, didn't I have the same thing happen to me once? I was nuts about a girl over on Tenth Avenue, bugs about her, I'm telling you, and I even had the money saved up to buy her the ring, and the way she cuddled up to *me* was nobody's business . . . but what did she turn around and do? All at once, without one lick of warning, she threw me down for the homeliest guy you ever laid eyes on, a guy without a cent in his pocket, too. It's no use figuring them, Al—it can't be done."

They walked down the street and still vented their grievances against girls, with now and then a gloating over the "loose" girls whom, in their fancy, they had used for purposes of revenge. To an appreciable extent, the whole battle was a corruption engendered by their environment to stifle their anger against the host of inflictions and obstacles in no way connected with sex. They boarded a subway train and rode to Central Park. They knew that the girls, whose names were in their cherished notebooks, would not be apt to be at home on this warm, clear summer night, and they were intent on making a pick-up after they reached the park.

The time was a bit after ten and the pallidly lit scene was a hive of animal relaxation and respectable disapproval, buzzing in and out, interwoven, above the grim bodies of workers and job-hunters hugging the lawns on all sides. Sailors, with round white linen caps slanting down to one eyebrow, scuffled, walked with their shoulder-hitching roll, always on the make for girls, to feel good again after the gruelling hours of service on ships and submarines.

Women in singles, twos and threes, tripped along with hard-eyed, wary miens, or tried to compromise between caution and attitudes of moderate invitation. Other women were openly attentive to possible overtures, and still others sized up the passing males and rebuffed most of them, waiting for the exact blend of natty attire and facial outline to which they were susceptible. A few of them loitered along the edges of the drives, to catch the signals of amorous automobilists, but there was little open solicitation among them because the tongue-in-the-cheek strictness of the police squads had forced the widespread prostitution in the city to maintain itself sneakingly, through bribes and in camouflaged apartments, five-cent dance-halls, lesser cabarets and drinking hide-outs.

Nelson had a flask of rye and the boys sat down to consume part of it. As McCormick drank, his reddish face, with its extended jaw and twisted nose under the auburn hair, became tight and quiet in an animal crouch, while Nelson was smiling as he fought the palpable gloat around his mouth. A girl seated herself on the opposite bench and the men examined her. She appeared to be just under twenty, bluntly curved close to stoutness, and the beauty-shop wave of her bobbed, black hair peeped from a cup-shaped, yellow straw hat with a pale blue ribbon circling over the short, slanting brim. Under the smear of red and white her face was tired, suspicious, hardened a little, particularly in the protuberant eyes and the large, parted mouth. Continually fiddling with her long, corn-yellow sateen, her glances at the two men said: "Oh, keep on staring at me—who cares? . . . Maybe I'll take to you but more likely I won't—wouldn't you like to know? . . . You're entirely too fresh, you big one over there, with the twisty nose, but you certainly look like you could take care of yourself, if looks count . . . and anyway, I'll bet you haven't nerve enough to make a play for me—both of you." The pitiful fluctuations of a girl tired after nine hours as a waitress in a hot, noisy lunchroom, longing for the small pleasures, which she could not afford, thrown between sexual temptation and 'moral shame' because her life offered no other outlet—this mixture betrayed itself in every flitting of her eyes.

The men surveyed her with veiled lust and conversed about her, in undertones.

"How does she look to you, Al?"

"She wouldn't be so bad if she had a decent nose on her."

"Well, she's kinda handsome even at that."

"Oh, she'll pass, but she's handing us some funny looks. Did you get that one? . . . I don't know whether she wants to be picked up, or whether she's just leading us on so she can get a kick out of slipping us a chunk of ice, if we walk over there."

Nelson, veteran of many flirtations, attempted and successful, chuckled.

"Both, kid, both. She'll make up her mind after one of us does the talking. Just leave it to me—you'll see."

He ambled over to the girl, with a slouch which he considered to be nonchalant, and she averted her head.

"D'you want to sit with a couple of nice fellows, Miss, uh—uh—pardon me, but I don't think I remember your name."

The girl still looked away—cross, indecisive, secretly attentive.

"I hope I'm not bothering you, but there's no harm in a little conversation, you know."

The girl turned her head and tried to look insolent above her amusement—'he talked smooth and not so flip, his clothes were alright, and after all, she *had* come to the park on the chance. . . .'

"Yeah, I think I heard that before, freshie."

"Oh, come on, be a good sport. We're not going to eat you up."

"I'll say you're not."

"You look sweet enough at that."

"Oh, stop the fried mush, please"—her voice had grown the least shade softer.

"Well, I'll admit I don't really know you. I'm just telling you how you look to me."

"Yeah, I know . . . freshie."

In the following pause the girl was more relaxed, though still partly removed, and Nelson, scenting victory, screwed up his mind for a resumption of the "line"—the semi-sugary kidding supported by the would-be careless boasts of a man 'who had plenty on his staff but was enjoying an off-night.'

"No fooling, I broke a date tonight because I had a hunch she was two-timing me, and that's one thing I never stand for. You look like you might be a square-shooter, Miss, uh—darn it, I can't remember your name for the life of me. I was going to buy a new notebook and put it down when I first met you at the Van Astor's last week-end."

The girl smiled-forced, warming a trifle.

"You're a quick worker, aren't you?"

"Oh, I wouldn't say that. There was something about you attracted me, honest. I'm just trying to get acquainted, that's all."

"Well, I haven't chased you away so far, have I?"

Nelson grinned.

"Now you're talking like a regular girl, um, and say, can I call my friend over? He's a fine fellow right down to his shoe-laces, no kidding either."

While talking to Nelson the girl had been absorbing McCormick, inch by inch, with side-glances, and approving his muscular tallness, his straight mouth and the lower jut of his face—a servility toward physical prowess but also, the stir of abused youth toward health and competence of flesh in the other sex. Still, she had to pretend to be hesitant—it was allied to the sorry game born from the atmosphere of rackets, verbal dodges, experiences with men, who became roughnecks whenever they drank too much.

"I'm not sure. I don't think it's safe for a girl to be with two men at once."

"Oh, stop the worrying, babe. We'll treat you like a couple of gentlemen all the time, and besides, he's a good pal of mine and I don't want to leave him flat, see?"

"Well, alright then—but remember what you just said."

"And how—leave it to us, babe."

Nelson signalled to McCormick and the latter joined the party. Nelson rattled on and Al made short remarks, barely polite, at times almost sullen, as his mind reverted to Allene. Why couldn't a man get the one woman he wanted, instead of pick-ups, tarts, and dumb-heads? Another quick drink, surreptitiously. 'Aa, he worked hard all day for damn little pay and swallowed bawlings-out, playing favorites, from Mac, that damn loading-supe—pile you up so heavy, in the afternoon, you'd be bound to drive back an hour late, with not a red cent for the overtime—and the sweet, little old night meant that he was his own boss again and he could down some booze, swing from the hip, if any guy bothered him without cause, and make a play for any dame he could interest. What else was there to living, anyway? Romance was alright, sure—even a hardboiled fellow had a little sugar in him, but in the meantime, hell, grab anyone he could get, if she wasn't too old and homely . . . and now, maybe he'd cut Nelson out with this jane—no rough stuff—just talk to the girl and see if she would fall.'

"Think you're good-looking, cutie?"

"That's for you to say."

"Oh, I've seen them worse than you."

"Puh-leese, don't strain yourself."

"Yeah? I do enough straining every day, loading up and handling the wheel."

"What kind of work d'you do?"

"I'm on a delivery-truck for the Wanman store, kid, and you've got to have it in your arms and legs for that kind of job, believe me you."

During the pause, the girl, Rea Adams, was shifting respect and resentment in a confusion slowly moving, nevertheless, in the direction of a primitive, sexual response. Her mind was too tired and browbeaten to function along the finer degrees of choice and rejection, and sex was the only major promise possible within the narrow confines of her social and economic existence. 'Geez, outside of a strapping, wise lad and, well, just a little something to drink, and a puncture-proof dance, and once in a great while, aw, who could help it? . . .'

"Let me feel your muscle, will you?"—Rea pressed her fingers against McCormick's tensely doubled right arm.

"Ooo, you certainly are a strong fellow, no kidding. It makes a girl feel safe to be with somebody like you."

"Oh, can the syrup, babe."

"But I mean it, really."

"Al's there alright, no doubt about that"—Nelson, feeling that he was "losing out," uttered the words as a perfunctory amiability and was already scanning the girls continually tripping past, in the hope that one of them would give him a relenting smile. Rea and Al were in the flurry of a sham fight, in which his surliness, transparent over sexual desire, annoyed and stimulated her contradictory emotions—the artificial desire for "a gentleman" versus the stronger pull toward a slam-bang physical ability and domination, and a slangy species of unserious attack and independence, which formed her version of a desirable male.

"Don't you ever surprise yourself and throw out a compliment?"

"Yeah, on Sundays, when I'm feeling good and rested."

"Is that so? Well, I'd love to teach you a lesson, big boy."

"Yeah?"

"Yeeaah. I think I'll trot along and look up one of my girl-friends, 'cause you're too darn fresh for *me*."

"Aw, stick around a while. Al doesn't mean everything he—"

"Keep your mitts out of this, Art"—McCormick was friendly but the syllables were hammer-taps.

He looked at Rea with a first smile, flint-rimmed but more openly admiring.

"For Christ sake, don't you get enough ice cream and sticky goo from all the fellows you know?"

"Suppose I do, what about it?"

"Well, take it straight from the shoulder for a change. You're a good-looking girl—I don't have to tell you that. If your head got too conceited, it might float up like one of those toy balloons—see?—and I want to keep on looking at it."

Rea smiled back, defiantly. The rough flattery, clipped to a minimum, made her 'respect the guy for not going down on his knees,' though she had not abandoned her hope of inducing Al to finish with supplications and love-words, which she might accept, or reject . . . tralala, lalalallala, who cared? and if the man was beginning to be appealing, perhaps, tralal, lalee . . . though he had better keep any tricks to himself, just the same. A queen rising from overworked, bossed obscurity, courted by men and teasing them on to prolong the sensation.

The trio rose and strolled over the grass to another bench which had been carried from one of the walks to a plot of shrubbery at the top of a knoll near the moon-dappled, squealing, oar-splashed lagoon. McCormick, who had his own flask and had bought some paper cups from a candy and soft-drink cart, urged Rea to take a drink of rye, and after gradually lessening expostulations—to preserve his "respect" and because she knew that the liquor might make her "too easy"—she consented with: "Well, alright, I will, but just a little one, please. Honest, when I drink too much I start to sing all over—"

"Yeah, I know—I'm not a good singer myself."

"Oh, shut up, freshie."

"Sure, anything you say"—McCormick had now become adept in a mixture of trivial slams and padded repentances. Nelson wandered off to resume the hunt. He returned, a little over half an hour later, with a full-blown woman nearing middle-age—a nurse, Magdalene Ecklund, who worked in a city insane-asylum and was having her weekly night off. Magdalene, with the ebbing of symmetrical lines still visible on her Scandinavian face, looked nerve-worn, expectant, wary, in the great misunderstanding between her stumbling mind and the desperation of her emotions, the desire to remain proper because 'it paid more in the end'—impulse of mistreated flesh and blood struggling for some compensation, some moonlit duet, against a sordid environment and its moral shibbo-leths. She had fat-rolled cheeks and a mouth of pure bitterness. She was forced to abuse the inmates at the asylum with the crack of wet towels, lengthy cold-showers, strait-jackets, and slaps on face and breasts, because the few nurses, who were lenient, invariably lost their jobs on some pretext or other, but the necessity sickened her and made her anxious to "step out and forget it" on each blessed night-off. The ill-temper of the sane prisoners, railroaded by schem-ing, or deluded, relatives, brought her no actual revelation of cause and effect, but she did believe that "something was wrong some-where," and that she was helpless and could only hold her job and be sneakingly kind to some of the women when nobody was watching.

She accepted a drink, with the remark that she could only die once and, besides, she wanted to bear up against the terrible heat. She fussed with her bottle-green, pleated dress, as though she were praying with tender finger-tips for something unformed and immi-nent. She told stories of the brutal ward, in which she worked, which Nelson tried to divert with intendedly humorous prattle and grunted assents, since the liquor in his veins had no desire to contact with realities, to achieve anything more than the physical closeness able to blot out the distaste of the past day and ignore the submissive and yet grumbling hustle and sameness of tomorrow.

Rea and McCormick were spooning, and as he kissed, heavy and eager, he touched her body in a childlike, fumbling way. She squirmed, pleaded, reproved, and yielded momentarily, in a fight between skin-thick inhibitions and the fire of the rye digging into her exhaustion, the young, bludgeoning muscles of a man upsetting her even more deeply. Nelson held Magdalene's hands, planted his lips on her partly averted cheeks and felt "the big, bad wolf" tugging within his chest, since it was hard to do more than ape the real ten-derness which was either a slushy counterfeit, or nonexistent, in the brisk, endured routines of the only life he had ever known.

"What d'you work at, Mister—"

"Art's alright with me."

"A-artie—gee, I think I'm getting silly."

"I'll keep you company."

"Stop it, please. Be a good boy for a minute, won't you?"

"Alright, I'll keep my eyes glued on the wristwatch, hon'."

"You're positively foolish . . . but tell me, what kind of work d'you do?"

"Aw, I'm a grocery-clerk—one of the Cheeves stores, and believe me, it's no soft spot to stand on your feet nine to ten hours a day for the lousy pay we get."

"Ow, don't mention *feet* to me. Honest, the way I have to race around that ward of mine, I'm just about ready to fall down when eight o'clock comes. That's the trouble with some of us nurses out there—we know we're getting a raw deal ourselves, so we get sore and then we take it out on the patients."

"Yeah, I know it's a tough world, no matter how you look at it, but what the hell, if you've got brains you can make money and be a big shot, and if you haven't, there's no sense kicking about it. I'm not going to be a clerk all my life—I'll get a chance to go into business on my own hook, some day. Don't worry."

Nelson's compulsion of hope swaggered to evade the fact that there was no specific basis for it, and Magdalene, who had been married and divorced twice, cuddled against him for the first time, with her lips beginning to loosen, her eyes softening, out of the general, hardboiled expression, which faltered and reappeared, jerkily. In her thirty-sixth year, she was still longing for a final jag and ultimatum of sex and sentiment—a last, pitiful burst of mature enjoyment and the glamor of a loyal attachment, and she liked Nelson's ambition "to go higher in life," and his youth made her jealous and anxious, and she told herself that she might even hold a man like this, if she let him go just far enough but no further on this particular night, and her cynicism retorted that a man never respected a woman whom he could pick up and instantly drink with, and the remains of her illusions fought to survive. 'Look at Madge Connally, nurse in 7 . . . about February it must have been when she married that stunning kid in the hosiery business, and then she admitted to the girls afterwards that he had picked her up at the Roseland dance-joint months before . . .'

Magdalene was half on Nelson's lap and he jammed her head just below his shoulder and kissed her as often as he could hold her face still, while she pulled at his veering hands, half-heartedly, and could not possess her thoughts and emotions in more than a slipping, and, for moments, barely objecting manner. Rea and Al had their mouths together, scarcely moving in a physical response far more genuine and direct than that of the other pair, since it was mutual youth in a surface attraction, without despair, or any desire for safety. Insects hummed and buzzed through the air, which, despite occasional puff and twirl, drifted heavy with the smell of growing, raw-fresh things and the more artificial odors of a city combined and neutralized. A blackish-silvery light trickled through the apertures and chinks within the foliage which canopied most of the bench, and in the distance, the sprinkles and rows of light dominated the hardness of tall buildings softened by night and a dark sky but still perceptible. There on the bench, nurse, delivery-truck driver, grocery-clerk, and waitress, squeezed and drained by a vicious, material claw and mouth, tried to escape from the imminent reality of an approaching day and exchanged their little rye-soaked touches of flesh, their intervening apology of sigh, hesitation, and foolish words.

Then, when Al was close to having Rea, she began to free herself with snaky retreats. The liquor was still skidding through nerve and blood, but she was not drunk in any definite loss of senses and control of her limbs. She was afraid of protruding policemen and the peering of passersby, and with two others on the bench, a wisp of modesty, like a feebly plucking but insistent hand, contended against the opposite exhilaration, and one voice within her shouted that 'whenever a guy got a girl on the first night he laughed at her, to himself, and tagged her as a pushover for anybody, and then she never saw him again, or he went with her for a while and then suddenly gave her the air.' The other voice told her that she wanted this boy because he was so strong and his fingers burned her soft flesh without giving her pain, and so far he had been just right for her taste, 'blarneying the least bit and yet showing that he wouldn't let a girl step on him, and hi-de-hi . . . di-ho, ten hours a day at the Roscoe tomorrow—rush two-thirds of the time and a dollar plus tips, sure, sixty cents all the past day, and for what? Just to remember that she'd been a good girl tonight?'

The shout, fright and vanity compressed, and the equally strong whisper, interpenetrated, whirled, and stopped short, expelled again by the man who was using his muscles to gain her legs and her breast, not gently, but in an active pleading never repulsively rough, and then . . .

"Al, cut it out—there's a cop out there watching us."

McCormick slid back, slowly, with a reluctantly handcuffed ill-temper. Liquor and physical desire eyed the nearby club, the concealed gun and blackjack, and became undecided. 'Aw, what the hell—wait till he passed. Instead of nosing around and spoiling people's pleasure, why didn't some of those cops go after some of the big gangsters circulating all over the city, damn them.' Nelson and Magdalene had also drawn apart, and he eyed the policeman with a hate nervously disguising itself, while she, who had been only half desirous, appreciated the chance to regain her control, pat herself because she was still the uncaptured prize. The policeman walked over to the bench.

"Listen you, all of you . . . what do you think you're pulling off? You're in a park—get me?—a *park*, and not a room with a coupla beds in it."

"Aw, what were we doing?"—McCormick, holding a handkerchief, shielded a scowl as he pretended to mop his face.

"You know damn well what you were doing."

A pause.

"Don't pull it again, that's all I'm telling you, because if I catch you, I'll run you in, the whole pack of you, see?"'

"Christ, can't a fellow spoon a little with his girl?"—McCormick's voice was almost openly hostile.

"Not the way you were doing it, and what's more, I don't want too much lip out of you either, or I might sock you one."

The four remained silent. Al was crackling, withheld only by the knowledge that he would not have a fraction of a chance, either now, or in the subsequent court-room. Nelson rationalized his fear —'kid the cop along and then get together when he was safely out of sight—use common sense. Cops were needed for law and order, though most of them were only too eager to be insulting and bossy unless they knew that a fellow 'was in with the boys, damn their hides anyway.' Rea felt that she was ashamed of what the cop might have seen, but the feeling was only a tremble in the sneer which she tried to keep from her face—'certainly, they went after girls on benches and women without pull, but when did they ever bust into one of those swell pent-houses and pinch a gold-digger living with some rich, old fat-belly, yeah, when?' Magdalene was flustered white under the cosmetics—the least dab of scandal and her job would disappear, and didn't she know it!

After he had gorged himself sufficiently on the unwilling silence from the others, the scowling policeman snapped a last warning and strode away. Rea stood.

"I'm not going to hand any more free kicks to the Peeping Toms around *here*. Let's go some place, Al—I feel like dancing tonight."

Al took out his watch.

"Eleven-thirty now."

"That's not too late."

"Late? Say cutie, this night hasn't even started with me."

"How about Roseland—that's open until three"—Magdalene felt lowered to herself—'bawled out by a policeman for displaying . . . my, she must be positively out of her senses'—and she wanted to leave the park, quickly. Nelson, amorously tantalized and still hopeful, chimed into the dance-hall suggestion, and the four stepped across the close-cropped, moon-washed lawn to a distantly curving walk. As they approached a corner where the square-lined cement was intersected by a sharply turning driveway, Nelson spied Allene and Ray squatting on the grass beneath a beech sapling with its leaves stitching the bare motion of serenity into the dwindling heat of the night. Nelson, the bad boy, thoughtlessly malicious, wanted to avenge himself because McCormick was more powerful with most women.

"Al, look, right over there beside the tree. See? There's your girl-friend sweetening the pot with Bailey—see her over there? Boy, that fellow sure is a wizard with the girls—I wonder how he does it."

McCormick yanked Rea's arm, halting her, and stared at the pair on the grass. He was combative, confused because Rea and his recent contacts with her made a jealous anger even more confused, and urged by his drinks to show that he was a man refusing to let another man rob him of a favorite woman, despite the grumble which told him that he was absolutely unjustified. Wouldn't he be sore, if he was sitting there and Bailey walked up and butted in? Aw, the hell with that. Bailey had probably slammed him plenty to Allene . . . told about seeing him with other girls, or the night he almost broke the glass door at the Celtic Grill. Allene hadn't sud-denly become cold for no reason at all, and when a man was nuts about a girl he used every trick he knew, to cut the other fellows out—it was in the blood of his sex alright.

"What's the matter, did you catch somebody cheating on you . . . dear?"—Rea lengthened the last word, with obvious sarcasm, and began, in a low voice, to sing the chorus of a song called "It's The Talk Of The Town," a hit in which one lover reproached the other for having made his desertion a subject of common gos-sip and implored the unfaithful one to return. The taunt decided McCormick—'what was the other dame to him, except a fairly good-looking pick-up, and now she had the nerve to . . .' He walked over to Allene and Bailey. Rea, Nelson, and Magdalene followed, uncertainly, with Nelson whispering hastily to the women in an effort to give them some inkling of the situation. The greetings were humorous. Al, groggy at the sight of Allene, spoke to her with an abashed swagger—respectful desire making the roughneck strive to follow his notion of a gentleman enriched by liquor—and ignored Bailey after he wrenched politeness of a "hello, how are you, kid?" Ray answered, stiffly, and felt murderous, laughed at the feeling and still found that it was clogging him in a scattered way, like a broken ax with its pieces wedged into the most sensitive parts of the heart. Nelson was fidgeting, just perceptibly affable, to be on McCormick's side and yet seem to be reasonably neutral. Outwardly, Rea showed the acme of sulky unconcern, beneath which she bared her teeth at Allene, without knowing why, except that the new girl might be too sure of her ground with a swell boy, to whom Rea, in her opinion, had first claim—'a man was obliged to stay with a girl, right after he had handled her so darn intimate too, and this blondie here had better . . . watch . . . her . . . step.' Magdalene, recovered from the fear of arrest, was alone naturally stolid—if the dances and, well, another nip, materialized, she didn't care how large the party became.

"Why don't you sit down and join us awhile, Al?"—Allene's emotions made a crazy-quilt covering the duplicates of words which she could not find.

The sight of McCormick, with another girl grasping his fore-arm, gave her a mixed-up pique and insincere resentment, like that of a child, who didn't actually want the candy-shelf and yet had no desire for the new child to want it so much that she herself might be compelled to attach a renewed value to it. Artifice had been drummed into her since her birth—admonishings from her mother and other elders that no courting male would be consider-ate and faithful if she revealed her loving reliance too plainly—the warnings which the flutter of a coquette, within her, had always accepted, smilingly. Again, McCormick's unvarnished manners, never seriously violating her idea of refinement and backed by straight shoulders and strong arms, had given her a physical agi-tation, growing and weakening, by turns, until Ray's advent had brought her an even greater sexual drunkenness and an inarticulate reaching toward him, 'because he had ambitions and was tramping the streets so patiently, and kissing him was like sipping brandy without getting a hangover, and he was ill-tempered about certain things but always cut it short with such a nice line of joking, and . . . but those weren't the reasons. Something turned on the music and the electric light in the dark room, that was all that she knew, and yet . . . . McCormick was a fine boy too—so strong, and seemed to know what to do with his hands, and he had a blaze in his eyes never standing for nonsense.'

She was still talking to McCormick, who had pitched himself on the grass beside her, with Ray on the other side, Rea balancing her slanting torso with one hand, inches to his right, and Magdalene and Nelson perched behind the others. Ray's face worked, like an angry man chewing gum to remain nonchalant and failing. Flirts, every damn one of them . . . almost. It was tiresome. A man didn't want a woman to crawl to him, in chains—if the woman was young and good-looking, the temptation to act rotten toward her, to revenge himself for slaps given by other women, was too powerful in such a case, and it made him thoroughly dislike himself afterwards. No he didn't want any woman to crawl, but by God, the other extreme was even worse. So, Allene was deliberately indicating that there might be an even chance of losing her, that she couldn't control the desire to make other fellows hop to her tune and hope for her approval, just after she had pasted her mouth on his face over a dozen times on this particular night. Well, ignore her, sure, and play up to what's her name, Rea, he guessed. He hated to make it a game but he wasn't going to be trampled on by anyone. He talked to Rea. She was scarcely friendly at first—casual, vexed, forced in her smiles—but her attitude became more and more intensely naked, increased by dagger glances at McCormick when she thought that Ray was not watching her. 'She hardly knew this Al chunk—he might even be a prize slice of cheese, too—but no man could hug her, agree to take her out, and then turn straight off to another girl and get away with it, not if she could help it! If she got up and walked off, he'd know that she was angry over him and feel big about it, and this other fellow, Ray, looked like a pretty competent customer, probably good and sore at Al for crashing in, as he had every right to be.'

McCormick and Allene were busy in the trade of words.

"What have you got on for Sunday night?"

"I think it'll be my rose crêpe de chine with the velvet tassels and . . . oh, a few other things."

"Stop the kidding, will you? I want to take you out Sunday night."

"I can't, I have another date."

"Well, Tuesday then. How about Tuesday?"

"I don't know. Maybe, Al. Ring me up Monday evening and I'll tell you definitely."

"Listen, that's not fair and you know it. You don't have to stall *me*, Allie—I can take it. If you don't want to go places with me any more, you can just hand me the bad news and we'll both forget about it, see?"

In the silence now, Allene was rattled down to her bones, self-preening—the least bit—and dismally repentant as she threw a quick look, over her shoulder, toward Ray. She was in love with Ray, almost sure that she was, but McCormick was physically pleasing and his insistence flattered her because she knew that he was not unpopular with the girls of her neighborhood, and he could take her out to shows, treat her to a midnight-lunch and a taxi home, while Ray, poor dear, could never do anything except walk around with her and love her on a park bench, or the few times when she took a chance slipping up to his room . . . and it *was* sweet just the same . . . but a girl wanted a good time so much, so, so much, and she just got sick at heart when her own lover could never give her more than an icecream-soda on the quarter she slipped him below the counter.

"You're a good kid, Al."

"That's not answering me."

"Well, phone me tomorrow around seven then, and I'll let you know positive."

"It's oke with me . . . sweetness."

"Get along with you, I'm as sour as . . . as sauerkraut juice, these days."

"Oh yeah? Not to me, you're not—but what's wrong, Allie girl?"

"Oh, it's that darn, nerve-wracking, finicky office of mine. It was absolutely boiling there all day long, and they simply won't put the fan right behind my desk where it would do some good, and the way he yells if I make the slightest mistake—"

"Fan, huh? That's a hot one, to me. Why say, listen—I sweated nine hours today and the only fan I had was the supe's tongue fanning me plenty because I came back late from the route. They expect a man to cover twenty-five deliveries, get out of all the traffic jams, carry a load of blankets and camping outfits for a bunch of lucky stiffs going on their vacations, yeah . . . and then drive back in time for the afternoon haul. Baby, I'm telling you—what they don't expect isn't in the books!"

"Well, I haven't the muscle to do your work, but if you think it's a bed of violets to strain your eyes out and pound the keys all day long, with an old growl-patch giving dictation so fast you can hardly take it—well, try it once, that's all."

"Listen, I'm not one to look down on brains and I know you've got to shake the old bean alright, but I still claim a guy can't carry a fan with him when he's piling it on and off the truck. Believe me, I've been sweating off a pound a day this week."

McCormick grinned, with respect and a relaxing affection showing through the cruder lust brought by his drinks, but the grin was also the effort to disregard defeat—a man, only a hireling, seeing no clear escape, no future promise of any kind, and posing to himself as one among many exhausted, sturdy kings, who worked their hides out because it proved their manhood and gave them a little money for girls and fairly decent clothes. 'If he threw over his job tomorrow, he wouldn't starve—don't worry, he knew the ropes.'

Allene swung her head toward Ray, fearful and yet hoping to joke it away, and said: "Hey, Mister Bailey, d'you know that you've been neglecting me terribly?" Ray, talking to Rea at the time, feigned that he had not heard the words, or felt Allene's fingers on his wrist, and Allene smarted, started another remark, changed her mind, and wanted to convince herself that she was being ill-treated—'after all, she had known Al for months and gone out with him time and again, whereas Ray was scarcely acquainted with the other girl, and furthermore, if he still doubted her loyalty after she had risked a howl of a scene with her parents by slipping up to his room twice during the past week, he must have a smaller nature than she had imagined.' Stung and guilt-ridden in a femininity too tired to think much on this night, her head tossed as she turned and resumed the hiding and banter with McCormick.

Ray and Rea were imitating a furious interest in one another, joined by the desire to retaliate against their respective partners, but in Rea it was only irritation and chemical attraction toward another, glued by drinks—a man whom she might never see again—while Ray was actually hurt, with all of his cynicism, so artificially nourished by the past, pinning down the more trusting resistances in his heart. 'Here she was, sparring with McCormick and on the verge of making a theatre-date with him—the girl who had been promising to love another man throughout the present night—*almost* love him, what a dodge that was. He'd heard it several times in *his* day. It *almost* tempted a man to believe that love was only the word they signed at the bottom of the profit-side of the ledger in Tin Pan Alley, for after all, he had really loved three times in his life—the genuine, hot-and-cold, heart-splitting article—and what had they given him? Maria Alten—what a fine name to make him thoughtful as well as gloomy. It was nine years ago, a little more than nine, and when she found out she had t.b. she disappeared completely, without even writing a letter—poor, sweet, timid *Maria-kind* . . . his nickname . . . and she could talk more with her black eyes, in one second, than other girls could in a hundred . . .'

"We were all going to Roseland tonight, but maybe it's too late."

Ray shielded his nickel watch before he slipped it back to the front trouser-pocket.

"I think there's still time—it's only twelve and the place stays open until three, you know,"—Ray cursed inside.

A man in New York without a cent to his name was in a prison-cell with a rope tying his ankles together, even though they seemed to be giving him the privilege of walking down the streets.

"D'you dance a lot?"—Rea gave him an inviting look, as she wielded her lipstick.

"Oh, whenever I have a chance."

"I'll just bet you're a dancing fool—I can tell every time."

"Well, I wouldn't say exactly that, but I haven't any glue on my feet either."

"Gee, I wish I could shake this crowd up to doing something—it's a shame. I'm not going to sit here and be bitten by 'squit'es all night, not me."

A pause.

"Are you working at anything?"

"Am I *working*? Honest, when I get through behind the counter at that darn lunch-room of mine, I feel like I'd been playing football in a Turkish bath, and I mean it. What kind of a job have you got?"

Ray checked himself on the verge of a petty lie—what would be the use of bluffing, with only a dime in his pocket?

"I'm not doing anything now. I'm just waiting for a good opportunity to come along. I've done a lot of work clerking in different hotels."

"Well, let me tell you, you're lucky if you can afford to wait. Down at the Roscoe where I am, they fired one of the girls the other day and then they put an ad in the paper, and honest, I never saw anything like it in all my life."

"Like what?"

"Why, the rush they had was simply terrible. Even after they hired the first one, the poor girls kept on trooping in all day long.

There must have been at least thirty of them, and honest, it made me feel down in the mouth just to see them walking in and out, all the time."

The portent in her words, emphasizing the possibility of another day of fruitless tramping, forced Ray into a vaguely expressed and yet frantic optimism.

"Oh well, there's one blessing anyway—things can't become much worse, and they're bound to get better with the good, old N.R.A. putting it over. Shorter hours and more jobs, that's the tonic we need alright, but . . . of course it's bound to be a slow process of recovery. The whole country was in bad shape when Roosevelt took hold."

Rea was silent. Her lunch-room had an N.R.A. card in the window, but its only import in her life had been a raise of two dollars a week—fifty cents deducted for cleaning the aprons—and an eight hour day stretched to nine, or ten, by devices such as a tacit hint "to come down a little earlier, if you can," and unpaid overtime work classified as "voluntary service for the good of the business." Besides the three letters represented a deep subject, to her—one of the little understood schemes and announcements issuing from the shadowy upper world of rulers, to which she gave a weak and frightened awe because it was so far away from her and yet so potent—the talkative dignitaries at Washington, the police-heads and generals whom she had seen parading down Fifth Avenue. She was out for a night of fun and she wanted to forget "deep things" and the yelling, stuffy, hurrying lunch-room day awaiting her.

"Oh, things will improve, I guess. They've got to"—her voice was stagey and impatient.

She turned and pulled McCormick's sleeve.

"Say listen . . . are we going to sit here all night? It's getting late, and I thought we were going to dance somewhere."

Magdalene and Nelson had already risen, followed by Ray. McCormick, muddled and self-accusing, despite his equally tense desire "to cut Ray out" with Allene, thought that a dance-hall would be a good change of scene, in which he could continue his play for her, and if the night ended in a fight with Bailey, 'he'd take care of that guy, never worry.' He jumped to his feet and grasped Allene's arms, helping her to rise. As he performed the same service for Rea, Ray was boiling over—the sight of McCormick's hands pressing into Allene's arms and the fondling, reluctant way in which he removed them brought a hot uproar to Ray's chest, to his mind.

"I think I'll be leaving you now, Miss Baum. I don't believe you'll miss me much, and I hope you'll have a pleasant time dancing tonight."

He started to walk off, with bitterness twitching in the forced calmness of his face, but Allene, dizzily remorseful, self-hating, and almost frightened—jerked from the coquettish ether back to the reality of sharper emotion—darted after him and tugged at one of his shoulders, during his first few strides. He wheeled, with an elaborately affected surprise on his face, to ease the tortured pride.

"Ray, you're acting like a school-kid, honest."

"Yes? Well, if I am, you're carrying a slate under your own arm too, old girl."

"I'm sorry if I've hurt you, Ray. I didn't mean to."

"Oh, don't mind me—go ahead and have a good time."

She drew nearer and lowered her voice.

"Don't be jealous, dear—you know what I feel for you."

"Yes, I thought I knew but you certainly have a poor way of showing it."

"You mean talking over a date with Al?"

"What else could I mean? And not only that, but you seemed to forget I was alive, the minute he walked over."

A faltering silence held them, with Allene miserably hunting within herself for some utterance that would be loving and yet not abased, in the intense desire to placate him, while Ray, shifting on his feet, clung to the frown to hide the turmoil of inward hesitancies. McCormick watched the other two with a suffusion of scowling embarrassment interfering with his possessive plans, refusing to admit and yet being overborne by the suspicion that Allene was really 'nuts about the other guy': remembering Rea with disdain and guiltiness interpenetrated: and saying to himself—his brain surfaced by the wiseacre journalese of his time—that most dames, by God, were so damn fickle they made a pair of bones look like six percent, guaranteed Government bonds. Rea spoke.

"What are *you* in a trance about?"

"Oh nothing."

"Nothing is right, with blonde hair too."

"Keep your opinion to yourself."

"Alright then, I'll be seeing you some time next year if that's—"

"Aw, I didn't mean to insult you, funny-eyes."

"You better say that, believe me, because *I'm* not going to be a parlor-rug for any man."

"Alright, alright, don't blow about it—I took it back, didn't I?"

Magdalene was begging Nelson to leave with her and without the others—still fearful of even a hint of trouble in its relation to the possible loss of her job—and Nelson was undecided, not averse to departing but afraid of McCormick.

"Ray, you've simply got to be reasonable, please. I like Al, sure, but that's positively, cross my heart, positively all he means to me."

"Then why do you shine up to him every time you meet him?"

"Ray, you're not being fair. You won't let me pay for your tickets to a real show, and if I go out to the theatre with another man, it's just because I can't afford to pay my own way. Honest, that's all there is to it."

Ray softened a bit, with his anger still justified to itself but beginning to be pushed out by the desire not to risk losing her.

"Well, we'll talk about it later—there're too many ears around here to suit me."

They returned to the others, Ray trying to be sullenly composed and Allene relieved but still a little apprehensive. McCormick and Ray gave each other a straight look for the first time since their cut-and-dried greetings on the lawn. Al was tight-jawed and peeved, in the imminence of defeat, but unable to find a reason more specific than that of a checkmated jealousy. Ray frowned without decision, feeling that Al, because of his rude intrusion upon a loving pair, deserved a good shellacking, but by no means certain that he was powerful enough to give it to him. Nelson, slapping Al's back, made an effort 'to smooth things over' because, after quietness came, he might find a pretext for slipping away with Magdalene, after which he could culminate his resolve "to make her" at all cost, to revel in a delicious postponement of the grocery-store ache.

"Why don't you two fellows make up instead of being sore-heads?—let's all have a good time dancing and cutting up, what d'you say?'"

The blunder made the quarrel a recognized issue between Al and Ray, and induced them to quicken their pugnacity, since other-wise they might have sulked, measured each other up, and waited for additional excuses, until the later hours of the morning. Al coveted Allene because he considered her to be a regular girl and yet a respectable one—willing to fool around in a physical way, to be a good sport, but refusing to yield herself entirely until she was certain of the man's fondness and her own, since, if a man went seriously with a girl and even thought of marrying her, he wanted her to be "lively and fun-loving, and yet not too easy," in Al's outlook. 'Damn it, Allie was like butterscotch melting . . . now why the hell did a guy, pretty tough on the whole, put on his baby-clothes whenever a girl really . . . mm, say, it might not be a bad idea to wipe that nasty look from Bailey's face. Bailey thought he had the upper hand now, so he was starting to sneer, was he?'

"I'm no sorehead, but I know who is"—Al's eyes were riveted on Ray.

Ray grew hot inside—'after he had forced himself between a pair, sweet and all by their lonesome out on the grass, and played up to the woman, this fellow, knowing that he had lost out, for the night anyway, was trying to pick a scrap now—the lousy sport. If it wasn't for the advantage McCormick had in reach and height . . .'

"Are you talking about me, McCormick?"

"No, it's a brother who looks just like you."

"Yeah? Well, just imagine he's here now—don't let me stop you."

"Ray, please, honey, please—let's be moving along. It's getting terribly late and I don't want to waste the whole night out here"— Allene, snatching his hand, was scared without confessing it to herself, and angry at herself, too, in the swing of quickening heart-beats. Ray pulled her hand away, scarcely hearing her words and concentrating on McCormick with fear and rancor struggling near the brink of decision. Magdalene, yanking every part of Nelson's coat which she could reach, increased the intensity of her whispers and implored him to hurry off with her, but feeling delightfully safe, he enjoyed the prospect of watching a possible fight between two other men—as much as he denied the relish in his conscious mind— and also, with a moderate, hang-dog loyalty to Al, his resented but adulated superior in muscles, he hoped to see Bailey wind up flat on the grass . . . 'that guy thought entirely too much of himself.' McCormick spoke again only because his fists were waiting for a more direct insult.

"That's a swell idea, Bailey, and now I'll ask *you* something— why didn't you slam me to my face instead of waiting until Allene chased after you?"

"Ray, *please*, we've got to—"

"Don't bother me"—Ray interrupted Allene, without turning his head, and wrenched her fingers from his nearest arm. He was exploding from vein to vein but still the least quivering fraction apart from action.

"Listen you, I wasn't knocking you to her, even after she stopped me, but I'll start in right now. You're going to get your face burnt some day, sticking it into other people's business."

"Yeah? Who's the bird that'll burn it for me—you?"

Rea intervened. Fuming at McCormick's neglect she had been smiling meanly, with her glances circling the distant lights and buildings, to convey indifference to him, but she realized that a fight might only be a matter of seconds now, and she remembered the shady bench, so recently deserted, and close to the pent-up tremors of youth in her hardboiled breast—'gee, but he had been nice and soft to her, this bruiser, and never too fresh when she wouldn't let him . . . the roughneck boy . . . and the other girl must be a former sweetheart of his, and *she* had led him on plenty, too, the whitish haired cat.' She stepped in front of Al, squeezed his chin.

"Al, I don't want you to fight him, it isn't fair. That blonde-haired meeow over there was doing her darnedest to make both of you jealous. Oh, I'm wise to her alright, even if you aren't."

McCormick believed that Rea was attempting to protect him, with the idea that he would be defeated in any fistic exchange with Ray, and the imagined slur was added fuel.

"Say, if you think I can't lick this guy"—he spun Rea back with such force that she staggered and would have fallen, if Nelson had not supported her.

Ray and McCormick were now only inches away from one another, and Allene, her eyes rotating between each man, locked her fingers around a little cambric handkerchief and was close to hysteria.

"Well, get busy, guy, I'm waiting"—McCormick's lips were rubber bands against the gritting of his teeth.

The men swung uppercuts. Ray missed, and McCormick's right thudded squarely under the left side of Ray's chin. Reeling back, Ray clipped a left to McCormick's chest, but the blow lacked steam, and in a savage rat-tat Al landed a left and a right flush on Ray's mouth, sending him to his haunches, with blood squirting from a swollen lower lip. Ray attempted to regain his feet, but his head felt like a fire in a brickyard, and he struck the turf again, with a thump which twisted one of his ankles. His face was a study in stunned but unde-terred enmity as he pawed feebly at the grass, still hazily obsessed by the longing to get to his feet, because, though he lacked the kill-er's insensitivity reputed to be the only full measure of animal cour-age, he was nevertheless relentless in the defensive instinct to strike back as long as a wisp of consciousness remained—the only actual approach to bravery.

Allene was convinced that Al would stay until Ray was on his feet again, and that the fight would continue and result in the further beating of her lover, and the hysteria within her died, suddenly. If Ray had stood over the recumbent body of Al, now, she would have been almost neutral, deviating only in the flick of a salute to his muscular competence, but his dangerous position produced within her the reflective calmness of an erring mother—practical, unscrupulous, and determined to repent for her recent flirtation by rescuing the prone child. It was in her nature to feel enviously inferior to a man in his physical triumphs and at least lightly sympathetic toward his defeats of the same kind, unless she was beginning to love him, in which case the sympathy became intense and alertly loyal in every fibre. She hastened to McCormick, leaned slightly against his side.

"You mustn't hurt him any more, Al—oh, you mustn't. If you do, I'll never speak another *word* to you all my life—and I mean it. You ring me up at six tomorrow, at the house—I wish mother didn't have this bug against my going with Gentile boys, but slip down to the drugstore and ring me up anyway, six sharp, and we'll make a big night of it, oh, a honey of a night, really we will . . . but you've got to leave without me now. He's my escort for tonight and I simply can't ditch him now. I'd be such a rotten sport if I did, Al . . . you understand."

Rea overheard the words and stepped forward to hand Allene 'the tongue-whipping of her life,' but checked herself with a wry look. She wanted Al to herself—if only for the pleasure of slapping him and then disappearing, she hadn't decided—and so, 'if this deceitful, rotten little trouble-maker wanted him to leave, too, in her effort to keep a hold on both men, well, so much the better.' Al was flattered, surfeited with success, and—with the effects of the booze slowly decreasing—he had even a germ of patronizing sympathy for Ray—'the poor, windy boob had been sore and jealous, naturally, and he'd remember *those* socks for some time to come, the bastard.' Al was not innately over-cruel, but the excess was super-imposed by his life—taking commands and abuse from men over him and straining his flesh for a relatively scant pay-envelope, with necessities, booze, girls, devouring it before the end of each week, he had been forced into the only importance remaining, which was that of the iron-knuckled, rollicking master among certain kinds of women, and the fistic challenger of all men except those actually ruling his wrenched-out existence.

"It's all the same to me, Allie—if you want to stay with a combo of a glass jaw and a big mouth, you go right ahead. I'll see you in church tomorrow night—we'll have to press the buzzer four short and one long before we can get in, but that's the fault of the cops. They don't know that the guy who runs it used to be a preacher in one of those little burgs upstate. I'll be seeing you Allie—ring you at six on the dot, and get your best rags out too, what I mean."

Smiling at what he considered to be an excellent, all-around joke, he grabbed Rea's arm and marched her off, just as Ray wobbled to his feet. Magdalene and Nelson had started a few seconds previous, after she had hurried away first, thus compelling Nelson to follow her. Ray lurched in the direction of McCormick, who was already several strides distant, but Allene, wrestling and supplicating, blocked his progress, foot by foot, until Al and the others were no larger than doll-figures in the palely murky electric lights over a far-off walk sprinkled with tree-tips and indistinct shrubberies. Then she made him walk forward, slowly, and she rubbed his mouth, gingerly, with her little 'kerchief, and continued her efforts to pacify him.

"I'm sticking with you, Ray—always. Don't you ever, ever worry about that, honey dear."

"Stick to *him* for all I care. You're going out with him tomorrow night anyway."

"I am not—that was just a stall to get rid of him."

"Oh, it was. Well, why didn't you leave that job to me when I wanted to get even with him just now?"

"Because he's so much stronger than you are, Ray, and I didn't want to see you beaten up any more, oh, I couldn't see it, Ray, even if you were brave enough to . . . to want to chase after him."

"Stronger, hell. He clipped me a lucky blow before I could get the old machine started and he was crowding me so much I couldn't land a good return, and not only that, but if you must know the truth, I haven't had anything but a cup of coffee and a single dough-nut all day long."

"But Ray, you told me you had a meal late this afternoon."

"Sure I told you that. Don't you think I get sick and tired of sponging on you all the time?"

Tears gathered in Allene's eyes, without dropping. It was not so much pity for him—men, until old age, were expected to prove their worth by fighting adversities and "coming out on top," according to the message driven into her by her elders since her birth—but it was the beginning of a realization that she, Ray, and so many other people, were held down, and soured, and pushed around, by just one thing, lack of money, money, money—the great, sickening tom-tom, flesh-pulverizer, the grinning siren always chased by millions of calloused hands with broken, dirty fingernails, always pursued to the last swish of heart-beats and cruelly evading them, or cap-tured only in tantalizing bits with no hope of increase, no incentive except the lure of "saving up enough to start a business." 'God, her own father had been forced to give up his little tailor-shop, years ago, when the gorilla crowd over in Brooklyn kept on smashing his windows because he couldn't afford to pay them fifteen a month. Hurray for America, for its government and its institutions too— bet your boots on that—but still, New York was crowded with too many smelly raw-deals, too many mean rackets, to suit her taste.'

As they walked along, she plucked at Ray's nearest hand, inter-mittently, and his only reply was to widen the distance between them. He thought that Allene pitied and yet despised him as a rel-ative weakling, whose mouth was much faster and stronger than his arms, and that she was hiding the totter of her love because she felt that he had already been sufficiently hurt on this night, and his mind and heart held a swirling obsession now—corner Al McCormick before the end of the week and pay him back . . . with compound interest and right square on his dirty face, yep, right in the middle of it.

III

MORRIS BAUM had a jellied, backward face with a brown moustache trimmed to a string, sparse lips straightened by worries, and a nose shaped like the droop of a morning-glory, and the lightest tap on the nose was sufficient to draw blood, as Morris had rediscovered earlier on this Sunday afternoon when one of his nephews, a boy of five, seated in his lap, had struck him, playfully, and spattered his white shirt. In a clean shirt now, he was rendering an old, popular waltz, "Three O'Clock In The Morning," on his piccolo, with a machine-like gusto, as though the mouthpiece held a message far beyond the minor, silken lilt of the notes borne from the nickel stops by his fingers. He was a nightlife blade leading his fellows and their girls on, forever revolving, dipping, fusing, until the floor became a plateau and the dancers assumed an ownership over the entire earth and proved it in every motion. He was back in 1909, long before the Irving Berlin waltz had been created—frisky, steel-knuckled, struggling for kisses in dim parlors, and bursting out with material plan and hope. With his piccolo, at night and on Sunday afternoons, he could blow himself, briefly, far away from the past and present facts of his life.

Through a period of twenty years he had conducted nine small tailor-shops scattered through Boston, Philadelphia, and New York, and each of them had failed—bankrupt-closures, dishonest partners, sessions in a hospital caused by liver-trouble and overwork, and years previous, the systematic wrecking of the last shop by a politically backed hoodlum whom he had chased out of his shop, with a pair of shears, because the latter, one evening, had made a drunken entrance and attempted to squeeze Allene, then only nineteen. In between these ventures, he had worked in garment-lofts as a cutter and stinted himself and his family to save, painfully, another two hundred dollars for another dream of success, ham-strung almost before the start. The family reins had slipped from his hands now. Fanny had been conducting the Chelsea rooming-house for five years and had amassed nearly two-thousand dollars, which reposed in a neighborhood bank, and Morris labored only three days a week at reduced wages, a situation in which he could no longer remain the boss because, in his world, the male parent was no longer respected after he had proven himself a failure as a provider, money-getter. In such a finale, he might still be treated with tolerant affection but he could not expect the silent attention and strict obedience, which he had formerly received. It soaked the very air of his environs. Money alone was authority and the broken-down pursuer of it, stumbling well into middle-age, could not hope for more than an occasionally irritable leniency, even from relatives and intimates. On an average of twice a week, the familiar quarrel resumed, with Morris berating Fanny for her refusal to loan him enough from her bank-account to open a small shop and Fanny stridently citing his past defeats in this line and asserting that she would rather "put a match to the money and have it over with." The "aunts" and "uncles"—a brother and sister on each side, living in New York—sympathized with Fanny and thought that Morris was likable and yet too much of an easy-going, piccolo-tooting *schlemiel*, and of the entire family, Allene alone, in her attitudes toward him, was moderately different. She sighed over his lack of shrewdness and sometimes chided him for it, but she was convinced that he was generous, and as honest as his life had permitted him to be—two relative qualities which she admired and the other members of the family despised while pretending to admire them. In this regard, of course, she meant larger honesties, contrary to the little over-charges, false eulogies of quality in goods, and persistent bargain-drivings, which she accepted as part of the matter-of-fact deception in "business-life."

The semi-basement had two bedrooms, a parlor, living-room, and kitchen leading to the backyard where a plot of nasturtiums and fringes of grass were weakened in their contrast with a pile of empty crates and cardboard containers with wood-shavings curling out, a high wooden fence unpainted and engraved with dirt around the knot-holes, and bits of rubbish which some of the roomers persisted in throwing from their windows, since they had no incentive for treating, with any loving care, the drably cramped abode in which they lived only because the rent was cheap.

Rose Kirstner poked her head through the gray and orange flowered, cotton-print hangings which divided parlor from living-room. Four years under her brother's forty-five, her face was a joke on girlhood, with lips shellacked in crimson, cheeks rubbed near to the hue of wax apples on a white tablecloth, and plucked and darkened eyebrows under the bob of blondined hair streaked with brown strands growing again, and the short fulness of her body bound by brassiere and girdle was forever in a flounce in a chase of the sugar-dripping idea of romance, which still pestered her, hidden within all of the clutchings, the irritations and practicalities of her life.

"Morris, I swear, we can hear you so loud out in the yard we can't hold it even a good conversation! D'you hear me, Morris?—stop playing for a while. You're driving us crazy!"

"Noo, I wouldn't have to drive you so far"—Morris's smile indicated that he was joking.

"Not with you around."

"Hmm, music you don't appreciate."

"One solid hour of the piccolo, that's enough to appreciate. Give us a little rest."

"But when you hens sit around the parlor here and cluck-cluck-cluck my head off, I have to listen, don't I?"

"You could take a nice walk then, Morris—nobody would stop you"—Rose had trotted into the parlor and was biting her lips, crossly.

She noticed a stain on her long, skittishly low-necked, pale green rayon dress and she scratched it in an accompaniment to her words. Morris sighed and deposited the piccolo on top of the old, upright piano, some of whose keys had lost their ivory pieces.

"I could play chopsticks on the piano. Maybe you would like that better, Rose."

"Go out and buy us some chop-suey, Morris, and never mind all your chop-stick foolishness."

Morris had risen and was looking at her, annoyance courted by intended humor.

"Only three hours ago you ate a meal like a horse—mmm, what a meal you ate, and now you would be willing—"

"Oh, shut up, I never—"

"No wonder you have to wear girdles, Rose—"

"Shut up—I lost over two pounds this week and what's more—"

"Are you sure you put both of the feet on the scales?"

"You are not funny, Morris, so please be quiet. If you are so anxious for music, you can take us up to 'The Capitol' where we could all enjoy ourselves. They got a swell picture on—'The Right To Love,' with Mila Marbo, and we heard the orchestra there last week and it was positively wonderful!"

Morris filled his pipe and sought to feel genially bored, to circumvent the formless, unrecognized weight, deep, slow-growing accumulation in his heart.

"You want to go to a movie on a hot day like—"

"But they have the air-cooling system, just like taking a trip up to Canada and yet you are sitting snug in your—"

"Hmm, better they should invent a system for paying the money for the tickets. Seventy-five cents is too much to pay for a balcony-seat, especial in the times we got now, it's too much, and besides, they are always boosting up the prices on Sunday because it's the only day a poor workingman can—"

"I didn't come in to hear you talk politics."

"So what did you come in for—to nag me?"

Rose lifted and drew back her hands, palms outward, in a smiling vexation on the verge of not smiling.

"Well, it certainly wouldn't hurt you to be more attentive to the family, Morris. You never take *Allieschen* and Fanny out any more, and if they are invited to a nice party, every time, ev-er-y ti-ime, they got to drag you by both feet. All you want to do is read the paper and make the neighbors holler with your old, squeaky piccolo, or maybe a game auction pinochle and then you sit—"

"Hold your tongue, you make me sick"—Morris was suddenly infuriated.

For years on end he had wielded the needles, shears, flat-iron, and steam-press, in the determination to support his family, and had even made them gifts of modest furs, adornments, seats for popular musical-revues, during the brief times when his shops were going good. On the whole, he thought that he had been a decent man, despite his very occasional, outside trysts with sex, after Fanny had begun to grow fatter, with gathering lines on her face, and after the impact of her coal-heaver's voice forever burying him under the accusation of stupidities and business-failures—'God, a man was human, wasn't he?—and now this sister of his was also rubbing it in because he could no longer aid his family on the eight, or nine dollars a week, which he earned, while her own man had political pull and made at least seventy-five a week and was one of the main assistants at one of the Home Relief Bureaus—a good man to his family, but a high-class crook otherwise, if there ever was one.' Unaware of the larger causes behind his predicament, Morris translated them into a spleen against the entire feminine sex—'the women!'

Rose, who had been babbling complacently, according to habit, with her mind scarcely operating, and with harmless irritations serving, principally, for purposes of entertainment, became equally furious, and a torrent of words resulted.

"I make you sick—a fine way to talk to your sister!"

"Is that so? Well, I repeat it. Just because your Looie is in with all the grafters, you think—"

"You leave him out of it. He's got a head on his shoulders and that's more than you've got, and besides, every week he takes me out—"

"Yup, he could afford it, with the soft snap he's—"

"Oh, shut up, will you? You are trying to excuse yourself by knocking my Looie because he is so much smarter than you are. Don't tell me. You are angry because my Looie has a pile of swell friends, some of the real, big people of the city, but you, who do you know? Nothing but a bunch of failures just like yourself—a bunch of cheapskates, that's all they are. You make me tired. Look at poor Fanny—she works like a slave, like a *slave* every day of the week she cleans all the rooms and the hallways in the house here, and yet, never once do you take her out, never once do you give her a little pleasure, and *Allieschen*, she has to sit by the typewriter when other girls—"

"Enough, enough!"—Morris was appalled by the flow of words. 'Who could compete with a woman's tongue, no matter how right he was? They had absolutely no use for a man when he stopped making money, and he could be the worst robber on earth but he was still an angel to them, as long as he didn't get arrested. Over twenty years ago, this sister of his was calling him a smart boy and asking him to run down to the telephone on the corner, Twentieth and Second Avenue, so she could tell one of her boys she would be late—a ride was a big treat then—so she could fool the strict papa, God rest his soul in peace—but *now* . . . the sight of Allene calmed him, partly. When she waded into him it was usually playful, he thought, and she didn't try to smother him with lying words but she went after some of his real, small weaknesses—his continual losses at cards, his table manners, or jokes a little too raw—yes, Allie was a good, sweet girl and yet, even with her, he couldn't stand the way she ran around with *schakitz* fellows and came home sometimes

at four, or five, in the morning, fine hours for a respectable girl to
be coming back! and he suspected that she was having something
to do with men, only once in a great while, but even then, it wasn't
right. A girl could fool around with boys to a fair extent, certainly,
but if she went farther, she was definitely bad then, no matter how
much she hid it, and there was always the danger of getting a dis-
ease—Doc Rosalsku had told him plenty about some of the rotten
boys in *their* neighborhood!'

Allene had succeeded in pacifying the contestants to a stage
where Rose was sniffing, mumbling half to herself, and against all
the vacillations of an inner grumble, telling herself that, after all,
Morris was part of her own flesh-and-blood circle and must be for-
given, especially since he had always been decent to Fanny in one
connection—never ran about with other women on the sly and
never a heavy drinker, cursing and breaking up the furniture early
in the morning—yes, that much she would have to say for him. In
her life, clannishness and material spites, moderate affections and
their snoring, unconscious counterparts, engaged in a free-for-all
far more subtle, at bottom, than all of the smug-shallow layers of
her conscious self dared to perceive. Morris was once more uncertain, thrown between his dying spleens and the desire to wallow in
blessed rest on this late Sunday afternoon, far from defences and
frictions, from the numerous questions, both specific and vaguely
massive, which he could neither answer nor, at best, quite dismiss.

Allene, in her long-skirted, white satine with elbow-length
sleeves and "old-fashioned" broad ruffles at the bottom, together
with the shortness of her body, looked like a high-school girl about
to step on the platform and deliver properly praising inanities in
behalf of the graduating-class and the secretly bored faculty. She
was nervous, filled with hidden thoughts and doing her best to
cover them with a smile, as she spoke to her father.

"Now, honestly, don't you think you're silly, pops?"

"Sure, to a woman a man is always—"

"But that's not it. You know what I mean. Every time Aunt

Rosie comes down here you two always wind up by tearing into each other, and what for? You've had it out tens of times, both of you, and it doesn't make either one of you any happier."

"Well, if he can't talk with a little respect to his own sister who—"

"Get out, you're just as much to blame as pops is. When pops was making money he used to take us out, regularly, but he can't do it now and he's too darn proud to let us treat him, the old fatty. I know him."

She pinched her father's cheek and he said: "Get away with you, who was talking about pride?" but his voice was grudgingly pleased and the small, straight lips rubbed against one another slightly. Emotionally starved and hindered, he lingered on the savor of the sentimental crumbs. Allene, on her part, had only been uttering words emptied to a resemblance of sweetness, to chase away a quarrel so familiar that it was now only a farce, to her. Rose, fanning herself in the squat, black leatherine armchair, which had withstood eight years of family use with only one of the springs protruding, looked at Allene and Morris with a rueful simper, the sign of another flitting truce between her malices, never visible to their own outpourings, and the fidelities of blood poisoned, sugared with artifice, woefully jumbled and expelled in every beat of her heart.

"Well, he shouldn't be so foolish then. I always did say it—it's certainly not a disgrace to be poor and Morris should realize the whole family is only too willing to help him out. I bet you everything I've got that Looie would be only too glad to make him a loan so he could start in business again, but if he don't ask, what then? Looie isn't a mind-reader, y' know, and I couldn't say anything myself without Morris's permission."

"Why should I take it from him, when Fanny has it in the bank and could easy give it to me? That's nonsense, that I should go begging to my brother-in-law when my own wife turns me down"—in spite of the aggrieved syllables, Morris manufactured a glow, told himself that his sister was more thoughtless than mean, and after all, it was natural for a woman to feel big and important when her man had a good position and could keep up a nice home, and bring her expensive presents, take her to some of those mahogany nests on West End Avenue, spin her out to the country in a fine, polished car—women were the delicate, the soft sex, and, of course, they liked a fine surrounding to set them off, like a ruby on a swell, gold mounting, maybe. The dull, cheap effort to poetize—not cheap to itself in the depth of Morris's need—spent its devices. The glow was killed by Fanny's loud voice travelling from the living room.

"Yes, I got it safe in the bank, and that's exactly where it belongs."

She waddled into the parlor and surveyed her husband with a belligerent pity, which was in no sense a contradiction within her spirit. Years of jawing, exposure, and mutually drained opiates had brought her a familiarity, which was careless, derogatory, and yet saturated with a compulsory sympathy. In the main she had been a practical, penny-weighing woman growing more so with the years, and her impractical husband, easily deceived in business-deals, business-tactics—unable to rob persistently, with legal astuteness, and on a large scale—angered her because he had proved himself to be deficient in the minutely alert cruelties and graspings, which, in her environment, became whitewashed under the phrase "a good, sharp businessman." It was tacitly understood that a man drove his competitors to the wall and knifed them, even his best friends, though in the latter case, his verbal reluctance, at least, was always supposed to be on tap and ready for use. It was also understood that a man repented for these practices by being kind to his family, his relatives, and the intimates whom he had known for a long term of years and who were not direct competitors.

Fanny continued to defend herself as she leaned against Allene, almost in a prayer for support, a confession that her strident profuse talk was an escape from uneasiness.

"Look at my hands—I got hands like a coal-driver, not like a woman. Positively, when I go into 'The Blue Bird' around the corner, to get me a manicure, I'm ashamed to sit down at the table, I'm *ashamed.* I didn't get through fixing the rooms until twelve o'clock this noon—those bummers upstairs always sleep late on Sunday and then they got the nerve to act sore if I don't make up their beds—the lazy no-goods—and now you want me to throw away two hundred dollars, two hundred dollars you want me to throw away when you know you are not a business-man and you never will be. Not a penny of mine will you ever get for another tailor-shop—not one cent, and that's all there is to it."

With the clack of loose slippers, Morris had been trundling around the parlor, apparently, to locate a match for his pipe but, in reality, to relieve himself, hold back the recriminations bothered, against their will, by compassion.

"If you work too hard it's partly your own fault. When I am laid off and I offer to help you, you chase me out of the house. You want to be a martyr. Again and again, Allie and me, we have begged you to let us chip in and get you a maid, and you could afford to hire a woman yourself, but no, you will never agree!"

"That's absolutely true, Mom, every word of it, and besides, you know it would make Pops happy to start a business again, and this time, maybe he'd be able to make a go of it. Pops is popular with a lot of people here in Chelsea and there's a good location, too—a nice, vacant store right past the corner in the next block. I passed it only yesterday"—Allene, sipping a glass of ice-water, regarded her mother with a bare tolerance not far from a version.

"Certainly, Fanny, why should you slave yourself down to the bone? It's ridiculous! You should get yourself a good, strong girl and you should take it more easy. After the hard life you have had, believe me, you are certainly entitled to a rest. Why look at Gladys, the black one I've got—she does all the washing and ironing, and she cooks the meals, and she keeps the flat so neat you could eat off the floor, I swear it, and all I pay her is nine dollars a week and her food, that's all"—still fanning herself in the armchair, Rose smiled, oblivious to the fact that she was overburdening and underpaying a domestic worker: feeding on this worker and giving her a pittance and the bare right to exist.

Boasting of her good-fortune in this process, Rose was voicing what was, to her, the inevitable law of life made and accepted, often without thought, by the class to which she belonged. If a person was obedient and "not smart," not terrifying—neither a string-puller nor a gangster—it was taken for granted that he was to be used and abused, with occasional, tiny favors and charities passed out to him, to produce at least the semblance of friendly relations between himself and his employers. As Fanny toddled near the piano and confronted the family, she was bitter and yet nonplussed because the bitterness had become less valid to itself. Her squinting eyes held enmity toward Allene. In the first place, Allene was 'too much like her father, refusing to take advice from anybody and spending money as though it grew on trees,' and in the second, 'she wouldn't stick with her own sex, take her mother's side against the bossiness of the male,' and in the third, she suspected that Allene was still running around with Gentile men, despite her denials, and once in awhile, doing bad things with them—'a swelled-head and a cut-up, from top to bottom!' She wagged an index-finger as she drew nearer to the offender.

"It's easy for you to talk, you make hardly enough to buy your own clothes, and as for Morris, he doesn't even bring in that much. Hire me a *maid*, hmmm, it sounds nice, doesn't it?"

"No, it doesn't, to you, because if we did it for you, if we really did make the sacrifice, then you couldn't tell us how ill-treated you are and have an excuse to yell our heads off day and night."

Standing beside Fanny now, Rose spoke to defend her because, though she felt herself to be above Fanny, socially and materially, she admired the other woman's conservative, nickel-squeezing, hard-working motivations, which represented, to Rose, the indisputable, unsparing, argumentative essence of life itself, where extreme sentiment was permitted as a luxury—in personal existence and not in staring at a honeyed movie—only when it failed to interfere with more serious, material greediness and concealment.

Again, 'if Fanny did get a maid, what would she do with her time—idle people had to spend money, and poor Fanny's two thousand wasn't a fortune.' Her own comparative idleness failed to interfere with this trend of thought—'after all, she had a husband who was getting higher and higher up in the world, mixing in with politicians who liked him, who might even run him for office one of these days, so *she* didn't have to worry, but poor Fanny.'

"Never mind, Fanny, you got a perfect right to be mad, and you shouldn't back down either. The only fault is, you are working yourself to a nervous wreck and saving up the money so you and Morris could have something to live on when you are old people, and maybe you could buy the trousseau for Allie when she gets married, and what credit do they give you for it? None, ab-so-lute-ly none, and it's a shame too."

Hands linked, these two, short, dumpy, middle-aged women, one in pleated apple-green above absurdly high-heeled pumps, to make her look taller, and the other bundled in gray, snug over big hips and buttocks—these two, suddenly, had a comical and yet sordidly ruthless appearance, to Allene. It was difficult to believe that they had ever been young, and though Rose still 'fixed herself up' for half-discreet pressures with men, at house-parties where her husband adopted the same liberties with other women—a wrangling but fairly steadfast understanding—it was still a dreamless middle-age unwrapping the dollar-bills from last gasps of hilarity and sex.

"You're painting a lovely picture, aren't you, Aunt Rose?"—Allene looked at Rose with a candid disdain. "Pops worked his fingers off for years, too, but he never got any credit for it, and maybe he wouldn't have lost all of his stores, either, if Mom hadn't tried to butt in and boss him around every single minute of the day. The trouble with Mom is, she wants to have her way all the time, and then she can go around and tell people how persecuted she is. Why, only the other night I caught her telling one of the roomers upstairs she had a weak heart and wasn't going to live long because she had to work too hard."

"Get out, you are like your father—never have I gotten an ounce of affection from you"—Fanny advanced toward Allene and sawed the air with right arm and hand.

"That isn't true, Mom. I do love you, but it's hard to show it to you. You're always shrieking about something, or other—always."

"Certainly, with you I've got plenty to yell about. Look at that nice boy, that fine, Jewish fellow you met at Rose's last Sunday night, and he was paying attention to you again and again, but you wouldn't even give him a tumble. He wasn't one of those *Goiyim* cake-eaters, those no-goods you are always running around with."

"That's my business and not yours! When he wasn't stepping all over my feet, trying to dance, he was telling me all about the wonderful success he was making in the furniture business. I like a man who can talk about something else except I, me, and myself—once in a while anyway."

"Of course! You can't stand a man with brains, who is making good in the business-world. A truck-driver, or maybe a corner-loafer, suits you much better, I know!"

Rose had fled out to the yard—'after all, why should she always mix into their squabbles, and be the target for all of them, when she couldn't help them in the least and she had so many much more important things in her own life, which needed attention?' Morris, shielding himself with the comic-sheets of the Sunday paper was relieved and troubled in varying proportions, as he sought, vainly, to concentrate on the pictured fortunes of Little Orphan Annie, who was battling against Silas Pinchpenny, miser and murderer, to restore justice and serenity once more to an imaginary village known as Cosmic City, and to rid this village of the only vile employer and mortgage-holder which it possessed—varnish, gush, and harmless melodramas, to veil the sores of a prevailing economic system with infantile chuckles, detective-fiction suspenses, brought to the eyes in the colored, pen-and-ink puppets of a comic-strip—the Sunday-dope of two-millions. This time, however, the favorite dope failed. Morris was glad that the load of contention had shifted from him to the women-folk, and he felt a loving gratitude toward Allene for her support, but still, her sexual life worried him, gave him twinges of resentment, because he longed for her to marry "a good, Jewish fellow" and settle down to the venerably approved tasks of house-keeping and child-bearing, directions to which she seemed entirely indifferent. The failure of Fanny to give birth to a son had always been a canker to Morris and the vision of petting a male grandchild, who would perpetuate his blood and perhaps avenge his thwarted life, was sweet and urgent.

Out in the yard, the three children of Rose Kirstner were chattering, frolicking—Freddy, Cecelia, and Harold. Freddy was a goggle-eyed, chubby kid of five, and he displayed long trousers of thin, dark summer serge, and his bluish black hair ended and stood out in an abrupt curve high above the shaved neck—the penchant, among certain middle-class mothers, to make their little boys as ugly and pseudo-masculine, in appearance, as they possibly could. The dun-gray canvas swing, spotted and unravelled near the edges, was occupied by Cecelia and Harold. A chit of fourteen, Cecelia was restless and sexually precocious. She could giggle, sniffle, and jabber about nothing in particular for hours unbrokenly, because her environment, with all of its slyly draped, sexual goads and fears, had never shown her any other outlet, and also, because her naturally slow mind could feign to be swift and self-sufficient in all of the outpouring of noise and wriggles. At her High School, where she was a first-year student, over two-thirds of the girls studied, erratically, or barely enough to "get by," since the pupils at this particular school were, in the main, from comfortable homes, and the very air was soaked with premature, whispered, toilet-scribbled sex, the one subject never mentioned in the fake propriety of the classrooms. Periodically, one or another of the tabloid-papers would print a lurid, suggestive, half-lying account of the conditions at this and other High Schools of the city, peppered with headlines such as: "Secret Orgies Discovered Among School Pupils," or "School-

Students Lured By Sin And Rum," and then promptly drop the matter before it assumed anything remotely resembling the proportions
of a serious investigation, while the schools attended by poorer children remained unnoticed by the mud-sheets in question.

Cecelia was starting to be fully blown, with a prominent nose,
fat cheeks, and a stumble of black hair down to her shoulders, and
she was forever pertly fiddling with her scarlet dress dropping well
below the knees, or twitting Harold, who was seventeen and much
taller, with bulky chest, and face dark, lip-puckered, studiously
complacent. Harold used a liquid concoction to glue the strands
of his blackish brown hair to a hemisphere with the shine of polished furniture, and wore shell-rimmed glasses, his weak eyes alone
preventing him from becoming an athlete. He was in the last year
of High School and he affected broad-cuffed, narrow-vested sports
clothes and had his mind set on becoming a politician—leading
the school-debates with eulogies on the President of his country:
the blessings of true democracy, where everyone had a chance to
become wealthy and, at the smallest, thrifty and respected: and the
dire need for a large army and navy, to protect the United States
from any possible invasion. Once, in the school-auditorium, a freckled girl, with tenseness on her Irish face, had risen from a rear seat
and heckled him, asking why her father, a shoe-worker, had been
forced to strike for higher wages when billions of dollars were avail-
able for the building of new airplanes and battleships. The principal
seated on the platform—an elderly man with a spade nose, peevish face—had immediately replied, in a voice almost barking with
anger, that the question was unpatriotic and irrelevant, and that the
mentioned strike was being peacefully settled by the local N.R.A.
Board. Entirely undismayed, the freckled girl had piped back that
the Board in question was conducting an arbitration largely in favor
of the shoe-repair shops and manufacturers, and the principal had
denounced her as a falsifier, and in the ensuing uproar, she had been
pushed from the auditorium by the school-janitor. After this incident, Harold had risen on the platform and proudly reiterated the

President's assertion that the wild horses of the country would have to be corralled and everybody must put his shoulder to the harness, to lift the country out of its depression. Afterwards, Harold had learned that the girl had been expelled for her outbreak during his talk, and on the suspicion that she was a member of a radical group known as the "National Students" League, and he had declared that 'it served her right and girls like her were really a menace to the country.'

He scuffled with Cecelia now, while Rose tried to be chiding but failed because she doted on her children.

"Ma, make him stop tickling me."

"Harold, what *is* the matter with you today? I can't understand it—you're usually such a serious boy."

"She started it. She can't keep still to save her life!"

"Well, I want both of you to behave yourselves, d'you hear me? You are not at home, you know."

"Oh, ma, why do we have to come here every Sunday? I'm getting bored, honest."

"That's not a nice way to talk, Ceelie!"

"Well I am, just the same. All they ever do is fight with each other, and I can hear Aunt Fanny's voice right out in the yard here. Why can't we go some place, to a movie maybe?"

Rose was undecided—siding with the children and, yet feeling that it was her duty not to encourage them to talk so disrespectfully about their kinfolk.

"You shouldn't be talking so sassy—I don't like it one bit. Your Aunt Fanny is a splendid woman and your Uncle is a fine man, too—he's got a good honest character, even if he's not so high up in the world."

"Oh yes? Then why did I hear father calling him a funny, old sucker the other night?"—Harold, who had risen from the swing and was scuffing the sun-baked dirt of the yard with his heels, looked jovially owlish and bartered eye-winks with his sister, who was fussing with her rolled-up stockings and throwing sly glances in all directions, to see whether any of the males in the nearby yards, or windows, might be watching her, so that she could hastily lower the dress and put a reproving sniff on her face.

These children were not innately vicious. They could be kind, even a little thoughtfully frank, sometimes, but the ever-denying snobbery and material deceit of their environment beckoned to their acting-ability in the most elastic years of their lives. Rose screwed up her face—flustered, half-heartedly loyal to her brother, and angry at the lack of wisdom which her husband had shown. In any crisis, she would have rescued any of her relatives from starvation, or jail, or physical danger to their lives—shocked, for a time, out of her customary complacency—but otherwise, they were frequently objects of sneers and indifferences, 'when the children were not around,' because, with the exception of one brother, who owned a large hardware firm in a Western City, the other two—a younger brother and sister, and their offspring, in addition to Morris—were all tied to respectable poverty, or a condition bordering upon it.

"Hush up, Harold—you mustn't repeat everything you hear, and besides, your father was only joking because Uncle Morris loves to play pinochle, and yet he's such a poor player. You're such a silly boy, Harold. You ought to know, by this time, your father never means half the things he says!"

Harold and Cecelia were unimpressed, anxious to switch the subject. They felt that they had "put their foot into it." The atmosphere of concealment was a thinly worn trifle. Harold loved his father and patronized Rose, who was, to him, merely a maternal echo of the bright, worldly figure, which his father represented. Cecelia was afraid of her father because of his moral admonitions always chiming, insincerely, to her ears, and because he had once whacked her, mercilessly, across the rump and legs, with his walking-cane, after he had caught her and a boy of the same age showing sexual curiosity toward each other, in one of the hallways of their apartment-building. Using the desire for a movie as an excuse, she was eager to return home now because she had arranged to meet her present "beau" on the roof underneath the water-tank of the expensive, uptown "Buckingham Manor," in which the Kirstners lived.

They trooped back to the front-room where Fanny and Morris were seated alone, Allene having departed a few minutes previous. Harold and Cecelia liked Allene because they had observed that she was a nimble fox-trotter, proficient in the Lindy Hop and other, newer steps, and that she kept up a smart appearance in her dress, told them near-risqué stories of cabarets and night-life experiences, in whispers and with the warning that they should not repeat the tales to their parents, or reveal the source of information. Also they suspected that—if only very occasionally—she had taken the full sexual contacts, branded as illicit, which they had only commenced to have, quaking, in deserted parlors, dimly lit hallways, with the threatening figures of their elders continually hovering over them.

"Aw, I wish 'Lene hadn't gone out so quick"—Cecelia was petulant, her mind still riveted on the tall, stub-nosed boy, whom she was scheduled to meet, and who always hugged her right away, without asking.

"Sure, who *wouldn't* like her—she's a peach!"—Harold, looking at Fanny and Morris, kept the dutiful mask on his face, while his mother beamed dubiously but made haste to substantiate the admiration.

After Rose had said goodbye several times, interspersed with strung-out, nervous cordialities and promises, to drive out the vague feeling that she hadn't been nice to her brother on this particular day, Cecelia and Harold, scarcely disguising their relief, yanked her through the doorway, and the Kirstners sped off in their little dark green sedan, with Harold at the wheel.

In the slumped-down contrast of quietness, Fanny and Morris looked at one another. Their eyes were reproachful but more sympathetic now. These two were joined by a common frustration. They had loved one another, long ago, before the slow host of frictions, tormented hopes, poorly compensated labors, and money-losses, had changed the love, largely, to a cat-and-dog fight—a misdirected battle between the sexes, to see which one would be allowed the lead in the gradual retreat toward an empty old-age—and yet, in any extremity, they would still have clung together from the dull but habitual compulsion of mutual protection. Fanny's tongue rested sometimes, but during her waking hours, her hands could never remain still for any length of time because the buzz and whine of her mind was never adequate to itself, and she drew a perverted relish from increasing both the real and pretended martyrdoms of her life, with physical exhaustion and its attendant complaints serving as the final importance of existence. The needle bobbed and the scissors clicked as she mended a green-and-white, checked house-dress, while Morris chewed on one of the costly cigars, brought by Rose from his brother-in-law, and played solitaire, and told himself, as he had for years, that he must curb his yen to bid up to three-hundred-and-fifty in the forthcoming, weekend game, simply because he had three aces, a chance for one-hundred-and-fifty, and a meld of sixty-queens and an additional twenty.

One of the roomers entered the parlor—Carrie Wilkinson—and after she had paid the rent for the coming week, sat down to chatter with Fanny. Carrie, at the finish of her twenties, was tall and scant-fleshed, with a slit on the lower part of her large, pointed nose—caused by a childhood accident—and small, sallow-pink lips turned inward. She worked as a "chamber-maid" in a large, Chelsea hotel—eleven hours of drudgery every day at a wage of twelve dollars a week, with Sunday her only time of rest. Her life was a tragedy. Homely, retiring, and with only a grammar-school education and one remaining parent—a father, who worked as a porter in a New Jersey roadhouse and barely kept himself alive—her life, generally, resembled the existence of thousands of other women in the City. Without the looks, which would have induced amorous males to treat them to night-life pleasures, and watching their youth gasp and slink away under the kicks of each day's grind, they faced only the conclusions of a drab marriage with a ground-down man, also in their general status, or a life of relatively isolated toil petering out to a dependent and disconsolate old-age. In the meantime, Carrie drank cheap gin, occasionally, because it made her feel big and wanted despite every contrary evidence, and on even rarer occasions, she gave herself to one, or another, of the male workers in the hotel, when the weight of sexual abstinence, in conjunction with the other facts in her life, could no longer be endured. Fanny liked Carrie because the latter was always willing to listen to her, with all of the brightness which she could summon, and was also reasonably prompt in the payment of her rent.

Carrie had a longing for Ray Bailey, to whom she had frequently spoken—in the hallways, or rapping on his door, on the pretext of borrowing some small article—and Ray's politeness, manifestly, not far from unconcern, had given her a meek resentment festering a bit in her heart. In the parlor now, malice stirred in Carrie—the reaction of a woman, enslaved and without brains, or courage, enough to direct her biles against any people except a few in her own stratum of life.

"Where's Allie?"

"Allie? Oh, she went out about a half hour ago. She's visiting her cousin, Esther, over in Brownsville. Esther is a fine girl, really a fine girl, and they're holding a beautiful shower for her because she is engaged to be married. But, d'you know, it's a shame, Allie went off and forgot the present she was going to bring over—a dozen, beautiful, simply beautiful hand-embroidered napkins, with the initials on them! Maybe she'll come back in the subway and get them. It would be mortifying, y' know, to come way out there with nothing, and then—"

"That's funny. I saw Allene right here in the hallway."

"Here in the hallway?"

"Why, of course. Right here, and it couldn't have been more than two, or three, minutes ago, because I'd just left my room to come down and pay the—"

"What was she doing?"

"Why, she was coming out of the bathroom on the top, and then she went into—"

"That's enough, I know where"—Fanny's face hardened, like an exclamation mark for the choked-off sentence.

She stumbled from the chair, with her stiffly doubled fingers opening, closing, in spasms. Her eyes rolled and then narrowed. Morris stood up, too—upset, but with the instinctive desire to shield his daughter, no matter how "derelict" she might be and in spite of the times, in which he had told himself that her conduct was hateful to the scores of prized but riddled inhibitions within him. Since the days of her infancy, Allene had been a feverishly guarded brightness in the brutal conflicts and disappointments of his life— deliberately sentimental, in part, but deeply lodged, never diminishing to a hairsbreadth.

"Now, now, don't hit the ceiling, Fanny! I am not going to have you shouting around the hallway here! You let me go upstairs and find out—"

"You'll do nothing of the kind! If she's up there in the room with that rotten *goi*, that lousy dead-beat!"—Fanny rushed to the stairway leading to the upper floors, and all of the thrice-mangled defeats in her life disguised themselves, became untouched, angrily victorious, to fly from the fact that she was a worn-out middle-aged woman poisoning herself without stint, or ultimate decision. Morris lumbered, lost one of his slippers, chased after her, plucked at different parts of her skirt, whispered hoarse pleas for restraint, and was thoroughly sick, agitated, and trivial, to himself, because the "moral" dictations, past and present, were obnoxious, to themselves, and yet forever rotting in the basic uncertainty of his heart.

Carrie had slunk to the sidewalk and was walking to an adjacent drugstore to buy an icecream-soda. She intended to sit in the drugstore for at least half an hour, waiting for the impending uproar to die down in the Baum house. Within herself, she cringed, muttered epithets against Allene and Ray but could not finish them, string them in order, make them imposing, because, in her life, the greatest stigma was considered to be that of a squealer. It was a cunning perversion of actual, close-lipped loyalty, in which men and women were commanded to remain silent concerning the tactics of their employers, the actions of gangsters, and the presence of plunder and fraud anywhere, and through narrowing it to include the more personal relations among the victims, the instigators strove to make it a complete and insidious device for their own protection.

Fanny had gained the top-floor and was banging on Ray's door, with Morris wrestling to hold back her arms. Allene opened the door and stood, smoothing her dress, looking at her mother with embarrassment and ill temper combined, less affected by the loud-voiced venom than by the fact that two other roomers—May Boswell, a sales-clerk in a neighboring bakery, and Powers, old night-watchman—had opened their doors, slightly, across the hall and were lapping up the personal revelation, which was a tidbit of "scandal" to their degenerated, browbeaten minds, and which, they imagined, compensated them for the boredom of a hot afternoon invaded only by the shallow clownings, sensations, and lies of the Sunday papers and the cut-and-dried music-programmes from a little, rundown radio-set.

Fanny's screams were almost incoherent, at first, as she accused Allene of dishonesty and sexual filth and called Ray a swindler, a loafer, a dog. Through lessenings in the screams—catches of breath—Morris's words sounded in a fluctuating rumble, a tortured pleading with Fanny to lower her voice. Ray, diving into his coat, could have murdered Fanny, and yet, certain now that he would be thrown out on the street, he glared, forced himself into silence, and then started sentences which he failed to finish, in a purposeless alternation. Fanny had pushed her way into the room and was pounding the rear frame of the bed. Morris, between jerks at her arms, frowned at Ray, inclined to hit the other man in the face, but withheld because his mind intruded on his emotions. 'After all, if Allie had wanted to be bad, it was her own lookout, but that sneak, that Bailey! No love, no marriage, certainly not, and God knows how far behind he was in his rent, but maybe the poor *schlemiel* had been afraid because he was out of a job so long, and it was certainly hell for anyone to be homeless, when he was looking for work and couldn't find it, and by golly, it was hard not to be afraid of Fanny's tongue because her tongue could be like a butcher's meat-ax, but Allie!—was she in love with this *goi*, had she given herself to him of her own accord?' The entire situation was a gulp of castor-oil, to poor Morris, and he could not decide whether he should fling himself on Bailey, or become more reasonable. Fanny was still raging.

"Get out of here this minute! I wouldn't even keep what you got—the rags you got, they're not even worth half a dollar! Two months rent you owe me, two months, but you can keep it, you dirty *goi!* You make a rotten woman out of Allie, you take her money! I know what you are! A dirty pimp, that's what you are! A dirty, low-down—"

"Shut your mouth, Fanny"—Morris drove his hand against her lips, held it there as he struggled with her.

"You had better pack up and go, Bailey"—Morris's voice was still distressed, trying to hate but finding it difficult. "You are not wanted here!"

"That's all right, I'll go, but you tell your wife not to call me a pimp again, because if she does!"—Ray swung his left fist to and fro.

The word had hurt him, cruelly, and his mind had surrendered to an itch in his hands and had almost ceased to function. Allene, who had been equally furious, became, suddenly, untouched, amused. 'Damn her mother anyway, staging a ten-cent melodrama, waving her corset in the air and calling it virtue, and all because she wasn't happy herself, never had been able to get one fraction of the things she wanted. If Ray had been a rich man, or even well-to-do, and she and Ray had been caught by her mother in a large, swell apartment with a servant hanging around, her mother might still have been sore, but she wouldn't have thrown any short, nasty words at him. It was always the same thing down at the bottom—respect a person, if he had money, and kick him in the face, if he didn't. Even her mother's hatred against Gentiles wasn't entirely fool-proof when it came to that.'

"Oh, ma, cut it out. Use your common-sense, won't you? If Ray and I want to stick together, you can't stop us. You're a dumb-bell, ma. Let's all go downstairs now and talk it over—all except Ray. He'll pack up and leave right now, if you're so set on it. Come on, ma, close up for a while—they've all got their ears stretched out in the hallway there!"

The only appeal that could affect Fanny was the realization, flopping like a wet cloth on her rage, that other people were listening, watching—people who might spread gossip concerning herself and her family around the neighborhood—because the collapse of the high, material estate, which she had once hoped for, had been superseded by the shamefaced desire to hold her head up, through a brand of respectable intactness, in which "nobody could say a single word against her." Allene tried to grasp Ray's hand, reassuringly, and turned, instantly, to her mother, because she was still apprehensive. Muttering and glass-eyed, Fanny allowed Morris and Allene to placate her, in the corner of the room behind the bed, and then lead her down the stairways. Disgusted and worried, Ray yanked his old suitcase from under the bed and began to throw clothes from the chest of drawers. 'One, thin dime in his pocket—where in hell was he going now? Drop in at the office where Allene worked—for a minute—if he couldn't make connections with her before he left the house now.'

IV

THE EARLY night at the end of September in Madison Square Park was, in the main, cheerless. The people stuck on the benches did not smile at one another. The others, spilling in and out of the walks, laughed and smiled sometimes, when they were in pairs and groups, but in such cases the humor was intended to be a personal secret, and audible snatches from the words, which followed it, often indicated ridicule and spiteful triumph—the glee of "putting one over" on another person, the glee of having witnessed his rejection, or confusion, in some small incident, real or imagined.

Factory-girls, shop-girls, on clattering heels, were kidding, frantically, to distract the slump of their bodies and the restricted freedom represented by the few bills, or coins, tucked within their flashy, shoddy pocketbooks. Bosses, managers, strode to their parked machines, to the subways, and laughed over the suckers they had trimmed in business-deals, over jokes about the women they had, or wanted; but the humor, generally, suggested insolence and lip-smacking more than happiness. Again, women in caracul and kolinsky coats—worn because a mild chilliness, a hint of rain, gave them a chance to flaunt the unofficial uniform of their class—lifted a brief, shrill laughter from soft, creamed faces that grew harder than chrome steel in the eyes and the subsequent setting of their lips; women hurrying to the costlier apartments of Madison Avenue and its immediate side-blocks near the Grand Central Station.

But these were exceptions. On the whole, Madison Square Park and its environs showed neither brightness nor comradeship. People flew along, looked at one another with suspicion, or aloofness. A frowning exhaustion was on most of the faces and many of the others—faces of drones, or worldly men and women in good clothes—were inordinately self-centered and showed not a scrap of interest in the human beings passing them, outside of a flirtatious stare at a pretty face, a neatly curved figure, a straight nose and squarely cut features under a black derby. Time and again, the swifter walkers were halted by slower men and elderly women—some, beggars, who lived only for liquor and sleep, but most of them unemployed, destitute, and forced to trample on their pride in the search for a sandwich and a bug-ridden bed. The people on the benches were discards, strays living on their wits, and workers of both sexes, who lived in the vicinity and had no other recreation, having already spent most of their small pay, or being compelled to hoard it for the direst necessities.

A clock in the tower of a life-insurance-company building, to one side of the park, chimed the quarter, half, and full hours, serenaded the slaves on bench and walk, and received anxious glances from humans late for their supper, or youngsters with blood and illusion still jumping within them, waiting for loved ones, courted ones, to join them. Later they would sit before the stale virus and dope ladled out by adjacent vaudeville and movie houses. Dry leaves scraped over the walks, and tapped against the erect statue of Chester Alan Arthur, twenty-first President, in frock-coat, stock, and high collar cut into bronze now blackish green with light green corrodings—an obscure, weirdly pompous figure in the history of past thefts, hidden bargainings, accepted as national service and statesmanship. Lighted windows stood, irregularly, in the blanket gray and dirty brown of the high and low buildings. Behind the windows, tired clerks worked overtime for their masters, and even a few of the masters themselves—ranging from aspirants and fly-by-nights to actual dictators—pored over papers, used telephones, to wind up their day of gouging, shiftiness, back-stabbing, in thousands of law-shielded ways. The pale green, single- and double-decked omnibuses lumbered on, with chauffeurs, conductors, in olive-drab and puttees, straining to avoid collisions and accidents, the lack of sleep showing, frequently, on their nerve-jerked faces. The groaning street-cars slid in spasms, hampered by darting, clotted machines.

The "eternal light" was perched over carved soldiers and sailors, to commemorate their death in the late World War, while some of their living comrades, trudging underneath, felt the bite of filth and hunger because the cost of furnishing the electricity for such lights was infinitely less than the millions of dollars once promised and then denied to them by the canny demagogues controlling the wealth of the nation. At the subway entrances and exits, squawking, beaten-eyed peddlers sold words to the most recent popular songs, the world's smallest playing-cards, and Japanese bulbs guaranteed to sprout and flower in water—backward men aping an opposite class, in the great dope-ritual of New York City, in the effort to remain, themselves, barely alive. Huge spirals of gray and black cloud were rolling over the sky, from the east, like screw-drivers which seemed to dig into the slits of the stars.

Allene was tired. Black and violet spots shook in front of her eyes.

"I went out with Al last night. We had a couple of beers, and we sat and talked for a while and then he saw me home and left me at the door, that's all."

Ray drove his knuckles into an iron rung of the bench, which served for McCormick's jaw.

"If you don't tell me why you're still seeing McCormick, and even if you do tell me and I don't like the reasons, we're going to split, and that's straight."

Allene was supposed to finish work at six, but on this day, as on many others, she had toiled an extra hour to revise and complete a selling-contract which had to be ready on the following morning. In such matters the theory was that she had the right to exercise her own choice, but Frederick Dulossi, one of the main bosses, always stressed the need of loyalty to the firm, always spoke of a raise in pay, which never arrived, and continued to pile the work of two girls on Allene's brain and fingers.

"You're talking so loud, Ray, and I've worked so hard today, my head's positively spinning and spinning and . . ."

Ray promptly softened. Fresh from almost ten hours in a large cafeteria, with a mingled stab and leaden clamping in shoulders and arms, a soreness in his feet, he relented in the common bondage, though the thought of Allene's possible treachery to him still rankled within him.

"Well, tell me the truth, that's all I want."

Allene bit her lip to quiet a sigh. What was the truth, when a man and a woman loved and so many things and people were shoving against them, knocking them in different directions?

"Sure, I'll try. You see, Al lost his job, about two weeks ago, and he hadn't saved up a single penny. He's been borrowing a little from a friend but he can't find another job and he's pretty much up against it."

"What's the matter with his people, won't they help him?"

"Oh, they're all out in Cleveland where he comes from, all except a sister here, and she works for the 'Sunlight Cracker Firm' out in Jersey and she only gets ten a week. They've all got all they can do to keep themselves alive."

As much as he had persuaded himself that he hated McCormick and must, eventually, avenge the knockout, Ray could not remain quite as dour to the other man now. He remembered his own weeks of tramping, humiliation, wrangling, and recurring hunger, before he had landed the bus-boy's job in the cafeteria several days previous. He remembered how, over three months past, he had parted with every cent of his savings in an all-night poker session and lost his job as an assistant-clerk in an uptown hotel, both events occurring within thirty-six hours—one stroke, sending him, with no trace of warning, broke and stunned, out on the gray, yelling street-levels of New York. Yet, he was also a man crazy to keep a woman, and the jealousy lost one of its legs but still balanced itself on the other. Besides, he had squatted on his haunches, sucking in the blood brought by another man's fist, and in his code no man could hold his head high until the situation had been evened, unless the other fellow was a powerful gangster and the victim knew that his own death might be involved, if he tried to retaliate. Close to hardness, with the fullness of it prevented only by uncertainty, Ray broke the silence.

"What's McCormick to you, why are you so concerned about him? God knows, after what I've been through in my life, particularly the last three months, I hate to see any fellow out of work and sliding near the gutter, but you're not coddling him just for that reason. If you were, you'd have to go out with about one million others in the same position, right here in Greater New York."

Thumbing the hand, which he drew away, slowly, Allene laughed—partly, at the glimpse of herself walking down New York streets with different regiments of unemployed men night after night, flitting in and out to console their need for a woman, and, partly, because her youth, bled and impeded, was alert for any excuse to relax, however briefly.

"I can't possibly locate all of them, Ray—have a heart."

Ray chuckled before realizing it, and then a lighter frown returned. In that moment, he thought that Allene might have laughed only as a first move toward inducing him to forget his questions, and though he dismissed the mote as too cheap, somehow, for her, his voice nevertheless grew louder.

"I still don't know the answer to anything."

"The answer is just this—at one time Al spent his last dollars on me, and he did all he could to give me a chance to enjoy myself, and it's hard now to slap him in the face when he's broke and out of a job. There are so many girls playing men in New York they'd reach clear out to Canarsie and back again, if they stood single-file, and gosh, I simply can't bear the idea of Al thinking I'm one of them."

"So for that reason you're going to keep on seeing him and then you'll encourage him to think—"

"That isn't true. I was explaining to you why I couldn't jerk away from him right off the bat, after he was knocking on my door, acting so sweet, apologizing because he could only treat me to a couple of beers but wouldn't I come and have a talk with him, just for a little while. Why, I'd have had a heart of rock, then, if I hadn't gone out with him. I didn't make another definite date, and the next time he finds me there, I'm going to invite him in, and then I'll make everything as clear to him as I possibly can."

"Does that mean you're going to give him his walking-card, once and for all?"

"What else d'you suppose it means?"—Allene was impatient, tender, bothered by her conscience, a little, as she slid the backs of her fingers under Ray's chin. Sore, without knowing why, Ray still believed that she had acted slippery toward him, whether it had been intentional, or not. Something in life was slippery, too, he thought, and maybe she was the victim of a factor which he could feel, but not see. The last few months had made him more thoughtful, but the thinking was still muddled.

"Have you ever told him you were in love with me?"

Allene pinched the navy-blue wool of her working-dress, tugged at the white, starched ruffles of the neck-piece, without immediately answering—not because she wanted to skip the question but because it could not be simply dealt with and she knew that no other reply would satisfy Ray. She had a vision of tired people falling into tired arms and reaching, tired, for escapes that would not have counted to them, otherwise—a process of hasty expedients springing from tiredness and then dying back upon it.

"I didn't tell him in so many words, Ray. It isn't easy, when a man proves he's really mad about you and you'd have to hurt him pretty bad. You see, I was almost in love with Al before you came along, and even now I think he has lots of good qualities in him, but I don't freeze and get hot again when he's with me, and I don't worry about him much of the time. He is a rough-neck and he believes he can fix everything with his fists, but it's not his fault. He was brought up that way."

"Never mind the rough-neck part. I can do a little swinging myself, especially when I know I'm in the right, and I'm going to show it to that bird some time"—Ray was still galled by the idea that Allene would never have tolerated McCormick again if the latter had not once split his lips and tumbled him sprawling. "What I want to know is—have you told him anything at all about your feelings toward me?"

"I did tell him you were the only man I had a deep attachment for, but he kept on saying he didn't believe me. Ray, don't you know your own sex by this time? When a man loves a girl, he won't admit it's hopeless till the very last minute, till she's actually living with another fellow, and even then, sometimes he keeps on trying. Haven't you ever done the same thing in your life—haven't you?"

Ray was silent in an undesired remembrance—Hannah Benjamin, with natural black curls and a wine-tipped, prize-winning face small enough to be masked in a man's hand with his fingers ending in the hair over her forehead. She had been one of the switchboard girls near the long desk behind which he had worked and sized up the patrons, scraping and salving to the more affluent ones until it had griped him, but following his orders from the hotel-management. Yes, it was true that he had chased Hannah for over half a year, though all the time he had known that she was visiting the apartment of "Chick" Seligson, on the sly, but that had been different. Seligson's father had owned the hotel, and "Chick," a sporty, smooth idler with an interest in a big roadhouse on the North Shore, could have spent a hundred as though it were a dollar bill, and did. He had longed to get the better of "Chick," show him he couldn't keep his pudgy hands on a girl who was really a fine skate down at the bottom, but her nerves got shredded, her back broke in two, from ten, and sometimes eleven hours, with only a few minutes relief every second hour, at a board where the calls never stopped racing in, and so she kept her job and wavered between her independence and the dizzy stepping-out "Chick" gave her every weekend. The rivalry with McCormick now was a damn sight more honest. They were, at least, a couple of working-fools with no unfair advantages, even if McCormick did have a bulldozing lousiness in his make-up.

"What's wrong, dear—have you lost your tongue?"—Allene, less serious because she seemed to have tripped him, was basking in the moment of peace, and yet the least bit worried.

"Aw, I was thinking. Are you going to make a clean break with Al?"

"I certainly am, the very next time I see him. I was just trying to make you realize how hard it's been."

"Christ, everything's hard when people haven't any money, and they're all set for loving but they get ill-tempered over every little thing because they're tired out and their nerves are all chopped to pieces"—Ray was surprised a second afterwards by the vehemence of his words, which he ascribed, ruefully, to a lack of spunk within him, and went on, much more evenly: "I know you've been sympathizing with Al because he claims to be nuts about you, and anyway, he's certainly no better off than we are. But this is a personal issue. I want to marry you, or else live with you, if you don't think the time's ripe for marrying. After all the times we've been close together, hon', you know I'm not just trying to get you and then throw you over."

"Yes, I do know it, Ray"—Allene kissed him on the mouth, quickly, shrinking in part from the passing eyes, and Ray poked his mouth against her temple and the flaxen hair still-rippled under the lower puff of her black velour beret. "I'm perfectly willing, Ray, but I don't think it would be practical just now. I don't want to marry you until we've laid a little money aside, and you know, the room I've got now isn't so large, and we'd be so crowded in it. Besides, everything is so darn uncertain—it makes me sick. If that Fred Dulossi keeps on loading me with stuff, like I was a truck-horse, I'm going to quit! I can't stand it much longer. He stalls me every time I ask him for a raise—'I've got to wa-ait until bu-usiness pi-icks u-up.' It never will pick up, if I listen to him. I know all the commissions they make on the sales and the rentals, and he knows I know it, but still he sits there and hands out the same old line, and he never blinks an eye, just because he's got to say *something*, I suppose!"

Ray groaned inside.

"Well God knows, I can't support you on what I'm getting, and say, there's one supervisor over at Johnson's, Norah Gallagher— she certainly gets in my hair, plenty! If she spies me catching my breath between the rush-hours, polishing the chairs and the woodwork kind of slow for a minute, she's right on top of me. She's sore because I don't smear it on the way the other bus-boys do, though I haven't got the heart to blame the poor mugs much—they're white under the gills, afraid they'll lose their jobs."

"Well, for Pete's sake, don't lose yours for a while"—Allene was irritated, to cover her own actual fear. "Outside of the three days you worked in the other restaurant, and that was more than a month ago, you know the hell you've been through. I understand, it must be pretty hard for you to trudge around and handle stacks of greasy dishes all day long, when you've cashiered and clerked in swell hotels and nightclubs—sure, I understand, but you've got to forget about your pride and stick to this job. If you don't, then the Lord only knows when we'll ever be able to live together!"

"It's not a question of pride. I'm glad to do any kind of work that'll bring me a living, but I'm not going down on my knees and swallow bawlings-out when I don't deserve them, all for a lousy ten-fifty a week, with three dollars off for meals."

"Oh, you'll get along till you find something better—don't be such a gosh-awful pessimist!"

"All right, I certainly hope so"—the smile on Ray's face revealed edges, like the flash of saw-teeth half buried in the flesh.

They were talked out, longing for privacy. They left the bench and swung south in the park. Fitful scurries of tiny drops, close-knitted, fell from the pallid ink of the sky. Ray and Allene hurried along, bumping into umbrella-points, spattered by machines through the start of mud near the curbs, and rammed by passing elbows. Allene had moved from her parents two days after the Sunday discovery on the upper floor, and was living in a room on East Twenty-Second Street designated as a one-room apartment because the inevitable, middle-aged, galvanized, prying landlady and her idle, cursing husband were both absent, with the tenants taking care of their own rooms and a non-resident janitor confining himself to the heavier outside work, such as cleaning the green-carpeted hallways, emptying the garbage, stoking the furnace for hot-water. Owing to the lack of restrictions, some of the apartments in the four-story, brick house were occupied by women, who received men-callers and staged drinking-parties at odd times of the night and day, and workingmen, neighbors, pounded on their walls, after

midnight, demanding quiet, without results. After repeated pound-
ings, some of the sleepless workers moved out while others, usually
the younger ones, made friends with the women and sometimes
joined their parties, to which other women had been invited. These
younger workers could be seen leaving the house in the morning—
blear-eyed, vacant around their mouths, scarcely remembering
what had happened on the previous night, waking from "a wild
party," which had held neither happiness nor physical restoration
but only the impact of bodies rendered almost witless by too much
liquor too hastily swallowed.

The brighter and more voluntary needs of sex and life were
absent from hundreds of like houses scattered throughout the
city—with few exceptions—because the people within them had the
nature of drug-addicts caught within an economic system, which
enslaved and stripped them under pipe-dreams of freedom and
the old bait of civic pride, patriotic fervor, to make them take the
hook with no great rebellion. Some of these people were waking
up, growling in the last convulsion of sleep, but most of them, as
yet, had not been able to see their mutual suppression and unite
against it, to avoid, eradicate, the myriads of agencies stultifying
their hearts and minds—the unending avalanche of bottles, legs
topped by pink frill, suggestive grin, morals and the lack of morals, both equally false, church prating and burlesque-show crudity
forever staging little sham-fights before shaking hands behind the
scenes.

The women in the house where Allene lived now were not prostitutes, in the open and strict sense of the word. They worked as
dress-models, movie-ushers, "beauty-shop" workers, dance-host-
esses, song-pluggers, window-demonstrators, anywhere from a
week to a few months and then loafed through similar periods,
depending on men to provide them with drinks, food, and room-
rent, and yielding to these men sometimes but refusing them at
others, in the vagaries of oppressed creatures turning upon one
another because they did not know the true identity of the oppres-

sors, or because they were without the courage to oppose them.

As Allene fumbled in her purse for the key to her room, a blast of radio-jazz, shrieks of laughter, jumbled talk and chair-banging, dropped from the next floor, and Allene said: "Honest, Ray, from about nine to one, or two, this place is as noisy as a picnic at a boiler-makers' union!" Ray straightened his shoulders, lifted his chin at an angle. Jazz-music, two or three drinks, and the girl you were hot about—that certainly was the one, reliable mixture to make you forget your troubles.

They were in the room, with the lights switched on.

"What kind of people live in this dump?—I thought the ceiling was going to cave in last time I stayed here."

"Oh, you know what I told you—the girls aren't exactly loose but they drink as much as they can hold and then they do a lot of heavy necking, and—"

"Sounds more like wrecking to me."

"But the funniest part is, Ray—most of the time they send the fellows scooting about two in the morning. They've got every single excuse memorized, I swear they have, Ray. Everything from illness to 'I'd love to have you stay, you know I would, but Frankie's a respect'ble girl and she wouldn't understand'."

"Well, I'm damned if I see how you can sleep much in this joint. I couldn't the other night."

"Oh, you know how I am—I could sleep on a street-corner, if nobody came up and bothered me. Besides, it's awfully hard to find the right room. The real cheap ones are just impossible—the gloomiest holes, and you can't have a male guest after eleven, and sometimes you can't have one at any time. And take a place like this—the rent's a little higher, and the accommodations are better, and you can do as you please, but—oh, that little, old but!—"

They were facing each other from armchairs upholstered in figured green with soft wood stained in mahogany—copies of better chairs standing in the high-priced hotels and apartments of the city. The chairs creaked, shook a bit with the movements of bodies, and in only another year, they would be ready for the junk-heap.

"I guess the only solution is to rent a couple of unfurnished rooms and buy your own stuff, slowly"—Ray snipped the end of a thread from his black pants recently mended by Allene.

"Dear, on what? You just take a look at the furniture ads in the papers. Nine-forty-nine, eleven-ninety-nine, and so on. They always get generous and take a penny off the round numbers, to give the impression of a wonderful bargain!"

In the silence, they needed to touch each other, leave the words, which were always inconclusive and nearly always leading to sordid, unfair problems locked against their vision. Confronted by a sordidness, which they had not made themselves, and uncertain concerning who was responsible for its extension on all sides of their lives, there was only one, guaranteed escape. They rose from the chair, eyes closed, and almost in marching-order. On the broad day-couch with its tan and purple-striped cover made faint by many washings, they kissed and hugged without stint. Their clean, innate urge— physical desire responding to physical desire—made all of the past quarrels negligible. Mentally, they were both caught in the same pit, clawing to rise out of its darkness to the little circle of light, which sometimes seemed thousands of miles away and sometimes drew nearer, for moments, and yet they were by no means happy. It was only a breathing-space, a strong need and pleasure, in which they still rubbed the bruise and fear, the anger and remembered stranglehold, deposited by a material struggle and all of its wiles and intrusions. Raising his head from Allene's breast, Ray looked up at the ceiling. "God, I wish that damn racket up there would stop!" Then he concluded, sheepishly: "I sure hate to listen to a wild party when I'm quiet and loving, myself. What d'you say? Let's do a little dancing."

"No, I'm too tired, Ray"—Allene pulled herself from the couch and went to a corner-closet to put on a pair of felt-padded slippers, as they still conversed.

Ray had risen, returned to the armchair. He noticed that a shade on one of the two, tall front-windows was up more than a foot, and hastily tugged it down. 'The-gold-fish-in-a-bowl wisecrack about lovers in flats certainly applied to New York, he thought. When their money was scarce they were lucky to have a room of any kind, much less the scrumptious privacy of a penthouse, or a suite on some fifteenth floor, or even an apartment with inside rooms.'

"How're the two bears coming along?"

"What bears?"

"Your mother and father."

Allene sighed, told herself that she was annoyed at him, and then gave it up as a bad job. She sat on the edge of the couch, to his right.

"They're still alive and kicking, if you're so anxious to know. I saw them night before last. I went over to see my father and get one of my dresses—I still have a few clothes there, you know."

Ray scowled.

"I wish you'd stop going there entirely. That mother of yours—"

"Listen, Ray, I know what she is and I don't want to hear it everlastingly. She can be the meanest, cruelest person on earth, but she has a good side—"

"Yeah, where is it—in one of her fingernails?"

Allene was pacing around the room, to cool herself.

"Please listen, Ray. I don't want to hate my own mother and I'm very near it sometimes, so I don't need any pushing from you. She can't see anything in life except money, money all the time, but it's not entirely her fault. When she was young she had her mind set on dozens of things and she thought father was going to be a successful business-man and get them for her. When he turned out to be just the opposite, she got more and more sour, and then she made a mistake and she thought, if she nagged him enough, he'd change and be what she wanted him to be. Why, I remember, when I was only a kid around twelve, there were lots of days when she'd sing and laugh in the kitchen, and when I had a birthday then, she spent the whole afternoon making icecream and a big birthday-cake for me."

"The only thing I can imagine her laughing at is a ten-dollar bill!"

"That isn't quite true, Ray—she was always selfish and narrow-minded but she wasn't nearly as bad as she is now. You can never tell what's going to happen. If we're still together twenty years from now, we might find ourselves right plop in another basement, quarreling over our kids and tearing each other's heads off for nothing, for just spending a dollar, or not having one. It makes me shudder to think of it, but it isn't impossible. I'm fairly sure father and mother started out by loving each other. They were both frightfully poor then, and from what I understand, my grand-parents weren't so keen about their marrying, either, because mother's father had a well-to-do match all arranged for her."

Ray sobered up, jumping from his chair and taking erratic steps toward Allene.

"Baby, you're in a hell of a cheerful mood tonight, aren't you?"

Allene approached him, held his head, kissed his cheeks.

"Oh, forget it, dear. I wouldn't be talking this way if I weren't all frazzled out."

"Nope, I can't laugh that one off. It certainly is hellish, what life can do to some people. There's something wrong with this world all right, but I can't put my finger on it. I don't believe in what those dirty Reds say—they're only out to smash up the country and let a few, long-whiskered Russians move in and take over the government—but something must be wrong when a fellow can't get a decent wage, can't tell when he's going to be fired, can't look forward to any promise of happiness. Something is rotten somewhere."

Allene was, substantially, in Ray's position. She saw the panorama—strike-news, gangster-crimes, prison scandals, people on Home Relief and in bread-lines, and the rumble of war-preparations from Europe and Asia—narrowed down to the slaps and barriers of her own existence and Ray's, but she swallowed the comfort and optimism of newspapers, felt that she was too uninstructed to cope with the huge mass hemming her in, and that, at home, most of the miserable conditions would be corrected when the people of her country woke up and elected honest and fearless men to office, everywhere.

"It is true, things are getting rotten all over, Ray, but all the papers say the President's doing everything he can, all except the out-and-out Republican sheets, and they'd be expected to knock him. I guess we'll have to be patient and see what happens, like all the other loyal Americans. The world's always been a question of money, Ray, and I know it's not going to change during our life-time, and after all, some people do fight it out and wind up snug and happy—it isn't hopeless by any means. We'll just have to hang on till we find better jobs, that's all."

"Yeah, hanging is right, with a rope around—"

"Ray, stop it this minute! We've got to use our heads and be just as hard as other people. It's a practical world and you've got to push your way up and not just sit down and talk dark, and complain about it."

"Don't worry, I'm not lying down for a long time yet, if I ever do"—Ray kissed her, tousled her hair, yanked her into a half-waltz, while she laughed, remonstrated. Sitting down later, while Allene was fixing some coffee in the screened-off kitchenette in the left-rear, he spun a nickel on the arm of the chair and it fell, rolled under the day-couch. He went down on his knees to retrieve it and, finally, had to push the couch away from the wall. The nickel was lying on a film of dust, with a sock resting near it. The sock was of blue-and-white stripes, obviously not one of his own. He picked up the objects and restored the couch against the wall. He was puzzled and intent, with a heaviness too sudden for any distinct motion. Allene appeared, with a percolator in one hand and cups held by the other. He waited until she had placed them on the large, pink blotter of a green-shellacked desk-table, to one side of the door.

"Say, 'Lene, have you gone into the haberdashery business?"— he twirled the sock around one finger.

Allene was blank for a moment, and then she laughed.

"Where did you find it, hon'?"

"Under the day-couch."

Allene stepped forward.

"Give it to me, Ray—it belongs to father. Ever since I packed up and left, mother's been quarreling with him because he always takes up for me, and now she's even carried it to the extent of refusing to darn his socks, and oh, well, he could do it himself—anything with a needle's pie to him—but I wanted to help him because . . . Ray, if anybody loves me, he does, in spite of all his prejudices."

"You're sure it doesn't belong to—"

"Ray, if you're going to be petty, you can go to the devil"—she snatched the sock, strode to the bureau beside the kitchenette, opening one of the drawers, flinging the sock inside, and closing the drawer with a bang.

Ray, who had followed her, quickly, noted that the drawer was filled, almost to the brim, with boxes, feminine underwear. Ray was undecided, not knowing whether to kick himself for acting like a wildly jealous sixteen-year-old suspicious of every mite, or whether he was justified in pursuing the matter, which he could not quite laugh away, inside. When Allene turned, he grasped her arms, prevented her from leaving.

"Maybe I am a jackass, Allene, but I didn't see any other socks in that drawer and—"

"God, don't be so small! I took them back the day before yesterday, and I was hunting for that one all over the place."

The bit of silence was like a string, cut and almost snapping, before Allene said: "Honest, Ray, I'm sick of it! If you're going to be so distrustful, so absolutely babyish, then we might as well quit each other right here and now. I suppose you're idiotic enough to think that Al slept here last night and walked out with one sock on!"

The picture made Ray release her and double up with laughter, but the laughter only caused Allene to become more furious. She felt that the aspersion had been small and stupid, and that Ray was "going cuckoo" and needed an unexpected lesson to lug him back to his senses, and his mirth also conveyed an over-sure attitude, to her, as though he thought that he could assail her at one moment and enjoy it at the next, 'just as though nothing had happened—oh yes?' These reactions, however, were no more than surface smarts. Underneath them she was riled by her life, by all of its present and past impossibilities, and, without the ability to reach, or even to locate, the targets in the far background of her feelings, she aimed at the one nearest to her immediate senses, trifling as it might be.

"Since you think it's so terribly funny, you can take your cap and trot along—cool yourself off outside on the street. You need it."

She had kept her back turned to him and the action made him contrite and serious as he passed her, faced her once more.

"I'm damn sorry, but it really was—"

"You get snickery and sorry a little too quick to suit my taste."

"But I didn't mean any—"

"I don't care what you meant. I'm tired and I'm sleepy, and I want to be alone—is that plain?"

"Yes, it is"—he was stung and his hands trembled as he whipped off, whisked his gray cap, ripped in the seams, from a hook close to the table, and hurried to the door. After he was half-way over the sill, with one hand on the outside knob of the door, he checked himself, revolved slowly, with the cap twirled between his thumbs to simulate jauntiness, in the old, proud manner of the male hurt too much by a woman. He was miserable, and the mistaken conviction that she knew it and still would not relent, caused him to desire to make her less certain of it, to talk once or twice more and then swing off, as breezily poised as he could.

"D'you want me to drop in tomorrow night, Allene, or will I have to see the rest of my harem?"

"No, please don't—drop in, I mean. You can ring me up, oh, perhaps Thursday around seven, if you decide to put thumbs down on your favorite crabbing and laughing act. Otherwise, please don't bother."

"All right, kid, and give my regards to McCormick tomorrow

night, don't forget."

He closed the door behind him, without undue noise, and the practised, renouncing, worldly airiness of his face disappeared, in a twinkle, to the simple hurt of a man whose sophistications were never more than frauds, self-defences as the man himself tramped down the stairs, pitched himself into the wet night. Ordinarily, Allene would not have been so severe at the end, would have run into the hallway and called him back, but the endless piling-up—day after day of overwork, brain-tax, choked resentments—fed her anger against Ray now, indirectly, and told her to be determined to 'teach him a lesson' before she showed him her love again, because, in reality, she wanted to attack the entire basis and force of her existence, and couldn't.

The rain had stopped and the street was dotted by black puddles reflecting the light in bars and spheres broken by ripples and closing again, with crumpled papers and pieces of refuse floating, or stuck, within them. The moist grime on the sidewalks showed a maze of foot-prints ridged and flattened in the drench of sallow light. The four-story houses coated with many layers of russet, dun, and yellow-cream paint to conceal the decay of their mortared bricks, their wooden window-frames, stood evenly wedged, some distance behind the grey-stone rise of office-buildings, twelve and sixteen stories high, with the angled dreariness of deserted jails waiting for morning to bring another mean activity to the returning wardens, and to the inmates transferred from the smaller prisons of their homes. Occasionally, machines sputtered and whizzed down the streets, carrying men and women to their pleasure, their secure destinations, in a flitting contrast to other men dressed in clothes little more than dirty bags and plodding toward the flop-houses and smoke-joints of the Bowery and its adjacent lanes, or poorly clad workmen travelling to the tenements east and just west of Second Avenue: girls with bent shoulders under crimsoned faces stiffly alert: girls with a brave show of cheap, brilliant-hued finery and an over-wrought toss to their weary heads: girls with the furtive sale of flesh stamped on every inch of their bodies and faces: men trying to act pugnacious, or supremely contented, under the betraying shine in their neatly pressed suits, the few coins, which they jingled, for reassurance, in their trouser-pockets.

Ray had borrowed a dollar from a counterman at Johnson's, several hours previous, and he still had ninety cents left. He was morose, limp, in every pore. He had never been a consistent drinker in his past, alternating his weekend jags with six days of abstinence, or sometimes, a highball or two, before he retired at night, and often he had avoided booze for weeks because his work had required a clear head, a ready tongue. Of late, however—unknown to Allene— he had been hitting the booze almost every night. So that his breath would not stink, he had been sucking lozenges and mint life-savers before he joined her. He had rediscovered what he had always known, that men, who would not loan him a quarter—bosses, sales-managers, small theatrical-producers, buyers, met during his few months of hotel-clerking in New York—were willing to order a drink for him, if he slipped into the uptown haunts where they hung out. They hoped that he would get drunk, slobber for more drinks, entertain them, run into a fight with someone outside of their crowd and give them a free show. Because he knew their swinish motives, always painted over with "good-fellowship," he had always sneaked out after the second or the third glass, drinking only enough to put a hopeful slant to his jaw, steadiness in his eyes, before he went to meet Allene. Now that he had a job, greasy, straining, and under-paid as it was, he found that most of the workers at Johnson's drank for another reason—they wanted to feel, for a time, that they were human beings, that they could yell and stamp their feet after the meekness of the long day of work, the idea that they must never stand still for half a minute, the supervisor, the assistant-manager, the manager himself, the visiting inspector, smiling, telling them that they were one, happy family promoting the welfare and the efficiency of the Johnson chain, and then cracking out with abuse for mishaps for which they were not to blame, driving the breath out of them, growing poisonous in the face at the barest mention of a raise.

Undecided, Ray loitered on a street-corner. The countermen, dish-washers, and cooks trooped into Max's, a spot behind a rubber-goods office on the second floor of a house between Fourth Avenue and Madison Square but on a Monday night the hangout would be emptier, since Tuesday was payday and the workers were always behind in everything—their rent, their credit at Max's, clothes bought on installment one dollar a week, the chiselling of coins from one another, until some of them finally reneged and were never seen again. Others paid up sometimes, cheated on the tricky luck of stud and blackjack games, plunged again, and then were cleaned out proper. They were not naturally dishonest. The load was simply too much for them.

Ray made his way to Max's. This world was still new to him. The world of white-collar workers was different. The majority of them were not so conscious of the steals, exactions, heaped upon them. Some of them were snobbish on the score of their better educations. Some were employed because they could be tactful—skin the victim, to the orders of the employer, and smear butter on the raw flesh. The process often ruined them. They fawned until they became managers, then bosses. Then they revenged themselves, bulldozed to forget "the climb." Many others, much less flat and scheming in heart and mind, hoped for this "climb" but never attained it. They worked through long years and wound up as dependents, living on sons and daughters, or lonely beggars drinking, gibbering in "Old People's Homes," to dim and numb the ending.

The cafeteria workers were not so deluded. None among them put on any airs. They knew that they could not arise to be sub-bosses and then owners. They had little education to fool them. Some thought that they were in a trap for the rest of their lives, but others were striking against this spurious fatalism. They shook their fists, held meetings to vent their grievances, cursed their drivers. It was only a beginning, but hate was crackling through the gags. The situation was becoming too clear to be accepted, misconstrued. Wages were being lowered to fixed levels, with minimum and maximum wage-scales. The maximum ones, almost never paid, were the jokers in the deck. The N.R.A. codes started with promises on huge banners and then grew yellow, full of loopholes, like hunks of swiss-cheese. Arbitrators in fine clothes arrived, told strikers to be patient, return to work, wait for a just solution. Then the arbitrators vanished, and the solution also. The workers were still held down by the fear of losing their jobs, fear of the black-list, fear of being thrown into unemployed ranks massed on all sides of them. The barrage of phrases from officials, newspapers, bewildered them, kept many of them tame. 'Pull together, with loyalty to your Country. Law-abiding citizenship Always. Peaceful methods of Protest Only. Sturdy, Christian virtues Forever. Respect for the Flag. Non-Partisan and Fusion Tickets to insure clean and honest Government. Obey the institutions of the Country and drive out the agitators and trouble-makers. Every one-hundred percent American should put his shoulders to the harness without grumbling.'

These phrases were still impressive, to Ray. He didn't know why, except that he thought it was American to stick up for his country and its laws and lawmakers. According to the papers and all that he had ever heard, there was only one public, one public interest. The division between capital and labor was admitted but, in the main, they were pictured as friends walking side by side for the good of the country. In the picture, capitalists spanked their greediest members and laborers drove the agitators from their ranks. The picture was still largely true, to Ray, but nevertheless, he had changed. His three months of unemployment had raised his bile, dug into his mind. The rebuffs, the sordid wrangles and partial hungers, never experienced for so long a period, had soured him. Night-club signs, photographs of society-people in mountain-resorts, and orders from cops to shake a leg, had made him frown for the first time. His dependence on coins from a woman had made him feel cheap. Bitter words, overheard from men on benches, from workers trudging home, had made him wince, wonder whether he did not echo them.

Since the base of the ideas refused to budge, the ideas themselves had to be revised. 'Capitalists were necessary, were often fine and patriotic, but the day-and-night idlers and revellers among them needed a good horse-whipping and a dose of Epsom Salts! The highest officials at Washington were honest, intelligent men but the lower ones, in States and cities, were usually lousy grafters ignoring the stupid men and women, who voted for them. The country was sound and wholesome, at the bottom, but the bankers, who had brought on the entire depression, were robbers down to the core and President Roosevelt would have to go after them with the old "Big Stick," and that went for some of the rottenest employers, too. The country was slipping from its good, old democracy and it would have to be whacked back to its senses—no doubt about that!'

Ray stood before the bar at Max's and voiced the last opinion to Ernie Hopkins, the counterman who had loaned him the dollar.

"Wait till Roosevelt gets after those bankers, Ernie!"

"Nuts. He's a wind-bag."

"But look at this guy, Pecora—tanning the hide out of them before that Senate Committee."

"Nuts again. It's a grandstand play."

"How d'you know?"

"How do I know I'm alive? They'll make 'em steal a few million dollars less. They're all in cahoots."

"But everybody's behind the President. All the papers say he's on the poor man's side."

"Who's everybody—the guys with dough, running those papers?"

"Yeah, but it took a lot of brains to make that dough, and maybe we haven't got them. Don't be a sorehead, Ernie."

"That's crap. They got the breaks and they were willing to tear anybody's belly out for two cents."

"Well, isn't it human nature to go after money?"

"Yeah, enough for a decent living, but you're not making a

million dollars honest these days, or any others. Not even a hun-
dred-thousand, pal."

"Aw hell, don't talk like a Red, Ernie."

"I don't know what I am. Go over to that café on Eighth Avenue and Thirty-Second, Felton's. Watch the cops come down on the
pickets and make them move along, 'cause the boss got one of those
injunctions against picketing, and then maybe you won't know,
either."

"Aw well, I can believe in my own country and still admit there
are some bastards in it, Ernie."

The girl beside Ernie, Laura Shires, interrupted.

"Say, Ernie, can this political argument, will you?"

"What's the matter, don't you agree with me?"

"Sure, but if I'm your heart-throb, like you always say, you
might pay me a little attention now and then, if it doesn't strain you
too much."

"Pardon me for butting in. I'm going in a few minutes anyway"—Ray shoved himself further down the bar and looked enviously at Laura and Ernie.

"All right, kid. See you on the mattress tomorrow"—Ernie
waved a hand, turned and applied himself to Laura.

Ernie had voiced one of the favorite jokes of the workers at
Johnson's, whose only sitting-posture occurred during their hurried meal-times. He was twenty-five with a blunt, spike-nosed face
and violent red hair. Laura was slender—hickory-stained skin and a
flat, small-lipped face under the quilted black hair. They had shared
the same exhaustions, same resentments, with only the minimum
of compulsory sympathy, which even the most self-enclosed among
the counter-workers shared with one another. When they had
walked out of Johnson's, they had forgotten each other's existence,
as far as personal emotions were concerned. Then one night, after
both of them were glum about losing their sweethearts, they had
kidded each other over being "thrown down"—throughout the next,
nerve-rapping day—and had walked out on the second night, in the

real start of a friendship. They couldn't think of marrying. Laura had a mother bedridden for years, and one of her brothers was serving two years in Elmira, for unlawful entry, while the other, in Chicago, contributed nothing except well-wishes and letters describing the illnesses, expenses, in his household. Ernie could scarcely support himself. They drank too much, sneaked up to Ernie's room once in a while. Two quarters, pooled, bought a bottle of gin at Max's, and so they began to deprive themselves of necessities, to squeeze out the quarters. The future was a blank. The present was fixed and slinking, endured with the aid of booze, though Ernie, becoming more and more a rebel, was forging a battering-ram, circulating among the workers at Johnson's and telling them to "get together, stand up for their rights."

Ray had retired to a table, with his half finished glass of rye. The place was nearly deserted, Monday blues. Only Max, the proprietor, Ernie and Laura, and another couple necking beside the machine, which played phonograph records, with a slot for nickels. Max slid up to Ray's table. He had a torso like a grain-bag sagging inward. He was short and knock-kneed. His face was a roly-poly smirk buttoned by the nose.

"Want to try a number?"

"Yeah, some time next year."

"Fagan, works in your joint, he raked in seventy bucks on it, last week."

"Yeah, I hope he keeps it"—Ray was listless.

"Well, how about it? You could always be the next one, y' know."

"I don't think I'll live that long, leave me alone."

Max, the professional jollier, yawned, and went back behind the bar. It was a variant of the policy-racket, twenty cents a number. The pari-mutuel prices on the horses at a distant track determined the winners of the numbers. The local "take" was handled by Gene Malloy, mobster. He turned it in to Constantini, a restaurant-owner on Broadway. Constantini gave it to Sol Kasoff, who drove to the curb in front of Constantini's, every 4 A.M. Kasoff tarried in his machine just long enough to grab the bag and speed uptown. The round-about was used to protect the leader, Frenchy Larosse, who was "hiding" in a luxurious house on the outskirts of the Bronx because the Federal authorities had indicted him for evading the income-tax. After a gang-leader, killing and extorting for years, became a household word, the Government, in some cases, suddenly woke up, with great fireworks of indignation, and admitted that it was aware of his activities.

Ray stared around the place. Flies snipped and circled over the bowl of pretzels, the cubes of orange cheese on a plate, at the end of the bar. The photograph of Roosevelt, rimmed by red-white-and-blue bunting, above the bar, had a big beer-spot on the left eye. It was an accident, the result of a wildly aimed glass in a fight one night. A mouse darted from a stack of beer-bottle cases and sped into one of the lavatories, through the chink between bottom door and floor. Gloomy, Ray reverted to McCormick. That bastard. Ray remembered his plight on the grass. Ten to one, Allene would never have allowed McCormick to be near her again, if that hadn't happened. Once more, Ray was knifed by the thought that Allene regarded him as a coward and admired Al for his bravery. What in hell had prevented him from getting back at McCormick? Well, in the first place, he had laid for Al on two successive nights, hanging around the house where Al lived, for hours, without catching him. The next few nights had been impossible. Walking miles in the hunt for a job and then staying out with Allene until midnight, and longer. After that, when he had caught sight of McCormick for the first time, Al had been surrounded by his friends, corner-guys almost as tall as he was, and the probability of their mixing in had made him hesitate. Those fellows didn't even know that fairness was in the dictionary, he had thought. Then also, Allene had kept on urging him not to nurse his grudge because she hated fighting between men, unless it was caused by stealing, or an insult to a woman, and even then, she thought that they ought to be sure that there was no mistake, before they swung. She had employed every argument she could think of, to hold him back—of course she had. That was always the line most women handed to a man. They were testing him out, wanted to see if he was a coward and would let them restrain him, even when the other fellow had it coming. They wanted to say they were shrinking from roughness, sure, and then what did they do?—they kissed it when nobody was looking. That must be the reason why Allene was still meeting McCormick. It couldn't be sympathy because McCormick was out of a job, and nothing else—he didn't believe it. Unless the issue was settled, it would last as a bone in their throats. He would lose her in the end.

He burst out of Max's, took the stairs, three at a time, went down the wet street in a lope nearing a run. He boarded a Twenty-Third Street car, rode to Chelsea. He was wedged between a fat woman and a child belonging to another fat woman. The first one poked him with her umbrella, the child kicked his feet.

He was in his shell, beyond physical annoyance. He jumped from the car while it was still rolling near Ninth Avenue. He knew the joint frequented by McCormick. The joints where the sheep tried to be wolves. Joints where they dribbled, staggered around, and asked to be sheared. The joints where the plug-uglies gave women Mickey Finns and carried them to rooms upstairs. The joints where workers were pitched into the street, with their heads rocking, every cent gone, to lurch along until cops questioned them, restaurant-bouncers flung them out. Then, when they were sober, they were tolerated again, yessed as good-fellows, prodded on to fight for the amusement of thugs, precinct-leaders.

They were crowded into Grately's now—howling, back-slapping, bragging under liquor, and trying to be happy with their women, who were watched by quieter, vicious-looking men ready to make up to the women whenever the escorts showed first signs of a slobbering loss of mind, or whenever they slumped over on the tables. Grately's was two steps below the walk. Ray peered down, to one side of the window. He could not see McCormick and was about to leave, when the latter, in the jam at the bar, jerked his head to talk to a man behind him. Ray ducked into the lobby of the rooming-house, to the right of Grately's and in the same building, and waited. He wasn't under-estimating the job. Al hit like a ten-pound hammer. Al was two inches taller, broader, had clipped men of the neighborhood, had chopped them down to their rumps. It was gossip that only gorillas had ever splattered him.

The pit of Ray's stomach expanded to numbness. His heart chugged like a motor that needed repairing. He had fought several times in his life, not counting school-boy brawls, drunks getting fresh with his girl, men lying about him behind his back, sore losers in card-games. He had stood up under the spark-ringed split, the near-paralysis of blows. Wavered. Found his spine to come back for more. Cursed himself for the involuntary shrinking, when blood spat from swelling mouth. Charged forward too blindly, his head lowered too much. Backed up, clinched, when the other man's blows were more powerful than his. He knew that most men were half cowards, half brave. They needed the raging feeling of being utterly in the right before they were effective. They attacked with their mouths first, to feel the other fellow out. In all of their anger, often, they wavered until the other man's punch brought the old insanity to pride.

Ray was too anxious to win, awed against his hate and will by McCormick's heft, his fighting reputation. But, looking sidewise through the glass door, to tab the men departing from Grately's, Ray discovered an emotion he had never had before. It was a hatred reduced to sheer discipline. It accepted the approaching fight as a practical task. Pain was the dirty side of the task and the worker struck to end it, flinched as little as he could, before exhaustion. It was like a day of work anywhere, with the slugging, the tension, confined to a minute, or two, made more concrete on face and chest. In another second, Ray saw McCormick leaving Grately's, and rushed out. No more ado than a machine started by levers and whirling the backward heart.

McCormick had been swilling ryes, treated by "friends," who

wanted his fists to be on their side in any impending tussle but made tens of excuses whenever he asked them for a loan of money. He carried a black overcoat. His dark red tie had almost escaped from a dark green vest. His pale blue shirt was loose at the collar. He picked his twisted nose, lowered the overcoat till the bottom grazed the sidewalk, tilted his black derby, and tapped the jut of his jaw, with right fist. He regretted that the jaw belonged to him. He was standing now, some two feet beyond Grately's.

"Hey McCormick." Al pivotted, saw Ray stepping toward him. Ray's face was calm, hands limp at his side. Al could kill a quart before he even commenced to lose his mind. He wondered. A guy wasn't always yellow just because you had flattened him and he had stayed put till you left, not unless you were there for some time. A sock with steam in it, flush on the button, could make a guy's legs rubbery, for three or four minutes anyway. Looked like Bailey was going to smile. God-damn funny.

"Yeah, Bailey. What's on your chest?"

Without answering, Ray plunged in, clenching hands as he lifted them, guarding face with right, driving left forward. Like any experienced brawler, Al raised arms a split second after the plunge. He was too late. The left caught him straight in the mouth. Off balance, his right dented Ray's stomach. Ray grunted, fought the stab in his wind, jumped back and waited. Surprised that he had not been crowded, in approved Dock 7 method, Al advanced slow—sore, but not as much as he wanted. Guy might be a punk but had a right to try back-payment. Get at him. Feinting, then Al's right on same side of jaw, Ray's on nose. Devil's dance of sparks, attempt at paralysis. Then clearer ache, for Ray. 'He could take it better now, fine.' Few men hit as hard, after crossing a certain drink-number, and Al was no exception. He tried to get in close. Ray side-stepped, guarded high. A right from Ray on cheekbone, muscle at its utmost now. The blow, helped by a trip on a crack in the walk, sent Al to right side, elbow prop. In a second he was up. A sweeping right glanced from Ray's fore-arm. It would have blotted him out, if it hadn't missed.

Wide open, Al got a right up-jolt, went back, still on his feet.

Ray heard voices, turned, left held straight behind him, right between shoulder and chin. Three men were pressing up the steps of Grately's. "There he is, the p—k, let's get him, boys! I saw him hanging around the window, the god-damn bastard!" Ray ran across the street and down Twenty-Third. Before rounding the corner, he saw that Al was kicking his derby into the gutter, from sheer anger, but was not joining the pursuit. The men were too drunk to run fast enough to catch Ray. They gave up the chase in the middle of the block. Ray subsided to a quick walk and caught a car held by the traffic light at Eighth Avenue and Twenty-Third.

Minus a gray cap, a dropped, Woolworth fountain-pen—who cared? Plus a stiff jaw, bruise on forehead, dull pain above the navel— who gave a damn? Hadn't been cowardice to run, when ganging was certain, though, to give McCormick credit, there was no blood-hound in him. Whatever his lousy faults might be, he wanted to scrap on his own, which was something. Odd, how he had been pulling at himself, like a fellow sweating over a rusty crank-shaft, just before he sighted McCormick. Lot of fool things said about bravery and cowardice. Perhaps the greatest bravery was when you felt sure you were going to be licked, in any immediate encounter, but moved in, backed up, careful and quick, waiting for the old ton of coal to crush you flat. Then, sometimes, it didn't. Guts, hell—how many times, outside of the ring, did professional bruisers, or gang-sters, go out with bare fists after their own kind? They knew whom they picked.

Yet, the elation died, even before he left the car at Third Avenue and walked over to the six-by-ten cell he had in one of those dingy, clammy, dirt-creviced hotels with the sign, "For Men Only," hang-ing below the electric name peppered by dead bulbs. Tossing on the knots in the mattress, he killed a couple of bed-bugs, and swore. In this case, the man who leased the hotel, worked as his own clerk, could not be blamed. He powdered and sprayed the rooms without end but the building was old, crumbled, and it would have been necessary to tear down every inside wall, to rid it of insects. It was one of many owned by a large corporation intending to wrest profits from them, make only a bare minimum of repairs, until the ceilings fell down, and even beyond that.

Ray was thinking on the bed. The quarrel between him and Al wasn't unique and it wasn't over sex alone. With enough money and a corking job, he'd be married to Allene, or living with her at any rate, now. And take men like Al. They didn't play fair and square, they went after everything with their fists, but who in hell had ever given them a chance to shake up their brains, instead? Tired after work, with not much jack, they stuck their chins up, craved to be yessed by other workers, lost their tempers, because they wanted to feel like great, independent mugs again. In a lesser way, he wasn't much better. High-school, one year at the U. of Chicago just to be lazy, root at the games, play shortstop and substitute right-end on the freshmen, snag after the roundest rattle-brains among the co-eds. Kicked out for flunking all his courses, because he showed no promise of being a star-athlete. Then white-collar jobs in Chi' and all around the middle-west, and finally, east.

His mother loved him and he loved her. His father was only the memory of a tall man with a Van Dyke and a booming voice, who had bossed his mother, with stern fatherly condescension, while she had cried, sometimes, but had seemed to adore it, mostly—a man dead almost twenty years. Now she was bossed by his sister and brother, damn them. She had lost all of his father's inheritance, through the manipulation of a crooked but legally wise trustee, and now she was supported by his brother, Sheldon. That snip-nose made fifteen-thousand a year, clear, with North Shore high-ups flocking to his Michigan Boulevard dentist-suite, but he groaned over every dollar he gave her, treated her like a servant, remembering that she was his mother only when other people were around. Then he kissed her and patted her hair, and she beamed at these crumbs of affection, blessed herself for having a wonderful, devoted son—poor mother.

She never realized anything that anyone did to her. She sure did live in a sentimental, babbling, fake-white world where everybody was goody-goody—Christ, would he ever forget the time his brother had refused her the money for a new coat, saying he needed every cent for new office equipment—he himself had drawn two weeks' wages and bought it for her, sixty dollars. Wonder if she was still going over to Hull House, making up study and hygiene courses for the mutts in the Maxwell Street district. A hell of a lot of good that did them, when what they needed was decent wages... Just the same, fellows like Ernie Hopkins were getting under his skin. They weren't right swallowing the stuff the Reds poured into them; and some day they'd turn and beat hell out of the Reds themselves, . . . but it was true that some of the higher-ups were getting away with too much. They ought to respect a limit to their grabbing. Life would have to become much cleaner and freer so that workers like McCormick, Allene, himself, would have a fair chance to be happy. It wouldn't be so long before the honest men and women from all sides, from millionaire down to scrub-woman, would have to get together and drive out the crooks and agitating fakers wherever they were found.

His optimism, however, was not as sure as it once used to be. God, the number of rackets, musclings, and scroogings, in New York City, in Chicago, everywhere. What was the answer? God alone knew. Well, Roosevelt was starting to clean house, if the reports could be trusted. He was a great man and maybe he would succeed, for God knows, the cleaning was certainly needed.

Depressed by these thoughts, Ray reverted to his family. His mother. During the cruel months, beginning just before July, he had written many letters to her, asking for money, and had torn up all of them, even when he had been griped, and his pride stretched flat. He knew that she would have had to plead with his brother, not once but often: that his brother would have parted with the smallest pittance possible: that Sheldon would have gloated over his failures: that his mother would have become frantic, and run into debt to mail him more money and urged him to come back to Chicago; and that his youthful sister, Frances, would have laughed and sent him five dollars with a letter of sympathy, but mote, jokes about 'why didn't he turn gigolo, with his good-looks, and should she get Irene, a former sweetheart of his, to ship him a box of socks and sandwiches, and he simply must return because Sheldon, the dear, was never himself unless he had somebody with whom he could really quarrel'—something like that. Any one of these stings would have hurt too much, but what his mother would have had to endure was the main deterrent. He knew that, secretly, he was still her favorite because, as she had often told him, he resembled her in being mushy and sentimental in refusing to accept unkind realities, in not being able to respect money and hold on to it the way others did. And she retained her secret favor to him in spite of her occasional weak scoldings of his little dissipations, his lack of "reliable qualities," and the profane ill-tempers he could fly into over little matters. The idea of her worry, her mournful conviction that he would never equal the sturdier success and virtues of his brother, had made him tear up the letters telling of his plight and substitute descriptions of a mythical job, his chances for promotion, plays which he had never seen, whose plots he copied from the reviews in the papers. The acceptance of coins and a seldom dollar from Allene, and very occasionally, from a man, who had once clerked with him in New York, had been less repugnant than troubling his mother.

Ray's pride, most of the time, was a bristling hindrance. Otherwise, it had to fall back on a nerve-drained sense of humor. To some extent his pride was vanity and magnified all the scratches inflicted on his self-respect. But for the most part his pride was a healthy reaction against injustice. Frequently, it had caused the loss of jobs, when managers had blamed him for errors actually committed by their stool-pigeon pets, and balled him out inhumanly, expecting him to take it like a whipped dog, or when patrons, accustomed to having the employees bend heads and race to their commands, however unreasonable, had found him turning upon them in protest . . . Dozing off, he recalled that he had once aspired to rise to a manager's job himself, and eventually, acquire an interest in a small dump of his own, or be an officer in a big one. Some of the patient, soapy-tongued, snooping clerks did it—the ones who yessed themselves blue in the face, worked just enough to get by—but not many. But what the hell, he wasn't old and crippled, yet . . .

He came to work at seven-fifteen, took his white, starched apron and jacket from a line of hooks to one side of the kitchen, with the other bus-boys, bolted two scrambled eggs and gulped some coffee. The workers had to eat in a far corner of the restaurant, segregated as alleged inferiors, even when most of the tables were empty. Their shift commenced at seven-thirty. The manager, in white linen pants and coat, was posted, with an elbow on the glass case filled with cigarettes and cigars, to one side of the revolving doors, checking the arrivals. If a bus-boy was more than two minutes late, he was docked half-an-hour's pay. Johnson's was supposed to have three eight-hour shifts, under the N.R.A., but in reality had only two, lengthened to nine-and-a-half and ten hours, with a few extras added during the lull-times from three-thirty to seven in the morning and kept on until the breakfast-rush was ended. Any worker complaining of this disregard of the sacred N.R.A. never lasted through the week— got fired on some cheesy pretext. If he went down to the N.R.A. offices and reported the violation, he was accosted by an information-clerk, filled out and signed a card, and was told that the matter would be investigated. After long waits and several trips, he discovered that the matter was still under investigation and the clerk much less urbane—others were waiting on business and he mustn't take up too much time. But while he waited he could see well-clad, uppish-faced visitors hand in their cards and win prompt admittance to the officials behind the opaque glass doors.

Johnson's, besides the manager, had three supervisors, women in white-belted wrappers stopping between ankle and knee above their street-dresses. One of them, Norah Gallagher, with a face as stiff as a board chalked in pink and white. She plastered the flat-pinned waves of her hair in henna, to keep the gray from showing. She was stocky, spraddle-toed, and her high heels gave her waddle a dipping motion. Her stub nose and small eyes, joined in an utterly mechanical peeve. She had tried to get rich running tea-shops, but had been forced to close the last one when her bank had crashed two years before, shortly after the beginning of the depression. The bank failure had left her stranded. She had been married and divorced twice—one husband had drunk up her profits, and spent them on Broadway girls, veiled whores; and another had run off with the cashier in one of her ultra-respectable, high-priced "Shoppes." She had the psychology of a middle-class failure dissatisfied even with the fair wages which she now received. Still drugged with her dream of wealth, she could not be happy in the reality, and felt herself lowered in the transfer back to the working-class from which she had started years past, even though her work now consisted only in bustling around, issuing orders, shoving a chair into place here and there, and putting on an alert, proper, chin-high look, as all of the supervisors were expected to do. Even the privileges of sitting down to chat when business was slack, eating at whatever table she pleased, ordering what she wanted, did not mollify her. The supervisors, nevertheless, had to be on their feet most of the time and were held responsible for scores of frictions and mishaps—that even a "higher" had to submit to hardships was distasteful to Norah. She felt herself abused beyond measure and took it out on the bus-boys, bus-girls, and workers behind the counter. She attributed her business-losses to a lack of practical instincts, though in reality she had always driven her own workers hard till some of them, cursing her, had walked out after the first week of their bondage.

She was not a monster, not unbrokenly selfish, but her life had strengthened a nature already selfish—years of scrimping, before she had opened the first, modest shop: unhappy loves: bankers refusing loans; the competition of other tea shops opened on her block had embittered her and she had whipped her workers on to the bone. She had not been able to see what she was changing into, a harpy, fluttering black wings among the larger harpies in her class. She was growing old. A final morsel of sex, invited by the rouge heavy on her face, and bossing the other workers, were now the only satisfactions which she could find.

The hour was eleven-thirty, when the mid-day crowd began, though the cafeteria was always well-filled. Workers, business-men and their subordinates, corner-touts and gangsters swiping the forks and knives to keep in trim, adolescents on their way to school, women in furs eating huge meals after their shopping-tours—all of them pushed one another around the ringing ticket-stand pre-sided over by one of the watchers, Phil Apfelbaum, a tall youth with dark puffs already under his eyes, working his way through a business-college and thinking that he had to act with a cool mask, a great assumption of worldly poise, changing from an obsequi-ous smirk to a sneery stare, according to whether the person was "under" or "over" him in the social and economic scale. The watch-ers were hired to prevent people from grabbing two or three tickets from the machine, having one punched for coffee and the others for heavy meals, and then presenting only the first one at the cashier's counter. Johnson's, cheating its workers, and customers, too, for huge profits, had no desire to have the practice emulated, in a tiny sneakery at its own expense.

The jam, clatter, and chatter, mounted. There was little real pleasure. Most of the eating was a stolid-faced, hasty stuffing. The eaters, unless they knew one another, eyed their neighbors, mainly, with disfavor, remoteness, covert wariness. The roughly dressed workers at the table were more companionable, but too tired to be really gay. The employees had to whip themselves to a frenzy, since their number was not sufficient to take care of the mob, without it, and because other workers, with only half an hour and less for lunch, had to hurry in and out, swarm and bump into one another at the food-and-drink counters, thus adding to the burden of their fellow-workers in the cafeteria. Ray hustled from table to table, with a metal tray upheld by a handle underneath, through which his fore-arm fitted. He had to remove the dishes, wipe off the tables with a wet, folded towel, put the condiment jars, salt and pepper shakers, back on the nickel table-holders, and straighten the chairs. The supervisors and managers were on top of the bus-boys and bus-girls, continually pointing to spaces cluttered with dishes, with new customers standing impatiently over them. If the trays were not piled high before the bus-workers made for the kitchen, they were reprimanded. Careful and yet hurried work—an impossible combination—was required to stack the plates, saucers, cups, and silverware, neatly, in high columns, racks, and yet keep pace with the ever-filling, ever-emptying tables. In addition, with customers knocking against them, when their trays were overloaded it was difficult to avoid dropping some of the utensils. Again, the plates were slippery with left-over grease, food, and hard to handle when the worker couldn't take his time. Ray had several narrow escapes, in these respects, and he cursed under his breath, as he had on the other days of the job.

Norah, in all the turmoil, seemed always to gravitate back to his vicinity, wherever he was moving. It was no coincidence with that old tub-face. She hadn't forgotten his remark yesterday, when she had followed him to the kitchen and said: "Listen, Bailey, when you polish the woodwork you're not supposed to be posing for a slow-motion picture—d'you understand?" and he had answered: "I'll try and be as fast as you are, Miss Gallagher," and left her standing, angry, but not quite certain whether she had been insulted, or not. She rolled up to him now, as he rested for a second against a table-front.

"Over at the end-tables, Bailey—can't you see?"

"No, I can't see everywhere at the same time."

He hurried away, with a glare. If they expected him to lie down and take anything, they were going to be surprised, though he dared not let his tongue go too far—the recollection of tramping, broken-spirited, bench-warming days, of nights with empty pockets and despairing head, was too close, and the threat of their return, too insistent. Then the inevitable happened, as it did at least once a day. A blatant-faced juvenile, in cream satin-back crepe trimmed with squirrel, a white turban with a little, black crescent at the front, swung around to chaff with her collegiate escort and rammed her tray against Ray's spine. Two of his cups toppled, crashed against the tile floor. Some of the girl's soup spilled on a cuff of her dress. Glowers. Remarks that Johnson's ought to pay for the cleaning. A nasty word from the man. Ray boiling, biting lower lip to keep from saying anything. A supervisor, Agnes Kramer, was instantly on the scene, shooing Ray off, after he had picked up the pieces. In such cases, the supervisors were instructed to be profusely apologetic to the customer, if he showed any front of clothes, and give him a short "sorry it happened," if he didn't. The workers were never rebuked on the outside floor but always had their ears tanned in the kitchen, to keep up the bluff of polite, tolerant treatment. Agnes was pretty in a softly oval, saucer-eyed, and yet business-like way. All of the supervisors were selected for this latter quality, which meant several things. They would spur the workers without mercy, forgetting that they were also wearing themselves out, and catch on to the art of making the workers regard it as "for the efficiency and advancement of everyone connected with the firm." They would help the manager weed out the "trouble-makers," the ones who talked back when assailed for slips, or strove to rally the other workers in protest: jolly the more docile ones, during the brief breathing-spells, try to make them believe that, at Johnson's, they belonged to one big contented family.

Agnes and Norah caught Ray in the kitchen. Norah rasped first.

"You're positively the clumsiest bus-man I've ever seen."

"Clumsy?—I'll say. Absolutely, if you don't catch on quicker than you have, put a real snap into it, you're not going to last long here"—Agnes piped, grim and matter-of-fact, as though she had been forced to notice him but barely knew that he was living.

In reality, he did have little existence, to her. Just another bus-boy, to be squelched in the day's routine, until she erased all of them and stepped out with her boy-friend, a hardware-buyer for a department-store. Ray fumed, controlled himself with an effort mighty to him.

"Well, it wasn't my fault. That girl walked straight into me while I was scooping the dishes up. I haven't got eyes in the back of my head."

"Never mind that. You're supposed to do your work and keep your eyes open, too. You don't have to be in a trance, you know"—Norah eyed him, as if she were examining a worm of some baffling species, and then flounced off, with Agnes.

Ray, burning under sweat, looked after them. He translated it personally, again. Who in hell were those two fat-wrigglers? Were they any better than he was? A dish-washer raised his back from the large, zinc tub, his red hands dripping greasy water. He was pock-marked, two front teeth gone, old in the middle of his thirties.

"Those god-damn tarts—they think they own the earth. They can't remember they're workers too, just like we are. The tarts! I'd like to splash dirty water on their uniforms and make them mop up the floor for a coupla weeks!"

"Couple of years, you mean!"—Ray went back to his rounds, still surly.

A bus-boy had to take such incidents over three hundred days a year. No wonder they got crushed and tongue-tied, if they stayed at the job. They ought to have a strong union, fight to be treated just as well as any other decent citizens of the U. S. A.—a patriotic union but not a wishy-washy one, either. And that flip wench in the squirrel collar—why was it, nine times out of ten, the swellest dressed babies were always most intolerant, had the worst manners? The workers at Johnson's were boisterous, when they had a chance to measure their breath, and poked the fork-prongs straight into their mouths, left the spoons in the coffee-cups, but most of them knew what human consideration meant. He was beginning to see that there was a hell of a lot of difference between fancy manners, put on for display, and plain helpfulness with no paint on it. Of course, a very few people had both polished manners and a considerate spirit, but they were rare birds, indeed.

One-thirty came, the scramble went down a fourth, and Ray had the opportunity to glance around now and then. Look at Viola . . . something, he didn't know her last name. Short and narrow-shouldered, with the skinniest arms he had ever run across. Her flat stomach was always bulging out, in the effort to hold up the heavy tray. She didn't have the strength for this kind of work. She couldn't be more than eighteen. A hell of a child-bearer she'd make, after three or four years of this work. And Bessie, the one with spec's—she was fat enough, but she had a grayish-brown skin with no life in it. Hardly any muscle either, just enough to get by—the grind gave them a little of it, even when they weren't healthy. After about fifteen trips to the kitchen, even his own arms had to tighten, so he could imagine how theirs felt. And Geraldine, the good-looking red-head—she was sturdy, clear-eyed, round as a peach, but about four in the afternoon her feet dragged and scuffed on the tile, her shoulders hunched an inch, or two. The stronger ones didn't show the strain so clearly, went out and danced at night, but how long would it last? If some of the bus-girls fell for any man under forty with a front and a car, it was to be expected. The respectable ones hoped for marriage, and those less so wanted a gay fling before the next morning's grind, but it was the same in both cases—escape, frightened, partly held back, or willing "to go the limit."

The bus-boys were all runts, too. Jim Cooper was a flyweight and Coffey wasn't much higher. They took them in their teens, or hovering around twenty, mostly, because they could get them for less—didn't want the bigger ones who applied, because they'd be more apt to go on the war-path and some of the customers might have thought it was curious that strapping men and women couldn't get better jobs than that. Why they had hired him was a mystery—must have found themselves suddenly short of help on the morning he walked in. The hour was two and the workers began to eat in relays of five, or six. They were only allowed a choice from the three, lowest-priced orders and coffee. They were charged extra for dessert, though three dollars a week was deducted for the food. Ray approached Hannah Rierson, the remaining supervisor. She was the fairest of the lot—a squat, long-faced girl with even, white teeth and a flow of chestnut hair to the nape of her neck. She was studying to be a cellist and worked to help support her family and pay for her lessons. After a bright remark about the weather and how she wished that she could be out in the sun, she gave him permission to go to his meal. Ray had the feeling that she would lose her job one of these days—'too chummy with the workers, and not just apple-smear either. When a fellow worked down at the bottom, he sure caught the knack of measuring the sincerity in the smiles of the workers above him in the scale!'

He ordered macaroni and meat-balls, and repaired to the far corner. One of the tables was occupied by Ernie, Laura, Cooper, Viola, and Joe Coffey. Ray slid into the spare seat. All of them ate too quickly, spoke with food in their mouths. In her black dress, black stockings and white canvas shoes, with the white, black-ribboned bandeau awry across the center of her mouse-brown, crudely bunched hair, Viola looked like a tragic ink-drawing come to life. Her face was apathetic, loose-lipped, not sub-normal but slow and hampered in her heart and mind. Cooper was slim, quiet, good-natured. Coffey sought to be loud and slangy, to rescue a head none too full with thought, to bluff away his stunted body.

"Why doesn't Gallagher stop picking on me?"—Viola's voice was thin, stoical. "She's a pain, that battle-ax."

"She comes out with her lousiness, anyway. Pilaky doesn't. When the rushes aren't on he joshes all over the counter, but baby, is he watching like a fox, is he? Put too much on a plate, or go inside and sit on a box for a minute, and see what happens!"—Ernie glanced, behind him, to be sure that the object was not within ear's distance.

Pilaky was the manager, a six-footer with a shiny, protruding forehead, front skull, wet ribbons of dark hair clinging to the back of the head, and a taut, creased face with smooth venom sometimes welling out from the habitual expression of the jovial "efficiency-man."

"Aw, I like Pilaky—he's always kidding the shirt off us but he isn't so terribly mean"—Geraldine, who had joined the table, was tuckered out but still invincibly flirty.

"Yeah, he'd take your shirt and sell it, if he could"—Ernie regarded her as a pleasant nitwit.

Laura slapped his upper arm.

"Atta boy, Ernie. Keep on talking. What's the difference? He's got you where he wants you, and you don't even dare to open your mouth to his face!"

"Sure I don't—that wouldn't do me any good. I'm going to get some of the boys together and trot them up to the Food Workers Industrial, one of these days. I've been up to their office on "X" Street a couple of times, already. We've got to organize, the whole bunch of us, or we'll never get anything out of the bastards running these chains!"

"Well, pick out a good union then. I heard those Industrial guys were nothing but a crowd of rat-tailed Reds"—Coffey scowled with his chin held up at an angle, as he thought a good American should.

Laura came to bat, her darkish, flat little face suddenly ablaze with the light from black eyes.

"Yeah? Well, when you get your ten-fifty tonight, you call up your best girl and take her up to Broadway, Joe Coffey. Then you'll be plenty in the red all right, tomorrow morning, figuring out just how you're going to squeeze through the rest of the week on the dollar you've got left, and the ashes you've got dumped in your head, too!"

"Aw nertz. Nobody'll ever catch me stringing along with a gang of long-haired belly-achers. They don't want to help us none. All they want to do is bust up the country."

"Get out; there isn't a guy up at the Industrial doesn't go to a barber unless he's broke. If you want to feed on hooey, you go ahead, but I'm telling you something—Johnson's'll walk all over a guy like you and make you like it, just because they're waving the flag in front of your mug. And listen, keep a close mouth about what I just said, and don't go blabbing anything around, get me?"

Joe was afraid of Ernie, so he subsided, still scowling, but the barest shade less certain of it. Sometimes a guy didn't know what was right, or wrong, he thought, but he did know the Reds were out to use a guy and get him to have his face smashed in for nothing, sure they were. Geraldine spoke.

"Well, if there's ever a strike in this joint, you can start right in and count me out of it. I've got a sick sister on my hands, all the time, and believe me, nobody'll ever worry about her, if I don't. What d'you say, Vi?"

"Oh, I don't know what it's all about. All I know is, I'll prob'bly have to keep right on working my back off till I marry some one"— Viola stroked her forehead, wearily, with the back of a hand.

Cooper broke in.

"You haven't any guarantees even then, kid. You're liable to get a crush on some fellow making fifteen a week and wind up breaking your back keeping house for him, and raising your kids. Rich guys don't go around marrying bus-girls, except in the movies."

"How d'you know? I've got the same chance as any other girl."

"Yeah, no chance at all."

"Sez you. Maybe I haven't got one of those dolly-wolly faces, but I know lots of fellows care a lot more about a girl's character, and—"

"Sure, I do myself, and I wasn't knocking your looks either."

"Oh, be quiet. You'll never win any prizes."

The others smiled, knowing that Cooper was sweet on Viola and sometimes took her to a cheap neighborhood movie and then back to the hallway of the building where she lived, since they had no other place in which they could be together. Ray was mixed-up as he spoke, feeling that an unshaped part of himself, hard to define, scarcely accepted, was walking a step in front of all of his previous convictions, while they continued their march, derided the thought of any possible division.

"I think you're on the wrong track, Ernie. That radical outfit doesn't give a damn about us. All they want is to get us sore as hell, make us go out and break something, fight the cops, and then we'll only wind up in the hoosegow with a nice, long time to think it over. What's the matter with the A. F. of L. instead? They're working-men just like we are, and they're not out to rip the Government to pieces, either."

Ernie pursed his lips to an ugly sound, like the tearing of thin cloth, before he answered.

"Yeah, I heard the main guys are busy right now, trying to put over a 'yellow-dog contract' with the Johnson chain. If they do, the chain'll have the right to hire union and non-union men, both at the same time, and the wages'll stay exactly where they are. Sure, the A. F. of L's got plenty of workers paying in thousands to the fat-bellied big shots running them. When those officers call a strike, there's only one reason behind it—the workers are so damn mad that the officers can't get out of it! And then what? They tell the strikers they've got to be nice and sweet, just like lambs, and leave the scabs alone, and ask the Government to arbitrate. Yeah, they arbitrate all right, but where I come from they call it picking your pocket, and if you're a wise kid—well, you know whose pocket I mean!"

"But listen," said Ray, "you'll find crooks on both sides of the fence, big and little, but I don't think the main guys at Washington know anything about it. They can't look into everything at once, that's the trouble, and sometimes they're just plain fooled about what's going on. When Roosevelt gets wise to some of those little crooks he'll clean out the whole, dirty gang of them and he'll make them see plenty of stars, too, before he's through."

Ernie started to answer and then checked the words, since he had detected Pilaky advancing within a foot of the table. Pilaky had meant to fire Ray on the coming evening, because Norah had recommended it, but he had heard all of Ray's last answer and looked at him, now, more approvingly. The fellow was green at the work and got a little grouchy when the supervisors nailed into him, but he talked safe enough. That was the main thing. If they were law-abiding and believed in the country, they soon got the feel of sitting on their tempers and settling down to harness without making any unreasonable demands, unless they were lazy, and this fellow did work his arms off. Might turn out to be a good cog at that. Gallagher was a prize bitch—if he listened to her, always, he'd be canning them right and left, just when they started to get the hang of things. She was a valuable bitch because she extracted every ounce of energy from the help, made them feel that they were being spied on every second, but she didn't realize that a dab of salve, applied at the right time, was just as potent as the worst bawling-out, in some cases. Pilaky suspected Ernie, from snatches of conversation which Eddie, the ex-pug' bouncer, had claimed to have overheard, but Ernie had worked at Johnson's for almost a year and was liked by most of the workers. In such circumstances Pilaky had orders from the bosses—who rarely appeared on the scene of activities—telling him to secure definite evidence before he took action. Back from the kitchen, he halted at the table, with the look of reluctant, "friendly," and yet steel-eyed whip-swinging.

"They're piling in unusually heavy now. Hurry it up, kids—it's one of those days, you know."

Viola and Geraldine piped "all right," immediately sprang up, but the others rose more slowly, in silence. They had all been talking, cramming food, less than twenty minutes. When Pilaky strode off, even Coffey thumbed his nose, quickly, lest he be discovered. Assigned to mopping the floor, afterwards, Ray meditated. Things were pretty stinko when a kid as decent as Ernie, got wild notions, raved against his own Government. Ernie was right and wrong. The fakers and blood-suckers at both ends would have to be wiped out. Maybe there'd have to be vigilante-squads all over the country some day—honest business-men, big shots, joining up with workers, everywhere, to elect men on the platform of a square deal for every one, rich or poor, and see that it was enforced, too. At five-thirty, Pilaky, making the rounds, handed the pay-envelope to Ray, gave him a brief: "Be good, Bailey." Hadn't been canned, even after the run-in with Norah and Agnes, hmm, funny. Perhaps they tried a fellow out, respected him if he couldn't be stepped on completely. Holding his head a bit higher, Ray left Johnson's, walked over to Max's and sat there until seven. Then he called up Allene, from a phone in the hallway of the ground-floor. The voice at the other end was an impatient, arrogant, feminine squeal, seemingly, a little drunk, with a latest fox-trot and faint haw-haws sounding behind it. "Wait a minute, cutie. . . . I'll see. . . Neeoh, she isn't in—she left word she wouldn't be back until midnight, but you'll get over it, cuteness, sure you will . . . bye-bye." Ray banged up the receiver. Another rye was the medicine he needed, and would all women kindly go to hell?

Part Two

NEAR THE middle of January in Boston, the waning afternoon was blinded by a ravage of powdered snow from a gray glare. The snow attacked in numbing whorls, flew straight in the blasts, charged around street corners, screwed against walls and rebounded, and rampaged in all directions when winds dove into each other and then scattered, like falling knives. The historic Commons with its levels and gradual slopes, slept under hillocks, mounds, ridged layers of white, pitted here and there with foot-prints and grazed here and there by the scurry of old, stiff yellowed newspapers and the flurry of a sparrow, flying low to avoid the wind. Sometimes a dog, bull-terrier or spaniel, rolled and frisked in the snow while its owner, fur-coated, gloved, yelled out an affectionate summons, all his or her attention for the dog, and completely indifferent to other men and women plowing past, some without overcoats, with hands thrust into pockets, some with holes and tears in the soles, the tops of their shoes, and some bending in scant coats under thin dresses, their legs, their arms, blue and pimpled with the cold.

Women could often be seen with wolfhounds, Belgian police-dogs, straining at the leashes. The dogs broke away at times, sniffed at the ankles of poorly clad passersby, but the women, sharply recalling them, did not share the curiosity. When the dogs trotted back, they received a loving pat, a reprimand. Then the women hastened on, with faces reddened and moist over cosmetics, necks and ears protected by high collars, bodies free-swinging under the drape of beaver, muskrat and other warm furs. They were women of the "athletic" kind, and, to them, the beginning of a blizzard was a bracing lark, a daring tingle, before the quiet reading hours or the festivities of the night. On the following day, if the snow were to halt, some of them would appear on the lagoons and duck-ponds, skating in tandems, circling with smiling, or wooden-faced, men. Others would sally forth, pulling the decorated sleds on which their bundled, rosy-cheeked children were perched, or walking along, with laughter and indulgent orders, while Negro domestic-workers performed the same service. Some of the fathers would participate in the innocent guise of this fun, chewing cigars, cuddling their delighted tots, but most of them were elsewhere, scheming and stewing behind office-desks, racking their brains to outwit one another, to tie up and compress thousands of lives, throw them around, speculate on the money which they produced, discard them without a grain of compunction. These ruling ones were from the Beacon Hill district directly fronting one side of the Commons and still uninvaded by an underworld pressing behind it, or from the Copely-Plaza—that large, "elite" hotel near the upper end of the Commons—where they lived in costly suites away from the summer-homes along the Atlantic, which they had boarded up for the winter. In the summer-time they departed, leaving the Commons to the workers, the unemployed bench-warmers, the sailors, the prostitutes, and the bands of toughs, apprentices or seasoned underworld men.

The blizzard on Boston Commons, however, had a different significance to the newsboys in front of or just inside, the kiosks leading to the underground streetcars at Tremont and Boylston Streets and at the opposite end of the Commons near the gray dome of the State Capitol. They stamped their feet, clapped their hands in cotton gloves unravelled to many a hole, and yelled the headlines of their wares—children from eleven to fifteen, with freshness already cheesed with adult wisecracks, with taunt and fist imitating the grown-up plug-uglies in their neighborhood, or the cheaply glorified, artificial gang-leaders, at whom they had stared, pop-eyed, from the balconies of fifteen-cent movie-houses. Their faces had already been pinched by "street-wisdom"—cheating to get coins; spying on women's legs; ganging after girls; sneak-thieving in stores; chalking dirty words on sidewalks and scribbling them on the walls of toilets. They were no longer boys but stunted men, raked by snow and cold, screaming the head-lines which announced that Mrs. Gilhooley, accused of killing her husband by slipping arsenic into his oatmeal, had fainted on the stand, under cross-examination, and had wept into filigreed handkerchiefs—a woman subsequently acquitted, hoisted on shoulders, carried in triumph outside of the courtroom, and then hired to tour the cheaper vaudeville-circuits of a nation doped by panderers, prayer-mongers, clowns, in the interests of the bigger exploiters.

The blizzard had another meaning, also, to the men in spotted, ripped clothes waiting for the traffic-lights to let them cross the street. Their faces stubbled, their hopes turned to scum, they were on their way to Salvation Army flops, twenty-cent hotels, the herded charity of municipal lodging-houses—places reeking with human servitude, with officious tactics near the crawl of vermin, with sneer and rudeness, tin plates scant with slop, coffee tasting like waste-fluid, cots digging into row on rows of spines, and pasty-smug men and women distributing tracts, gurgling about blessed redemption, whining of a worshipped God, to hide their miserable condescension. Then six A.M. and the jerk, the bark of their jailers, tumbling them out to renew the hunt for non-existent jobs, to beg for nickels, if the pride had been kicked out of them, or to sit on the benches of the underground street-car platforms, until they were ejected, or huddle in the waiting-rooms of the South and North Stations, until special-cops of the railroad-lines drove them out, or to stand in doorways beside restaurants and ale-houses flaunting N.R.A. eagles in their bottle- and food-laden windows. Yet, some of these men were beginning to wake up and were joining the maligned Reds in Unemployed-Demonstrations on the Commons, in mass-meetings for unemployment-insurance, for the extension of the C.W.A., for adequate relief—fighting back against the charges of the cops and aided by the hate and rage of workers in the unions supporting their demands.

The blizzard would have still another meaning, too, for workers who would soon pour into the shed-like, underground car-entrances, from the huge department-stores on State Street, the twine and dry-goods firms, the wholesale grocery-companies, the fish-markets, between that street and the docks—men and women, to whom the furies of snow and wind meant rising coal-and-wood bills, warmer clothes for their families, their meager wages dissolving, instantly, at the first invasion of this new horde of necessities. Other workers again would jam the cars to reach their single cells, facing the night of radio-croonings and optimisms—if they were lucky enough to own cheap sets—or "romantic," lip-glued posturings, hothouse melodramas, at a neighborhood movie, to dull the realization that this was Monday and they would be broke before the end of the week, would have to cut down on meals, deny themselves the smallest pleasure, to subsist, somehow, until their bosses handed out the next, comparative dole for days of hard, nerve-yanking work.

Shooting the elevator up and down in the Book Hotel, Ray, in spasms, reflected on precisely the same situation. Monday was pay-night, eleven dollars for six days, twelve hours a day. Six went for the room in which Allene and he lived, in a scurvy "hotel" on a side-lane just off Scollay Square, one of the main underworld and proletarian centers in the down-town part of Boston. Thirty-five cents for their breakfasts every morning, sometimes reduced to twenty-five for both of them. Twenty cents for their lunches, and damn little food at that price. Then supper in their rooms, thirty cents worth of food, usually, bread, sausage, and coffee, with some of the bread soaked in the coffee to make up for the absence of butter, which was bought only once a week. The total amounted to six-dollars and sixty-five cents above room-rent. It couldn't be done this week. Last week, Allene had secured three half-days of typing at The National Sales-Campaign Company, earning a dollar for each half-day, and so they had barely managed, including a minimum of incidentals such as newspapers, a package of cigarettes a day, between them, and one punk movie on Scollay Square. This week, however, threatened to be a nightmare. The Sales-Company had laid off its part-time typists with the vague promise: "Drop in about two weeks from now—maybe we'll have some more work for you then." Unless Allene found something else, part-time or full job, they would only have money to pay the rent and buy barely enough food to keep them in their half-hungry state. Then again, Allene's carfare while she was looking for a job, or even one cigarette a night for each of them before they went to bed, would be impossible. It was reducing life to the lowest ebb of physical existence! If she did land another part-time job, three or four bucks a week, the existence wouldn't be so damn much higher, either.

One of the elevator-men lived at home and had to fork in, to his mother, everything except three dollars for his lunches near the hotel, his carfare and other expenses. His lot was a bit better, Ray thought, but even then, how much money did he have left for any kind of pleasure, to take out his girl, to shoot a game of pool, drink a few beers on Sundays. The other two elevator-men had an even tougher break. They lived alone, without gifts and mendings of clothes from relatives, or home-meals, and the rent shared by brothers and sisters, as well as parents. One of them had confided that his steady girl had ditched him, recently, because she couldn't stand sitting night after night with him in the front room of her home, and some of the department-heads, in the loan-agency where she worked, were always asking her out to night-clubs, shows and swell dances, and so, one night she had gone hysterical, screamed and laughed in his face, and told him she thought love was only a big joke, anyway.

Ray tightened his hand on the brass control-levers, as he thought of this man, Leonard Drossi, running the elevator to his left at that exact moment. Leonard had openly confessed, on the noon of this very day, that he was seriously considering a proposition made to him by a young tart of his acquaintance, who had known him, spoken to him, for a year in the shady hotel near St. Botolph Street, where he had worked. She had paid for his drinks in a liquor-grill on one of the squalidly narrow, crooked streets leading from Edgar Allen Poe Square, ironically enough, and had unfolded the idea. College girls and others from well-to-do families often invaded the down-town section, in search for adventure. She would get herself introduced to some of them, be "refined" at first, drink with them and invite them to "sleep it off" in her room. When they woke up, late in the morning, she would not be there but they would find Leonard, in pyjamas, in the room. Hazy about the previous happenings, they would be eager to leave as quickly as possible, without raising a fuss if part of their money was missing, and without even being certain that they had not spent it themselves during the past night's revelry. If any one of them was friendly and stayed, Leonard's partner would reappear with a plausible story, after he left, and "work them" some more.

When Ray had assailed Leonard for desiring to mix in such a crooked sneak-game, Leonard had asked whether the owners of hotels were not crooked, using their employees, to make big money, and giving them almost nothing in return. Leonard had also asked whether the big shots, who had waltzed off with his girl, were better than sneaks, and how about some of the business-men and politicians of Boston, always grafting in a safe way, under cover, while the papers praised them as great civic-leaders? How about it? Leonard wanted to know. Ray had replied that fighting crime with crime only meant an eventual jail-sentence for the smaller guys, while even the bigger ones sometimes got it in the neck, too, and that it would be more intelligent to join a decent union and fight for living-wages. Then Leonard had informed him that a union-organizer, over two weeks before Ray had been hired, had been pounced upon by the private dicks in the foyer of the Book, beaten up and thrown out on his ear, and Leonard had demanded to know what was the use of a man's fighting, of his being honest, when the odds were so tremendously against him? The discussion had waxed hot, with Ray stubborn but growing weaker in his retorts. His mind couldn't shake off the matter now. It blazed in his head whenever he was waiting for the elevator to fill, listening for the starter's click. A man lost his desire to live, or became a crook outside of the law, if he thought the world was all wrong, and it wasn't all wrong by a damn sight, but parts of it certainly needed an out-and-out scrubbing, change! The workers would have to form strong, patriotic unions, and the honest business-men would have to unite with them and halt most of the brazen robbers existing in every walk of life down to the under-world. Yep, there would certainly be an uproar such as the country had never known, when the next Presidential election rolled along. Things were positively raw when fellows as hard-working as Leon-ard—not rats, but with a good, clear look, usually, on their faces—were tempted to enter the lousiest practices, in a preying on people with money, and all because they couldn't see any other way out of it. Some men and women were natural-born criminals, he thought, but a lot of the others had been and were still being kicked straight into it, just the same, and it was a damn shame, too. Yep, the hon-est people of the country would have to stage a clean-up, a kind of peaceful but determined revolution from coast to coast, and it would have to happen before very long, too. Roosevelt had started it, but there were too many skunks trying to undermine him, damn them.

His legs and feet felt a drag, his neck was stiff from craning toward the red, floor-signal lights in the rows of opaque, glass discs, and his arms heavy with the constant opening and closing of the iron-grilled cage-and-floorshaft doors, for the greater part of nine and a half hours, with two and a half still to go. Ben Weintraub, the starter, was a fair man, rotating the passengers, evenly, among the elevators, to give all of the operators a minute of rest on their feet, and overlooking it when they took five, or ten minutes more than the half-hour allotted them for lunch. He was also lenient when they left the cars to visit the lavatories, and this had drawn reprimands from Gallineau, the assistant-manager, who claimed that they were abusing the privilege. Weintraub was a tall, club-shanked man with high cheek-bones and remote bloodshot eyes—a man who had passed through the mill and kept his balance, precariously, since it was difficult to be just to the operators without risking "the can" and the loss of the moderate advantage which he had gained after years of cage-work. It was the invariable problem of the few workers who managed to secure promotion in their line of work. If they had honest spirits, they remembered their past grinds and resentments and tried to be decent to the men under them, and yet, if they were, they drew the censure of men still "higher," of the bosses themselves.

The Book was filled with patrons, visitors, who sat on the brown leather divans and armchairs, wrote letters on the desks of the balcony foyers, strolled over the thick, green-blue patterned carpets on the white flagstone floor between the palms in dark blue porcelain pots, met friends or waited for them, smoked cigarettes and cigars, held low-voiced confidences, laughing talks, in a purring idleness conscious of supreme comfort. Some were hard-faced toward strangers; some gloated as they spoke of business stunts; others, bored and restless, marked time until supper and the beginning of the night's enjoyments. People were already trickling into the glittering dining-room, behind the elevators, from which thumping, carnal bars of jazz-music thrust their way through the subdued clatter and tinkle of dishes, silverware, easeful voices.

The bell-hops wore red and gold-braid cadet-caps held by chin-straps, jackets of robin-egg blue cut high and level, trousers of the same blue with broad red stripes on the sides. The elevator-operators, were in like colors, with longer jackets, black peaks to their caps. As in many other hotels, they had all been rigged out in swank clothes with a military touch, to suit the ideas of elegance held by patrons and visitors, to present an appearance belying their actual wages and conditions and give the impression of "soldiers," privates, accepting orders and rancor of any kind without a murmur. The bell-hops received only three dollars a week and tips. This common practice not only saved money for the owners but compelled the boys, ranging from fourteen to eighteen, to be servile, race to the abuse and whims of drunks, remain passive to the snottiness of certain guests. Yet, servility being foreign to their sense of sturdy, growing manhood, many of the boys talked back to grouchy patrons and were fired in the end, while others derided and grumbled among themselves, in guarded voices, as they sat on the benches to the left of the elevators and waited for calls.

The marble counter with brass grills at each end held a seething of activity always padded, calculating, poised between genuflections and business-like scrutinies. Ray often cocked a knowing eye in the direction of the counter. The clerks had been easy for him to size up. Cassidy was the professional laugher, Biedenkranz was the college-man hired to ingratiate the more "cultured" patrons. Neumann, straight-nosed and square-jawed, was the clothing-model ad assigned to impress and jolly the women. Larrsen, quiet-mouthed and wandering-eyed, was probably the spy, gaining the confidence of the others, because he appeared reticent and trustworthy, and then reporting back to Gallineau and Seidendahl, the head-manager. Ray had applied for a clerk's job and had been interviewed by Gallineau, a bald, dwarfed fellow with eyes as tight and soulless as oiled bolts on a face once hard but softening from too much rich food and a passion for cordials, vermouth and chartreuse, always consumed, secretly, and away from the hotel, since he had to pose as a respectable hand-shaker to the guests and be, in verity, a penny-squeezing, never-relenting buffer between the workers and the "highest" officials, the owners themselves. Greatly altered during the past few months, Ray, in the interview, had found it impossible to be urbane and submissive, tempered by the bluff of man-to-man heartiness now and then—the mixture necessary to bag a clerk's job—but he had convinced Gallineau that he knew most of the tricks of the hotel-game, and the latter had finally taken him as an elevator-man, after testing him in the cage, with the promise to send him "higher," if he showed he was steady and reliable.

Ray caught sight of Gallineau now and snarled to himself, remembering the statement. Yeah, stick around a year, or two: age five years more in the worries, the half-rations, the almost impossible wrench-out for clothes, a room where the cockroaches around the wash-basin made a fellow puke—Christ, Allene had used a whole can of powder and still a few were prowling back—yeah, all that, and never fail to lick Gallineau's corns and act like a beetle when Seidendahl nosed around, and then, *maybe*, they'd make him a clerk, let him raise his chin an inch higher, invite him out for a drink—maybe, if they didn't have some relative they were anxious to shove in, or some guy didn't show up with a letter of recommendation from one of their business-friends, when the next vacancy appeared. He thought that the old days had been better, a fellow with a little education had had something of a chance then, but now, by God, the mob of white-collars waiting to pounce on the smallest desk-job was positively sickening. Sickening to whom—the other fellow, with his collar getting dirtier every week, trying to claw you out of the opportunity because he had to live, also? It was still too baffling for him, this goddamn scrambling-match everywhere, where fellows, who might have been friends, had to trip one another up, shove the other ones aside, if they could, and spring every foul play on the calendar, because they were frantic from being out of work so long. Some escape, to keep the fineness, the faith, in men and women, prevent them from getting so savage that they wanted to destroy their own country and its hallowed, democratic institutions, like Ernie, like Bill Randorf, with whom he had scraped up an acquaintance in one of the hasheries near Scollay Square. Randorf was a book-keeper in the offices of a huge clothing-concern, had worked there for three years with only a dinky, two-dollar raise, in all that time, and found himself now reduced to a couple of dollars under the wage he had started with, and why? The N.R.A. code. The concern had changed to a four and five-day week for the employees, hired a few more to fill in the gaps, and then hacked all of the regular book-keepers down to a minimum pay of nineteen dollars a week so it would not be forced to increase the sum-totals of the wages. What in hell was the good of having two full days to yourself and less money to spend for enjoying them? By God, it certainly was getting to be true—the common thug, who backed you into a doorway, poked a rod in your face and went through your pockets, was a damn sight more honest than some of those other birds. He didn't pat a guy on the shoulder and tell him it was all for the mutual interest and efficiency of the L. R. Snicklehoffter Suit and Overcoat Business, before he amputated him. Yep, something goddamn drastic would have to be pulled, sooner or later, when men like Randorf, pretty clean and straight boys, were already beginning to pound the table and spout Communism, running 'from one poison to another because they couldn't see any other way out.' Something goddamn drastic. Maybe a Third Party at the next election, headed by Roosevelt himself, to knock off the crooks on both sides of the political fence and chase some of the rats out of the necessary business-world, put real teeth in all of this N.R.A. hullabaloo.

Seven o'clock had come. Ray was putting on his street-clothes in a locker-room in the basement. Crates of canned vegetables, canned sea-foods, were stacked, unevenly, around the tin partitions walling the lockers—food which would afterwards be palmed off, in the high-priced Purple Room upstairs as "fresh string-beans, finest of the spring crop," "asparagus shipped daily from Long Island," and "crab-meat straight from the Atlantic foam." A small, electric bulb hung from the ceiling, on a braided cord, and the inadequate light strained the eyes of the men. Drossi and Weintraub were there, and also, Wally Stone and Alec Williams, the other two elevator-operators. Two of the bell-hops shouldered in—Don Schermer, Fred Countiss. Some of the workers dressed upstairs, in a room off the kitchens. A second locker stood near the boilers and furnaces in the rear of the basement. A free-for-all started in Ray's place. Men's voices boomed, sang and swore, loudly. Men repeated details, interrupted one another. They wanted to attack and forget the suppression of the dreaded "upstairs"—the cautious pleasantries to some of the patrons, who desired to show how human they were by handing out small-talk, or comments on political events, murder-sensations, prize-fights, hockey-games, and wanted, also, to have their half-pint opinions on these subjects yessed by the employees, to wallow in the belief that the men "under them," serving them, were "regular fellows," who knew their places but shared, in a general, comforting way, the outlooks of the hotel-guests. It was a "democracy" achieved at no expense to the babblers. It had its variations. A liberal professor, doctor, set out to be a half-hearted pal, for moments: a pie-eyed business-man wanted them to chime into Rosie O'Grady, or Sweet Adeline: a gold-digger became attracted to an employee's face and threw out hints of invitations after, or between, her more regular pursuits: a girl, "seeing the sights," looked, amorously, at one of the bell-boys: a baseball-reporter, assigned to the visiting nine, asked the employees into his room and suggested a crap-game, to pose, warmly, to himself, as a good sport among the rank-and-file of his fellow-men. But it was always condescension, conscience-stricken at its best.

Wally was a tall blond, with a split nose and hating eyes. Alec was short and hang-lipped, under the side-part of red hair. Don had a handsome, childish face and less muscle than a girl. Fred was chunky, broad-nosed, with the beginning of a glare in his blue eyes. Drossi had a slim body, a pale, steep-nosed face, with a sneer always thickening in the corners of the eyes. Ray chinned with Wally now.

"D'you get the rose-bud in 412 today? I didn't pipe her."

"Stink-bud, yeah. I'd like to have the do-re-mi she chucks on it. Smells like Eau dee Veeoletta—ooh la—the punk-tweezer."

"She slipped Drossi a come-on yesterday."

"Yeah, me too, day before. You see, she dropped her key just before I opened, and after I picked it up she said: 'I'd like to get you another one.' She never even looked at me. Just sprang the line and, zippo—gone."

Drossi, become the "wise one" regarding women, slouched up.

"I'll bet a soldier she's on a tear away from the double-chin. Don saw a photo on her dressing-table and it read: 'To my own dear, lovely carnation, the sweetest flower in the nation—Cornelius K . . ."

The men roared, loosening the stiff bodies. Drossi drove a light punch against Ray's shoulder.

"Would you grab her, if you had a chance?"

"No, I don't think so. I might catch something"—Ray grinned, absently, his mind on Allene and the ghastly problem of the coming week's budget.

"Well, I'd take her in a minute, and then to hell with her"—Wally spat, tried a half-clog.

"Same here. We press our dogs all day long, while dames like her hit the hay until noon, and then they gulp a good feed and start handing out the works. It would suit me fine, if I could make her and then slough her one on the jaw, for good luck"—Alec's eyes had points of youthful hate, softening, returning to hardness, beyond his knowledge.

"To hell with that stuff. They'd land you in the jug before you could say Mister. I'll give you the lowdown on what happened right here in this joint, about six months ago. There was a nice kid running the first cage, name was Pedderly. Well, there was a broad in 614, one of the niftiest eyefuls you ever took in. She had a guy from out of town, keeping her on the side and running in for the week-ends. So well, she kept on baiting Ped, for a week or so, and then he took a long chance and he hot-footed it up the stairs to her room, after seven. He got her all right, but she let out a scream over the phone and the house-dicks flew up. It seems like she slipped him a few drinks, afterwards, and then she got cock-eyed herself and called him a dirty name, and he clipped her in the eye. And what did she do? Set up an awful stink and claimed he forced himself into the room and tried to rape her! After the cops broke his smeller for him, they hauled him off, and then the poor kid got two, solid years in the jug. Baby, was he a sap, was he?!"—Drossi slapped a trouser-leg, to emphasize the last words, and his face had a viciousness, a sympathy, too tight together to understand one another.

"I'd have taken her to a room over near Scollay, some dump

where they don't come up till the ceiling falls down. Otherwise, nothing doing"—Wally, who was only twenty-one, sought to be mature and sly in coping with The Great Racket, which was most of the life he had ever known but whose class-lines were still semi-shrouded, to him.

Drossi kept a cigarette in the sneering curvature of his lips, as he spoke.

"You've got the wrong slant, Wally. The best thing is to play them smooth, get everything you can, their money, too. Who are the birds sitting pretty on top of the world? Who are they? Well, I'll tell you—they're the slick babies, all the time, the ones who pay the other fellow to run the risks, and then rake in most of it themselves. They never get rough unless the odds are one-to-sixty in their favor. They hire other guys for that, and besides, half of them haven't got muscle enough to chin themselves three times running on a bar!"

Ray studied Drossi with the look of a man dismissing his own blisters.

"Listen here, Dross, that's the line of every small-time crook I've ever heard, and what happens to them? Ten years in the pen, when they wind up, that's what. The guy who stays honest and keeps plugging till he gets a good job, he's a damn sight better off. Then he can marry the girl he's crazy about and settle down to a decent life, and maybe he won't have any cream an' strawberries most of the time, sure not, but he'll be a lot happier in the long run."

"Yeah, I'm on your side on that one, Ray"—Alec clung to the sentimental hopes of his youth, the more real sentiment under them, to avoid the opposite cynicism, which was slowly soaking into him, nevertheless. "I'm not going to bring any disgrace to my old woman, if I can help it—she's gone through enough, believe me, without me giving her any more. I'm going to marry a steady and I'm going to hang on to her. I'll take a loose hooker on the side once in a while, cert'. Hell knows, they're not good for anything else, but just the same, you're not going to see me chasing after them all my life."

"Well, I can't quite figure it out myself. If a guy works hard he gets next to nothing for it, and if a guy tries to get it easy and shady, he finishes up with the dirty end of the stick, anyhow, so what the hell?"—Wally made himself think that he was a careless fatalist now, filching his bits of pleasure whenever and wherever he could, and spending most of his time paying for them with as much submission as he could muster.

Drossi centered on Alec.

"Marry a steady, huh? On what—eleven a week?"

"Oh, I'll be snagging more before I'm through, and if I don't, she'll have to keep on working so we can make up the expenses, I guess."

"Oh yeah, I know a pair like that, right in the room below mine, and the girl's the keenest little jelly-roll you ever popped your eyes at. He pushes a cradle down on the docks, and she does some kind of work on children's dresses—I don't know exactly what. Anyway, I'll tell you one thing—when they come home, they're too damn tired even to go out to a movie. They douse the light about nine-thirty every night, and even on Sundays they don't seem to have any too much pep in them. They haven't got any kids now, but when they do—how are they going to take care of them?"

"Aw, I won't have any kids, not till I'm over thirty, and maybe not then. It's easy to stop them."

"No, you bet you won't, and you won't have anything else either, not until you get wise to yourself!"

Ray became angry, to squelch the morbid feelings.

"Cut it out, Dross—you're getting on my nerves. Don't go around trying to make crooks out of fellows. Have a heart. There'll be plenty of good jobs in this country, and good wages, too, the minute the honest people in this country stick together and stand up for their rights. All of the business-men aren't lousy, and that goes for the small ones in particular, and believe me, when they join with the rest of us, you're going to see a hell of a clean-up in the next few years. The Government's starting to get mighty tired of all this grafting and pick-pocketing, especially with Roosevelt at the head. He's got a tremendous job on his hands, but I'll bet you, before he gets through he'll do it, too, and he'll go down in history as the greatest President we've ever had."

"Yep, I think so too"—Weintraub stepped up and handed Drossi a nasty look. "It's a good idea to keep your opinions to yourself, Dross. There's nobody making you hold down a job, if you don't want to, and I hate to hear you taking the hope out of these kids. They'll all pull through, and they'll end up with a good wife and some fine children, too, if they don't let guys like you make them go haywire, instead of fighting their way up."

Weintraub was married and had three children, and he had butted in to encourage himself as well as to oppose Drossi with "the decent climber's" outlook, since his wife expected a fourth child soon and he was wondering where in the devil he was going to raise the money for the hospital bills. Drossi, still shaky in his "criminal" resolves, and divided between fears and the birth of a sneering callousness, back-watered.

"All right, I wasn't telling them what to do. I'm on the job at seven every morning, jerking the cage as good as any other guy, and that's all you have to worry about"—Drossi pulled his face to a blank, as he swung around and knotted his green-and-white patterned tie before the cracked mirror over the dirty white, porcelain washstand.

He knew the facts, and all of that hot air wasn't going to bother him any, he thought, but he didn't care to risk the loss of his job just now. Fred Countiss edged in between Ray and Weintraub. He ran his fingers through the side of his dun-colored hair, hammered Weintraub with his blue eyes, looked at Ray with an impatient aversion. These dope-merchants, he thought—they didn't even know what they were, who was selling it to them, and Christ, up to half a year ago he hadn't been much wiser himself, but he was beginning to spin his noodle plenty, now.

"Well, if that's what you think, Wein, then maybe you'll tell us something else. How are we going to get there without a strong union? I mean an honest-to-God union, too, and not a union with a bunch of labor-pimps taking in our dues and living on the fat, and then telling us not to go on a strike until they talk it over with the bosses. Yeah, they talk it over all right, and I know what they talk about, too—how they can manage to kid us along and make us think we're winning something. Why, the damn p—s don't even ask us if they can do it. They hold the confabs first and then they get real kind and they tell us about them, later on."

"Say, where did you get that line?"—Weintraub was uneasy in spite of the scoffing.

"Never mind where I got it, but tell me this much—are you in favor of a union here in this hotel? I mean a rank-and-file union with officers that'll do what we tell them to do. Are you?"

Weintraub squirmed. He had been told, in a special session with Seidendahl, that "a gang of stinking Reds were lurking around the hotel, trying to poison the men and lure them" into joining up at the gang's office on Huntington Avenue, and that every effort must be made to warn the employees against them. He proceeded to the task, but his heart was not in it. While he didn't believe in the Reds, as he often told himself, he was also forced to admit that the hotel had more than doubled its profits during the past year and was clutching this increase with might and main. Feeling like a straddler and a detective now, he worked himself into a contemptuous answer, to down the implications.

"Say, have you been approached by one of those unpatriotic rats down on Huntington?"

"Never mind that. Why don't you answer my question?"

"Sure, I'll answer it. I believe in a union, sure I do, but it's got to be the right kind. You're only eighteen, Fred, and you don't know what those fellows are up to. They're paid by another country to stir up trouble over here, the whole, crappy outfit of them, and you'd better be watching your step, kid. They tell you that decent, respectable men are no good, just because these men don't want you to smash up the windows and ask for forty a week, right off the bat. We'll have a union here sooner or later, sure, but it's going to be a decent, law-abiding crowd, when we do put it over."

"Yeah, sooner or later, about 1950, if the bosses have their way. Every time they want to scare a guy, what do they do? I'll tell you. They holler 'Red, Red,' at the top of their lungs! Sure, they're a decent bunch, all of them, and they're all waving the flag in front of our mugs, all the time, but don't get soft in the head and ask them for five dollars more. Why no, they couldn't think of it"—Countiss whipped a cold look over and reached for his coat.

Alec and Wally followed Countiss through the door, questioning him in whispers. Don Shirmer trailed behind, thinking of nothing except his date with a "cream-pie girl" in the Fenway Park section and wondering whether she'd stand for "a little more," in the hallway after the movie. Drossi was shaken a little. He'd always thought that those Reds were just a few crap-artists, trying to put their hands on the swag without one chance in a hundred to do it, but maybe he'd better look into them. Countiss was the second guy in the hotel, whom he had heard spouting in their favor—Phil Dakin, suds-diving in the kitchen, seemed to have caught the bug, too. Aw well, "Kittens" Robinson was a sweet proposition when she warmed up enough, and he was going to meet her in less than two hours. The shake-down scheme with her was still very much on the fire, after all, and it would feel damn good to have a few drinks and put his arms around her, after the twelve hours he'd just gone through.

Weintraub paced with Ray, tried to excuse and defend his position. Ray listened without much interest, agreed, partly, and yet felt baffled, as if the agreement were compulsory and yet failed to lead to any definite solution, or reward. Leaving Weintraub, outside, he was sullenly confused as he ducked through the snow-crammed wind and walked north on Boylston Street opposite the Commons. Hopkins, Randorf, Countiss—there were still only a few, as far as he knew, and yet they did seem to be increasing. At least one, or two, every place you worked. Jesus Christ, it must be a quarter to eight by now. Allene would be hopping mad, but she would get over it and be warm and unsteadying and heart-patting to touch, tickle her just under the side of her chin, huh, the way she always liked it most, the gosh-darn . . .

Allene was talking to Judith Hammond. Judith wore a washed-out strawberry bathrobe, none too clean because the laundry charged extra for such articles and it was the only one she had left and she couldn't afford to send it in more than once every two weeks, or so. Her feet were cased in yellow cloth slippers with darker oil-spots dropped from the two-burner gas-range in her room. She stretched her legs out close and clacked the heels in time to the jazz-hits, which she hummed, on and off, between her words. She was twenty-five. She had a mouth twisted almost to a compressed eight. The cheeks were clumpy, the eyes gray and afraid under boldness. Her body was fat, sweepingly curved, the left shoulder hitched a bit higher than the right. The soot-brown hair had a trace of the ripples left by a curling-iron. She was humming a radio-favorite, broke into the words: "I'm a slave to . . . don't you want the heart I gave"— snapped off, stared out, as if she were looking at a picture-puzzle nobody else could see, and then she went on speaking, to bring the pieces nearer, put some of them together.

"Well, as I was telling you, my old man croaked about three years ago and then my old lady, she popped out a few months after the old man. It was the day before Christmas—year before last, too. I had a darb of a Christmas that year. A tree full of doo-daddles and a raft of presents, and a turkey with all the trimmings—oh yeah, so did Murphy before they doused him with cold water."

"Gee, it certainly must have been tough, coming right at that time"—Allene sniffed as she lifted the lid of the tin pot on the two-runged radiator to find out whether the water was boiling for the frankfurters, which it contained.

The death of Morris, on the previous October, had backed all of the youth within her against the old, dark wall, brought it another year of maturity in the space of a few days, when understanding became too naked to lag, to dwell only on its own exhaustions. Judith hummed another chorus, sang, low, the words: "Did you ever see a dream walking? Well, I" . . . then hummed the next bar, stopped, and stared off again.

"Well, as I was saying, the old man croaked and then the old lady passed out. We weren't getting along so bad before that. We didn't have no money in the bank. The old boy was working as a night-watchman and he got fifteen a week. I was making ten slinging hash, and Tillie got nine bucks for pasting labels on the jars—you know, one of those dumps where they make vanishing-cream and cold-cream, and the darn stuff ruins a girl's face because it's got—I can't remember the name. Nitrate of—something. Tillie knew all about it. Anyhow, it's no good."

"It's like a lot of other things then"—Allene spoke as if she were spitting out pebbles.

The blizzard, screeching, rattling the panes of the two front windows, the shoddiness of the room, and Judith's ramblings, gave her the jumps. She felt overwhelmingly cheated, disliked herself for feeling it, for not being a "good sport." Judith squashed a cockroach on the floor.

"You can use a ton of powder and there's still a few left. They must have swell digestions, believe me."

Allen said, listlessly: "Yeah, they must." She eyed the pot holding the frankfurters. Franks were sticking out of her throat. Judith was nervous unless she talked.

"Well, Tillie drew in nine, as I was telling you, and Steve, that's my youngest brother, he was finishing high-school, and then Floyd, I told you about him—he was learning to be a baker and he got eight-fifty. It wasn't a lead-pipe cinch at that, but I guess it could have been worse."

"Did your mother have a job, too?"

"Yeah, she had one of those easy ones. You know, all she did was cook for the whole lot of us, and do half of the washing, and clean up the flat, and cross my heart, she plopped right into the downy every night about eight o'clock, just after Tillie and me finished helping her in the kitchen. I'm telling you, honest to Jesus, we hated like poison to see her working so hard, but what could we do? We was away all day, in the first place, and then when we got home at night, sometimes we didn't even have enough pep to doll ourselves up and go over to Silver-Grove—that was the big dance-joint out there, oh, about half a mile away from our flat."

Allene thought of Fanny. After paying the funeral-expenses, Fanny had hooked up with a male partner and was running a restaurant and beer-grill on the lower East Side. Allene had written to her mother only once since arriving in Boston and had received a letter telling her that she would be welcomed and loved once more, if she left 'that *Goi* dead-beat, that loafer, who had no use for her except to take advantage of her, but otherwise, she had made her own bed and would have to suffer for it. Still, if she ever got sense in her head and decided to come back to the mamma' . . . Something in life made women hard, made them work themselves down to the bone and groan when they had to hand out a penny of the money they had fought for, and yell, try to boss their own flesh-and-blood, because something was bossing them every day of their lives. What was it? What made it? Her mother had giggled over going to parties once, dressed herself up for beaus, used a much softer voice, an occasional backing-down when little disputes came up—she could almost remember every inch of the progress since her extreme childhood, trace the voice through scores of incidents, as it grew louder, more and more insistent throughout the years of her girlhood near it. Allene woke up, with a start, realized that Judith was talking again.

"So the cops came pounding on the door, about six in the morning, and then they told us about it."

"About what?"

"The old man. A bunch of yeggs backed a truck up to the fact'ry gate. They was out to load it up with silk-bales and make a big haul, and the other watchman, he saw them through a window and he beat it down to a boiler-room—the rat, but the old man stuck it out and he got the slugs right square in his forehead. I'll bet he didn't live a minute after they drilled him, the bastards."

Judith's face became rigid, less cringing. It was no longer mawkish and sneering, by turns. The death of her father had convinced her that life was merciless, wrong, "stinko," that she had no ability to cope with it and that her only recourse was to be a sneak, to get a small part of what was coming to her, by hook or crook, to be prostrate, or unsparing to anyone who had more money than she had and save her sentiment for the few whom she liked, the few men and women jammed within reach in her own exact level of life. Her mind spied the brutality around it but couldn't locate the source. Allene slumped on the bed, with one hand curved on one of the bed-posts and the other brushing against her eyes. Facing "the whole mess," sometimes, she felt like screaming, like a person out of her senses because she couldn't find a single clue to the entire proceeding, and wondered even, at such times, whether she had the slightest desire to live—the gang-killings, the mean rackets, the people straining muscles and nerves for such a paltry return, the church-bells, the movie-clinches, the riotous cabarets in one part of the town and the filthy, crowded, old tenements standing, mile-square, in the other. She had to steel herself, now, as Judith went on with the story.

"Well, the company gave the old man a swell funeral, and they was all throwing nothing but bouquets at him for being a brave man, because, you see how it was—a cop, he heard the shots and he came running, lickety-split, down to the fact'ry, and then he drove the yeggs off before they could make the haul. Yeah, they all said the old man saved thousands of bucks for the company, and they even ran a picture in some of the papers. You know, the old lady, all dressed up in her mourning-weeds and the head of the company standing there and handing her a check for five-hundred berries, as 'a test'monial of the company's undying gratitude'—baby, the way that guy stepped on the gab was something pretty, I'm telling you."

"Well, the check was better than nothing, I suppose"—Allene felt the compunction to say something, however hollowly it sounded, even to her own ears.

"Yeah, you're describing it perfect, that's all it was. Tillie lost her job and couldn't find anything for months, and Floyd went and got himself married and he left the shack, and then I got fired, too, because I had a fight with the boss in the beanery where I was working. He kept on piling the over-time on me and he never payed me a single cent for it either, the louse, and then he said we was getting more in the tips and we was holding out on what we raked in, so he'd have to cut our wages down from five a week to four. Can you imagine that? Honest, whenever I saw a tip as large as a dime in that joint, I rubbed my eyes to see if I wasn't fooling myself."

Allene had gone to one of the windows, had peered into the blizzard. Ray would have a terrible time getting back. She herself had slipped, crossing Scollay, and if a man hadn't caught her, she might easily have fractured an ankle. She had quickened her steps to avoid a taxi-cab rounding a corner, and after the hackman had put on his brakes, she had had the glimpse of a woman bundled against the upholstery—young, wearing what had seemed to be a Hudson Seal. Some women were as practical as the nail in a shoe, weren't they? They went out after every protection, every pleasure. No romance in a six-dollar room, for them, and as far as the rest of the world was concerned, it could go and hang itself ten times over, for all they cared. She came back, prodded the frankfurters again. Judith was still in the past. She was talking to herself and Allene's presence was only an excuse for the monologue, at this juncture.

"So after that we stretched out the five hundred as long as we could. Tillie got another job. She was learning to trim hats in one of those millinery lofts down on Gallivan Street, but they canned her after a while, because the slack season came on, and then she got tired of hunting for a job and she started running around the wine-dives over here on the Square, hanging out with all the gamblers, and all the cokies and the flashy boys. I never had the heart to bawl her out much. I was in and out of a job all the time, myself. I wouldn't stand for being walked on and I started to figure it out this way—if I had to be walked on anyway, I might as well get something out of it, but then, you know, a girl has it drummed into her, from the time she's a kid, how she'll never be able to look anybody in the face and she'll go straight to the bowwows, if she isn't a good woman—oh yeah."

The sneer recurred but it was apologizing for itself. Allene winced, for several reasons. A girl might feel that marriage was not inevitable, that as long as she and a man loved each other they could live together and it would be clean, and fine, and necessary, even if no one had mumbled a few words over them and they didn't have a slip of paper to prove it, and yet the question continued to plague her because, without marriage, the surrounding world seemed to be doing its utmost to make their union sneaking and ugly, literally, to force them into being ashamed of themselves. Even in the low hotel where they lived now, she and Ray had had to sign the register as Mr. and Mrs. Bailey, though the proprietor had surmised that they were not married and had explained, some time afterwards: "It's only for the dicks, y' know. They don't mind it so much; if it's only a fly-by-night couple, y'see, or just somebody up in the room for a few hours, but when you're staying steady here, week after week, it's got to be Mr. and Mrs. on the books. Just putting up a front, that's all." That was a lovely situation, wasn't it? Why should Ray and she take the responsibility of marriage when their lives were so uncertain, so bare of money, so far away from the real home which marriage demanded, and, even, so quarrelsome now and then, when they flew up over trifles, silly jealousies, because they were both tired out and worried, to impulses in which it was just impossible to keep their balance for the time being?

Judith went on: "Aw well, Tillie's living with a fellow over on Charles Street now—he lets out the back of his basement for crap-games and takes a rake-off on them, and well . . . I'm not saying what else he does. She isn't partic'larly happy with him because he hits her, sometimes, when he's good and plastered, but maybe it's better than wringing yourself out for nine and ten plunks a week, or walking up and down the stairs, looking for work."

Judith shrugged. "So what was I telling you?—oh yeah, the five hundred cheque. Well, after the five hundred petered out the old lady went down to Hurley, that's the President of the firm, J. H. Hurley, and she went and asked him if he wouldn't help us again. He acted like she was asking him for his upper and lower teeth, honest to God he did, but she was crying in his office, like she told me afterwards, and he knew everybody in the next offices was hearing it, so he didn't have nerve enough to turn her down flat. He gave her another hundred, and all of us, Stevie, Tillie, the old lady, and me, we squeezed it out for another two months. All I could get then was a part-time job, you know, around the lunch and the supper rushes, and Stevie had to quit school but he couldn't find anything—sometimes he'd get a quarter for running errands for the drug-store on our block, and don't get balmy in the head and think I mean a quarter for every errand. It was five nickels an hour and the poor kid was lucky to get it, too."

Judith had risen and offered Allene a cigarette. They smoked and she continued: "She hated to do it, but she was ailing and waking up in the middle of the night with her pains—she had something the matter with her bladder the poor thing, and she had to plunk down the old, two dollars every time she dropped into a doctor, the poor thing, because she'd gone to one of those clinics where they treat you free, and they told her, oh, it was nothing, she'd only have to rest up because she'd caught cold in her kidneys—the liars. So she hated to do it, but she went and applied at one of those home-relief bureaus they've got here, and the bastards in the place, they told her they couldn't do anything because Steve and me was working part-time, so the family wasn't destitute. Oh no, it wasn't—not much. There was nothing else left, so I beat it down to Hurley's place, tramped there at least six times, far's as I can remember, but Mister Hu-urley was always having a conf'rence, or he wasn't in, or he'd send some one out to see us in the ne-ear fu-uture. The old man saved them from losing thousands of dollars, sure he did, and he was a damn fool for doing it, too, and I'm telling you, right from the bottom—the whole thing certainly taught me a lesson, if I ever needed one, and you know what it is, just as well as I do. If you don't look out for yourself in this little world, all the time, you'll wind up with a crick in your back and not a cent to your name, that's what!"

Judith, with her hands on hips, surveyed herself in the mirror above the bureau, as if she still had an imbecilic kindness within her, which needed all of her vigilance whenever she liked anyone too much, or in any case where the other person expected her to believe his promise, make any extended sacrifice. When she turned, the face was colder, the eyes humorously jeering at themselves, the slangy guard once more on tap.

"Aw, I'm sick of jabbering my head off. I've got to dig up some dough this week—my clothes, pardon me, my wa-ardrobe, is down to nothing plus, and you know, I told you I've been out of a job since the last of January now. It's getting fierce."

Allene sighed as Judith moved toward the door. Then she had a craving to say anything that would be nonsensical, make life pleasanter, wake up to the "discovery " that a nightmare, created by her own self-pity, and Judith's too, had been mistaken, by them, for all of life itself.

"Oh, come on, be a scrapper, don't hang like a faded wrapper—now, am I silly or am I not? We've got a bad case of the jams, Jude, and no wonder, with this kind of weather, but I'll brighten up the minute Ray comes in, and you—how about your boy-friend, Harry?"

Judith, standing beside the door, grinned. It was the caricature of a grin, maligning itself, to hide from a pig-sty.

"Oh him? He's a good enough mug, but I've never been cuckoo about him. He hits the bottle too heavy to suit me and then he gets sore over nothing, though I can't blame him so much when I think of how he has to keep the fires up from seven to six-thirty, in that damn building of his. Anyhow, I'm going over to Tillie's tonight and I'm not coming back till I get what I'm after, plenty of it, too, and you don't need to be a mind-reader to know what I mean. I won't he so *darn* partic'lar about who it is, either."

Judith tossed her head and left, immediately after the last words. Allene rested on the bed. So, Judith was going to become a prostitute. A hell of a world, wasn't it? Judith had had some men in her life, that was obvious, but according to the stories around the hotel, no one of the opposite sex had ever visited her room except Harry Kollisky, and the other men in the place had shied away from her because Kollisky was a six-footer, with bridge-like shoulders, and Judith, outside of seeing him, two or three times a week, had given them a kidding tongue, sometimes, but nothing in any way resembling an invitation. But now it was going to change—just the old business-deal, any man who slapped his money down, ugh . . . nice, wasn't it?

Yet, it happened thousands of times, every night, in New York alone, in Boston, Chicago, everywhere, she thought. She had known of its existence ever since she was fourteen, and had swallowed the explanation offered by books, by people, telling her that prostitutes were always lazy, weak-spined creatures entirely lacking in the reserve, the shame, present, at least to a moderate degree, in every other woman, but the explanation had a rotten smell to Allene, now. The lazy and flat part of it might be the end of the story, but it wasn't the beginning of it. The society-girls, the girls from well-to-do families, who didn't have to work, and the other ones, too, with easy jobs, with high wages—what they did was outside of the story, entirely. If they took many men, it was only because they had plenty of leisure and were out to fill it with their idea of pleasure. If any of them were gold-diggers, it was only because they were exceptionally greedy and wanted even more comforts, luxuries, than the ones they already had. It wasn't desperation that started them on the road—it was boredom and sexual desire. When women took any man, who paid them anything above a fixed sum, she'd bet her last dress that all of them had been pushed into it! Perhaps most of them weren't really starving, but they got damn tired of scrimping, looking for a job, working long hours for a few dollars and living in holes, some of them worse than the one she was living in—some, damn tired, too, of seeing other women flouncing and riding past them, in expensive clothes, and reading, everywhere, accounts of how these others lolled around Miami, stepped out in night-clubs, took trips to Europe—what not? When these working-girls didn't become prostitutes in spite of it, it was a credit to their patience and their ideals, sure it was, but when they did, the blame was completely in the cruel lives they had been compelled to lead. Some of them didn't have the patience, the oh, the sheer stamina, to hold out against it. These moral people now, they were always asking girls to be decent, to get a husband and have children, and be happy in their homes, but gosh almighty, who was interested in giving them, and the men they loved, fine jobs, good flats and houses, and money enough to carry out these things? And here was Judith now, getting ready to go over to Tillie's dive, take a few drinks and pick up one of the winners in the dice-games run by Tillie's present man. One?— maybe more, for all she knew. Gosh, it was enough to turn a girl into a wild and woolly radical and then some! Maybe it wasn't the fault of the Government and the business-people and maybe they were just blind to it, but the day would come when they would have to wake up and change the whole darn situation.

Allene struck a snag here. Would they ever do it? Didn't most of them know what was going on? In the lack of either solution, or belief, she went back to cynicism. Ray and she would have to fight their way out by any means—flatter people, use their own wits to get better jobs, be sweet to anyone able to help them, in the smallest way, and chase after money in every possible manner, as long as they were absolutely sure that it was within the law and they couldn't be arrested for it. How could people, down and out themselves, rescue one another? What good would it do now, if she went upstairs to Judith, during the next hour, and tried to argue her into a cheerfulness springing from . . . what? Any person knew when he had reached the real limit, when his spine had snapped in the last bone and simply couldn't be mended again.

As she turned on the bed, from side to side, her mind reverted to the past few months. Look at her father—what had honesty ever brought him? And herself. She had quit her job at Dulossi & Sons. One morning Dulossi had piled two days' work on her desk, with dictations interrupting it throughout the day, and then, just before closing-time, had bawled her out because she had finished less than half of it. She had called him every name she could think of, and made a final exit. Then her father had died from hardening of the liver, after two weeks of increasing agony in the hospital, and afterwards, her own stony-faced grief, her feeling that she would have cut her hands away to see him alive again, fled before the conviction that he was a thousand times better off now, resting forever, still existing in a different world—the question of a hereafter had seemed humorous and flimsy to the point of nausea, in the face of all of the problems, the worries and necessities, in the only life that people knew. She had felt, also, that life had been responsible for his death—that it had only killed him a little earlier than its end to most people. He had been a simple man on the whole, willing to work hard, liking his beer and card-games, but he hadn't had the—oh, the everything-for-me spirit, the cast-iron nerve in playing people, the smoothness, the ways in which men pretended to be good-fellows and yet tried their hands at every kind of tricky grabbing.

Her calm but darkened face, above these broodings, had enraged Fanny. Fanny, weeping and shrinking inside as she remembered the many tongue-lashings, which she had given Morris, had directed her ire against Allene, claimed that her daughter was "worse than a chunk of lead" and that Allene, with her "carryings-on," had robbed Morris of at least ten years of life. Recalling the accusations now,

Allene smiled, weakly. It seemed that only death could make some human beings realize that they valued another one, immensely, and had treated him unfairly during his life-time. Her mother had been only too eager for a pretext to dim the naggings, the sordid rows, the ill-tempered stinginess, the ridicules for his lack of "smartness"—well, her mother might be much more selfish, more lying-to-herself than Morris had been, but then, life hadn't been any too kind, or beautiful, or thrilling to her mother, either.

Allene wandered to the events before her trip to Boston. After more than three weeks of searching—estranged from her mother—she had been reduced to accepting a job typing circulars and had been fired because the ad firm expected the girls to type five hundred circulars a day, and when they failed to reach the mark of this task, now and then—one which never gave them a chance to glance up from their machines, for a split-second—the firm "canned" the girls, since the actual motive was always to bring in fresh "human material" able to over-strain itself, for a week, or two. Then Ray had been dismissed from Johnson's, after he had burst out and told Norah Gallagher that she was "an A number-one stool-pigeon," and Allene and Ray had joined the regiment of the unemployed once more, often plodding, together, to the same places, the same curt rejections, until he had stumbled into a job in a *Bier Halle* in Yorkville. The owner, Hanz Stengledorf, who wore a swastika on his coat-lapel, had the "quaint" notion that his porters—three of them—should mop floors, polish brass-work, carry kegs of beer, cases of wine, and even pitch into some of the dish-washing, ten hours a day for thirteen dollars a week, and then contribute one out of the thirteen to a German "National Society" with nearby head-quarters. Ray had rebelled against the second week's extortion, and the job had promptly vanished—poor Ray, he had fumed back and forth in their room on that night, and had sworn that he would never give any of his sweat-soaked wages to any club of Jews, German Gentiles, Irishmen, or any other nationality. What did they mean to him, what aid were they willing to extend to him when he was wearing his shoes out on the pavements, day after day? Poor Ray, it didn't seem in his blood to accept the fact that independence was reserved only for those 'on top,' she thought—a quality within him, which made her admiring and fearful at one and the same time.

She frowned as she remembered the swindle which had sent her to Boston. Responding to a newspaper ad, she had been interviewed by a Joseph Q. Maybe, "division-head" of the Merit Magazine Distributors, Inc.—a semi-bald fellow with a face protruding like that of a scaled fish, without light in the eyes. He had spoken to her at length, tested her in dictation and typing, and, after calling her again, a day later, had informed her that a position as secretary was vacant in the Boston branch, and that he would be willing to telegraph the branch-head and advise him that she had been hired, if she cared to accept it. He had explained, also, that he was offering her this advantage because he had been impressed by her competence, intelligence, and personality, and wanted to assist her for that reason, since nothing was open for her at his New York offices, and the Boston job demanded some one with unusual qualifications. Lulled by his briskly jovial manner, the buzz of activity in the small but well-furnished suite of offices, she had discussed the matter with Ray and then decided to take the position. Maybe had given her a sealed letter of introduction and then she had gone to Boston, with Ray, on money borrowed from a cousin of hers in Brownsville. Then the hoax had revealed itself—one of those house-to-house canvassing propositions, for some of the "spicy" and "adventure-story" magazines, wherein the canvasser was armed with a certificate asserting that he was working his way through college, or business-school, and that the prospective buyers could perform an act of charity, for him, as well as secure these "thrilling, gripping, and entertaining magazines at greatly reduced rates."

The man in the Boston office, Kirkland—a pudgy specimen with spectacles and bulbous eyes—had presented suaveness plus, to the continual tapping of his pencil on the desk. 'Of course she would be given a little dictation in the mornings, for five a week, and she could also try her hand at composing form-letters for the other selling-campaigns, which the firm advanced, but in the meantime she would be expected to join the canvassing, on a commission-basis, and thus become familiar with the work and problems of the concern, preparing herself for the secretary's position, which she would receive in a month, or so.' In reality, the firm had been finding it difficult to secure canvassers in Boston, and was trying to obtain them from New York, openly, in some cases, and with rank deceit in others. It was calculated that, after the applicant arrived in Boston, with almost no money, he would take the canvassing in the effort to escape from his predicament. The work required a lying tongue, a profuse, brazen "line," and the ability to accept slammed doors and other rebuffs, so that the number of successful canvassers frequently ran out and had to be replenished.

Allene had exploded, threatened to take the matter to the police, but she had talked it over with Diana Henderson, a girl tricked in the same manner, and they had decided that any complaints would have been a waste of time. They had been offered actual, stenographic work for two, or three, hours a day, and Diana had told Allene that even the college-fake was protected, since the firm could always claim that it had been misled and that the applicants had really represented themselves to be students, or people eager to enter some school. Allene lingered on Diana now—she had been such a straight-eyed, trim-looking peach of a girl, well-educated, too, and had been forced to use her last dollars for a ticket back to New York! What on earth was the use of a good education when it failed to support the life of a human being, afterwards? Here was Diana, fitted for chemical research-work, laid off from a job of that kind, half a year previous, and now reduced to hunting for office-work, trudging the streets, answering fraud-ads which sucked up her last dollar, and all because—for the time being, at least—it was simply impossible for her to find anything in her chosen profession. Brr, sometimes life could make a blizzard look positively foolish, when it came to coldness, couldn't it? . . .

Ray arrived, stamping the snow from his shoes, shaking it from his old, gray cap and the black overcoat showing the cross-threads, in places, and starting to frazzle around the button-holes, which he had bought for four-fifty in a second-hand store in New York. She jumped from the bed, tripped and tumbled to her knees—laughing, a bit hurt. He dumped his overcoat on the floor in the haste to reach her. He picked her up, rubbed her knees, kissed her, poked his fingers against her cheeks, her mouth, and ringed his hands around her neck, lightly, on and off, and told her that she was his slave and he was going to choke her, to prove it. She took his hands, framed her face with them, climbed up on him and kissed his ears, the nape of his neck, and pulled the front strands of his chestnut hair down, over his eyes, and swore that she had had a vision, in which he had looked, longingly, at nine, beautiful girls during the immediately past day, and therefore, she intended to make him blind forever. They showered each other with trivialities, made unintelligible sounds—distinct and musical to everything still inarticulate in their hearts—interrupted, continually, in the odds and ends of a love-talk rendered profound, to them, by their need for each other, and tried, in every extravagant, kid-like way, to isolate themselves from an unpleasant world, from the profitless effort to fathom it.

Then the slump came. Ray slid, lower and lower, in the one arm-chair in the room, his feet spraddled, his forearms between his legs. The springs protruded behind the dark red leatherine thinned by wear, and after shifting his back, he clambered up, took a white-slipped pillow from the bed, propped it against his shoulder-blades, in the chair. Allene was spreading tissue-paper napkins, eating-utensils, on the chipped, golden-varnished, pine table, which tilted and dipped, an inch or so, because the paper under the uneven legs had become displaced. She squatted on the floor as she fussed with the wedges, strained to lift the table. He wanted to help her but his legs, straight out and wide apart, felt like iron shafts thick with rust in the joints. He jerked himself up a little, twice, with the intention of rising, and then fell back again. That pillow and chair held too much glue for his energy. On her feet once more, she glowered.

"You might have the decency to give me a hand once in a while. You know perfectly well that table weighs a ton."

"Well, I'm sorry, honey, but honest injun, if my feet don't feel just like a couple of hot bricks, then you can call me a liar."

"Oh yes? How about me? I was sludging through this blizzard all day long, up to five this evening, looking for something."

"I know, but it isn't as bad as jamming your soles and heels down without a break, hour after hour,"

"Isn't it though? Well, you certainly had to buck the wind and the snow around those street-corners out there, when you came home, and you ought to know better."

"Christ, don't tell me—it's one of the worst nights I've ever seen."

During the pause, while she was dumping the four frankfurters and some potato salad on the plates, she felt irritated at him, at herself, and at her own irritation, and he was remorseful.

"Still sore at me, hon'?"

"I don't know."

"Well, you stay that way, then. If you don't know I'm the least lazy person you ever—"

"Oh, let's bite our tongues off, Ray. I'm the unreasonable one and I know it."

She kissed the hollows between his nose and eyes. The prosy, gnat-like frictions, inevitable, occasionally, to any pair of different egotisms living together, were always more than tripled in the case of Allene and Ray, and usually followed by a relenting, in which the one immediately at fault realized it and sought "to make up." Yet, the sum-total left its deepening marks. Temporarily, they felt themselves powerless to change the lack of sensory enjoyments, the sinister anxiety over money, the barely endured room, and the temptation "to take it out on something" was often so insidious, so spontaneous, that they directed it against one another because, otherwise, they would have had the sense of being even more stifled, more handicapped by unwilling silence. Quarrels brought them a cheap relief, but afterwards they paid too heavily for it in the feeling that they had been small, cutting, beyond credence, and had thrown a doubt even on the strength and purpose of their love for one another. At other times, each one went to the length of persuading himself that the other had hateful qualities—excruciating selfishness, or unbearable rudeness, or the habit of always flirting with presentable members of the opposite sex and always, adroitly, denying it. Then, it was, in part, the entirely artificial bitterness springing from different varieties of blindness. Allene was less impetuous than Ray. She liked to pat her emotions, dally with them, stretch them out to awaken her anticipations, and then go into long periods of reserve, which Ray couldn't understand. She could be forgiving in larger impacts and insistent over little, personal, illogical ones which, to Ray, were scarcely trifles—the exact angle of his tie, the slightest spot on his collar—good lord, he had never been a slovenly man but he didn't have the time and the energy to be always scrupulously tidy now—or the fact that he had a passion for whistling one tune after another, that he used too many profane words, at times, when he "blew up" against some injustice in the past day of work. Sometimes, Allene melted to good-looking men just enough to make them attentive, hopeful, and then, quickly, became almost impersonal, but it was by no means coquetry pure and simple. She had worked ever since she was eighteen. After nine hours of clicking the keys, hunching her back, concentrating on too much involved material, and taking the tense disregards of employers, she had frequently gone home to find her parents in a screaming-match, had been forced to hurry out after supper, if only to restore her nerves. The streets, into which she had hurried, had not been much of an improvement. Pimply, and surly-faced youths had shouted, raised bottles, and children had shrieked, as they swarmed on the streets and dodged the machines, and overwrought mothers, fearing that the children would knock into their baby-carriages lining the walks, had often yelled: "Get away from there, you little bastard, or I'll break your neck!" In such a life, the sex within her had offered the only variety, the only deliberate inflation, and the zest of teasing men, listening to their compliments, leading them on to plead for dates, for favors, had become an infinitely precious one.

Ray had never been able to understand this attribute, in which she was not actually fickle and yet never exclusive and remotely loyal, when other men approached her. As they were finishing the meal now, he returned to the contention.

"Honest, we've been here less than a month and you're starting right in again. I still don't see why you were laughing so much with Konig, when I came in the lobby last Saturday night."

"Ray, you're positively an expert when it comes to raving over nothing. He's always been just pleasant to me, and he's never made any passes, and if he stops me and tells me a funny story, a really funny one, what am I supposed to do then—cry about it?"

"Well, there's no law that you have to press against a man's arm, either, while you're doing the laughing."

"I don't remember anything of the kind. I think you're absolutely insane sometimes, when it comes to imagining things—really I do."

"All right, maybe I am. Let's drop it"—the weariness in Ray, suddenly, made him abject, glad to leave the never-settled issue.

Afterwards he stretched on the bed, looking through the paper, while she read a mystery-thriller entitled "Murder In The Ardmore Mansion," which Judith had loaned her. Sometimes the story engrossed her, with its staccato account of a group of society-guests at a week-end party, on a storm-wracked night, and the host, an elderly broker, who had toppled from one of the bridge-tables, dead, without bullet-mark or perceptible wound, and the subsequent discovery of the guests that the telephone-wires had been cut and their machines had vanished from the garage, and most of the "servants" had disappeared, while unexplained crashes came from different rooms, into which the guests rushed, only to find the rooms void of any human being. In the midst of her creeps, however, she glanced around her own room, stared for a second at the window-panes, against which the actual blizzard was rapping and whistling, and heard voices in the hallway, just outside of the door—"Well, if he thinks he can get away with that stunt he'd better watch out for Johnny, because—." "Aw, the boss doesn't give a damn about either of them, and I'll tell you something else"—the harsh voices became indistinct as they reached the upper floor.

Allene closed the book, fiddled with the white, cotton trim on her navy-blue dress. Why didn't they write about what was going on everywhere? What was the idea? It was really true, she could walk into any book-store and pick up ten books at random without finding a single story that dealt with people like herself and Ray, real, flesh-and-blood people pouring out of the factories and offices, and the big-stores, and the booze dives, and what they went through, how they lived, how they dragged their feet back to depressing rooms, like the one she was in, and tried to make a dollar stretch like a six-inch rubber band, and soaked their legs in hot water to take some of the ache out of them. Only the other day, she had read a review of a book, in the "Boston Transcript," and the man had panned it, said that the author was a disgusting realist without any imagination, but according to the reviewer, the book had been about a cabaret on Broadway and the efforts of a gang-leader to win one of the girl-dancers away from an honest, young newspaper reporter, and how the reporter outwitted the gangster, in the end, and had him sentenced to prison for a long term, after his sweetheart, the dancer, had been killed, accidentally, in a sudden gang-fight outside of her dressing-room. Very tragic, sure, but what connection did it have with the day-and-night life of all the people whom she had ever known? No, their lives hadn't been particularly pretty, either, and as for creepiness, in their own slower way they had had all of the murder-mysteries on earth faded down to nothing, yet these writers never seemed to pay any attention to them.

Take the only two books she had read during the past month,

what had they been? The one called "Twenty-Eight Hours," in which
a small-time vaudeville girl had been murdered by a jealous man—
had played around with different men, in a flat over on Tenth Avenue, and had been killed, in his drunken fury, by the crook, who
had lived on her money and saw that she was deserting him for
another man. This prostitute was a million miles away from the life
of a girl like Judith—a hard-working, kicked-down girl, probably
already over at Tillie's now, drinking to steepen her nerve, to size
up the men in the dive and, finally, snuggle up to the one willing
to give her some of the money he had just won in the game. And
the other book, the story of "the Stacy family," living uptown in a
big apartment, and the father, a successful business-man, who had
always wanted to be an artist, and how he had wound up, at last, in
a studio, painting his long-hidden dreams on canvases, while his
practical wife had scooted off with another man and his children
had dissipated most of his fortune, all except one daughter, Amy,
who had clung to him, to the last page, and praised him for his
courage, for the beautiful way in which he had broken off from a
sordid business-life in spite of his forty-eight years—people of that
kind, how many of them existed, and why were they the only human
beings interesting to a writer? Possibly, the idea was that most of the
world down on the streets, and in the crowded shacks, in the work-
ing-places, the gin-mills, the heartless offices where a girl flew like
a machine, tugged her brains out over figures and statements, and
got exhausted for the smallest wages they could pay her—possibly,
the notion was that this world was too ugly, and, yes . . . squalid, that
was the word—too ugly and squalid to write of, but if it was, it certainly wasn't the fault of most of the people in it. They didn't seem
to have much of a choice concerning their own situation, their own
days of work, the homes they returned to, the pleasures they tried to
wring out. Something was behind all of this back-turning, must be
behind it, and though she wasn't certain regarding its precise shape
and aim, still, whatever it was, it didn't smell right to her nostrils.

    Allene flipped the pages of the mystery-thriller, once more, and while it still brought her goose-flesh, now and then, the creepiness became annoying, in its let-downs, as if dummies in silk and paint had been dropped into a thin, grisly plot and manipulated, cleverly, to distract her from, oh—from that hole in the bed-spread, that brown spot on the plaster ceiling over the wash-basin, from which the water leaked down at least once every night, that radio in the next room—they always turned it on too loud and the announcer was squawking, for the third time, his burning message that "Camels" were "fragrant, mellow, soothing, joy-bringing gifts, snugly wrapped, under the most sanitary conditions, folks, in the finest cigarette-paper obtainable, made of the choicest, inner-leaf, Virginia tobacco, without a single head-ache, or throat-ache, in a whole carton of 'em, folks. This mellow, fragrant"—for heaven's sake, cut it out. Tell people how to get the money to buy them, for a change.

Ray was absorbing the full-page ad of a film, "Viva D'Alvarez," purporting to be the breath-stirring drama of a bandit-chief, who had once ruled all of the north of Mexico, and the ad had the large-typed words: "Senors, we attack with the dawn . . . and because we are men the shock of battle will be sweet. . . . After victory there will be bread for our skinny bellies . . . bread for all of the poor . . . and for me, your Pedro, there will be a woman . . . a lovely woman!" "Ten months to produce it! One hundred cameras filmed it! Ten thousand people in its cast!" The shock of battle will be sweet because we are men—the writer of that film should have had his block knocked off, sometime, to find out how sweet it felt, Ray thought, and as for the bread part of it, it was becoming harder to obtain, all of the time, for everyone who worked his ten and twelve a day, everyone who wasn't gifted enough—if it could be called a gift—to twist out movies of strutting Generals below the Rio Grande, and fill his . . .

"Say, Allie, we've got to pare it down to the bone this week, unless you stumble on some kind of an opening."

Allene stared up from the paragraph where a bony, white hand had thrust itself through the black curtains and "gripped the softly bare, lovely shoulder of Rosalind Trevor, youngest daughter of the murdered broker." . . .

"Bone? . . . brroo. What were you saying, Ray?"

"I said, we'll have to go mighty slow this week, if you don't find anything and as a matter of fact, I can't see how we can make it even then and keep our strength up, unless you locate a full-time position and get some kind of advance before your first pay-day."

Allene threw the book on the bed. She felt as though she had been asleep again and Ray had whisked a silly dream, tinier than a fly-speck, from her head.

"You can search me, Ray. I looked through the ads in tonight's paper and I marked two of them, but they didn't seem any too promising. One was for 'a secretary with unusual intelligence and experience in a law-office'—it'll probably turn out to be a job typing contracts, and affidavits, and damage-claims for twelve per, maybe fourteen at the most, and there'll be at least five, or six girls ahead of me, unless I go down about five in the morning and camp outside in the snow, in front of the building-doors. That's the only way I'll ever be sure. The other one was for a 'sales-girl with personality and perseverance'—another canvassing-idea, more than likely."

Ray left the bed, stretched himself, and went to the closet just behind the bed, to retrieve a lone cigarette from his coat-pocket— one given to him by Weintraub before they parted. He had been afraid to buy a pack on his way over to the room.

"Christ, if they have to advertise, with so many people out of work nowadays, there must be something phony about it."

When he emerged, he continued: "And I need a pair of slippers worse than blazes. I'm dirtying my socks up, walking around here on the floor every night."

"You need? Of course, you need a million things, you poor kid, but what about me? I'm down to exactly three decent dresses to my name—the others simply aren't fit to wear any more—and if I don't buy some stockings soon—"

"Stop it, the boat's leaking, and if you don't think it's a stormy night at sea, you just listen to that wind bumping against the front-cabin windows, matie"—he tried to smile, to be self-sufficient in a blackness not fully admitted by his voice.

Plink, plink . . . plink. He shifted, eyed the washbasin, then the ceiling.

"Did you say *leaking*, Ray?"

They doubled with laughter, shook with its tumult. The tension, sometimes, had to be swept aside with any device, if their heads were to remain level. Afterwards, as they smoked in bed—cigarettes borrowed from the couple in the next room—they spoke more darkly.

"We were all chinning down at the lockers, tonight, and Fred, one of the bell-hops, well, Fred got into an argument with Weintraub over having a union in the hotel, and he told Wein the Reds were a darn sight better than a lot of the fellows knocking them. There's a bunch of them over in a union-office on Huntington and they're trying to drag the fellows to join up with their outfit. Of course, I know that most of them are foreigners, and they're always ready to do anything to stir up violence, sure, I know that, but the trouble is, Allie—they hand out a line that sounds honest and they tell the men, in plain English, that they've got to look out for skullduggery and stick up for their rights, and I can't blame the boys, if some of them fall for it. With the wages they get and the hours they put in, they're sore as hell, most of them, and of course, the Reds are trying to take advantage of it. If I didn't have a pretty good balance in my own head I might tumble for it myself."

Allene responded with the cynicism which she had nursed in her heart throughout this day, the feeling that life gave its material rewards only to people who were dishonest in every particle of their bodies and spirits but knew how to make it legal, cover it with myriads of hypocrisies, hand out the exact mixture of browbeating, crawling, and charity, that seemed to be the accepted standard everywhere.

"Well, I'm going to tell you something, Ray—I'm beginning to think the whole world's a racket, everywhere, no matter where a person looks. I'll bet anything the Reds are nothing but racketeers themselves, the leaders I mean. It wouldn't surprise me if they had their own cars, and big, secret bank-accounts too. Don't tell me. You can't be on the square in this world, Ray, you simply can't. The only trick I can see is to be crooked as the devil, but be crooked in a nice, respectable way. If we aren't, we're going to stay just where we are for the rest of our lives, or else we'll get a break for a while, get better jobs, and then what? We'll never know when we're going to lose them and we'll always be liable to come back some night and find ours right smack in the same hole again. We've got to do something about it, that's all there is to it, Ray."

Despite the enormous temptation to agree with her, Ray held out. He felt that every really sensitive man had smaller dishonesties forced upon him by life, and that sometimes he was even capable of them himself, but that, if he steeped his whole life in the larger ones, he would always hold a self-disgust in the still depths of his being, no matter how much he refused to confess it to himself, to others.

"I won't argue with you about the world. I think you're exaggerating about it, but I'll admit it seems to be a pretty lousy proposition sometimes. But Christ, I'd feel like committing suicide if I thought the only way I could get a decent living was to skin people right and left, and fool them, and get rich on it. I've been dishonest in little ways in my life—you know, peeking at another fellow's cards, or bragging about my wages and putting them up ten dollars, or well, cheating a fellow in some little deal—sure, I'm not trying to make myself out to be perfect, not by a long shot, but just the same, I couldn't make a regular game of it to save my life. I'm just not built that way."

"All right then, stay honest and see how much it brings you"— Allene's voice was cross but had a falter in it, since her cynicism was only skin-deep, and yet she went on, felt herself compelled to return to it.

"For goodness sakes, Ray, look around you, look at the wages they're paying, the butter-scotch they hand out, and look at all the people too, tramping their feet off trying to get a job. You know what happened when I went down to that C.W.A. place the other day. The office was packed with girls—I think there must have been at least a hundred of them—and what did I get? Nothing. Come back in two weeks, and now I read in the papers that they're going to drop the C.W.A. thing too. I'm telling you, it's enough to give a person the jitters. We've got to look out for ourselves, first, last, and all the time, and if there's any honest way of doing it, I'd love to know what it is."

"Well, what do you want me to do . . . read up the law-books and then think up a safe way to swindle people?"—he tried to be humorous, to ease the dark weight for a moment. "You can't even do that unless you have a little money to start with. Maybe you'd like me to start some fake mail-order game, something like that."

"I don't see anything to joke about, Ray. For instance, you know the hotel game from top to bottom and yet you've never gotten anywhere in it. You ought to make every effort to get on the good side of that fellow, Gallineau, no matter what you have to do, God, lick his feet if it's necessary. If you don't smear butter on people you don't rise up an inch from the sidewalk, not an inch. You ought to know that by this time."

"Yes, I know it, but it's damn hard for me to change my nature. I can be friendly to people if there's any reason for it, but Christ, how I hate to crawl to them. That's why I've lost one hotel-job after another. I liked the work, and I liked the idea of handling different people and, oh, the idea of seeing the whole country by proxy, you know, with everybody trooping up to the desk, especially in a big hotel . . . but I never kept any hotel-job longer than a year, and that was a record. Something would always happen—I'd get disgusted with the conditions and go off on a tear, or I wouldn't be a stool-pigeon, or I wouldn't be a stooge to the main cheese—something, always."

"Well, if you don't learn to hold your temper, and be tactful, and do anything they tell you to do, well, if you don't, I can just picture what your end's going to be."

"Cut it out, I'm an artist that way myself"—he arose, turned out the light, and came back to bed. "And how about you, kid—you're in no position to talk."

"Don't you suppose I know it? But believe me, the next full-time job I land I'm going to be honey and cream to all of the heads in the firm, and I'm going to rack my little brain for ideas on how to increase the profits. I don't care whether they're honest, or not. And what's more, I'll show the bosses I can carry them out myself, too."

"Oh rats, if you were like that, you'd have done it long ago. You wouldn't be starting in at this late date."

"Maybe, but I'm desperate now and I realize a person has to do those things, because otherwise, he hasn't a single chance to get ahead"—there was a quiver in her voice, which she tried to make more decisive than she felt.

For a time they peered through the darkened room at the patches of white frost on the windows pallidly drenched by a street-light, and then she said: "Ray, don't you think you ought to write home for money? Think of it, we could get married and go to your mother in Chicago then, and with all her connections, and your brother's connections, gee, you could get a decent job again, and maybe I could too. What's the use of always struggling, always getting nowhere, just to save that foolish pride of yours? Honest Ray, sometimes I think you're an idiot, I do."

He studied a long time before he answered. Examining the question again, he began to realize that his reasons for opposing Allene's urging were not only those of confessing that he had lied about his financial success, not simply the dread of being patronized and derided as a failure by his brother and sister, the sorrow, and embarrassment, and secret head-shaking, which he might cause in his mother, who had always cradled him first in her heart, always feeling certain that some day, in spite of his impulsiveness, he would be secure and "well-fixed," be respected in the only sense in which, innocently, she valuated the word. He was approaching thirty-one now and beginning to solidify in his heart and mind, though much more uprooted and dismayed than the possible average in his time of life, as he told himself. Why was he shrinking from Allene's words now, why did every atom of his being desire to ignore the easy escape which they afforded?

It was because the past half year had thrown him into a world entirely different from the one to which he had loaned himself before, a world that he liked, felt a common heart-swing with, in which he shared the angers and the rougher jobs of men and women who seemed, to him, to be much more sincere, and unadorned, and persistently struggling, than the ones he had previously known. His idea of success had changed. It was no longer the craving to rise, to gather money and leisure, to keep on rising until he found himself in a padded chair surrounded by obedient flunkies and dictating the working-conditions of hundreds, perhaps even thousands, of other men and women. It had never been more than a half-hearted craving, at that. He had never been willing to maneuver for "the pull," the favor, that could have elevated him. He had always doped himself into believing that he could make his way without these efforts, with the exercise of ability, acumen, and insistence, but even such a victory, were it possible, had become distasteful to him. It meant, to his vision now, the continual pitting of one's man interest against that of the others, who worked for him, and while he still thought that such a pitting was necessary and showed a superior brain on the part of the one who attained it, he realized that it would have been an uneasy, even unhappy ending for him—a position in which he would have been endlessly torn between his sympathies and leniencies toward human beings, on one side, and the commands of "hard, shrewd business-sense" on the other.

He was attached to a different world and different emotions now, and while he still believed that this world could peacefully adjust its disputes with the more honest members of the first one— still tried to believe it in spite of faltering, anger—he knew also that he was innately on the side of working men and women, that he had no longing for anything except a fairly good job, wages that would enable him to live in bare comfort, reasonable hours of work, and a liveable home with Allene. Ambition, as so many people defined it, was beginning to take on a heartless aspect, to him. If he went back to his family now, they would expect him to accept this definition. He would be once more in a world where the coveting of money and its attendant power was supreme, under every possible cover, protestation, frivolity, and connivance, and within it he would feel lost, disagreeing without any means of making the disagreement effective. He had a strong desire to see his mother again because so many of her small, personal traits were similar to his, in a softer guise, and because she had always been willing to defend him, because he believed that she had been born in a sphere of society to which she had never been sharply and consistently loyal, but he told himself now that this wish would have to be postponed until he could gain his feet, return without asking for charity, without having to make long explanations.

Irritated at his silence and dubious regarding its motives, Allene asked: "What's the matter, Ray? Every time I mention the subject of getting married and going back to your mother in Chicago, because that's the only way we could get married and have any prospect of security—every single time I mention it you haven't a word to say, or else you start in to hedge and you say you don't want to be made out a liar, but I'm beginning to think there's something else behind it."

He kissed her on the mouth, pressed his cheek against her face, for a moment, hoping that he might placate her a bit before the possible argument, the revelation. He had become sleepier now, drugged and gutted against his will by the long day of work, but he resisted because he knew that she was really hurt by his failure to confide in her.

"Listen Allie, it isn't my mother alone. She'll have to find out some time, but I don't want to tell her for the simple reason that I don't want to go back. When I see her again it's going to be on my own money and on my own hook. I guess I've grown out of the world I used to be in. I don't like it now that I look back on it, and I'll tell you why. The people in it haven't got any hearts. They can be as sentimental as the devil, sometimes, and they can hand out charities right and left, sure, but they haven't got any hearts just the same—oh, maybe for their relatives and some of their closest friends, yes, but that's where it ends. They're always flattering and working wires to get to the top, every single one of them, and when they get to the top and they've got their big bank-rolls, then all they want to do is hold on to them. I don't care to play their game any more, and as a matter of fact, I never did care to play it, and that's just why I wasn't successful at it. You can tell me the world's full of racketeers, but where are they? They're in the underworld or in the one upstairs, that's where, and we don't belong to them. We're working-people, and it's not in our blood to be dishonest in any big ways, and we might as well stare it right square in the face!"

He had spoken to her with equal seriousness before, but never so articulately, never with such an intense sweep in his voice. Her own cynicism was too weak to resist him and she changed to a feeling bordering on despair, a feeling that, taken by and large, working-girls had an almost non-existent chance for consistent happiness, and that, if they achieved it at all, it was only by drawing on inner resources, which seemed to fail her now.

"Then what's going to happen to us? We'll never get married, and have a kid or two, and enjoy ourselves . . . a little, will we?"

"Certainly we will, but we'll have to fight for it with all our strength, believe me. I'll get a better job some time, and you'll find one too, but we'll never know when we're to be fired, or laid off, or run into sickness . . . or something. It's a tough game for people like us, always, unless some relative should die and plop a few thousands in our laps, and even then, Christ . . . a bank-crash or a rotten investment . . . you never know what's going to happen to you in this messy world."

He hung on to the wobbly optimism because he was a man with

all of his beliefs crumbling under him and he found it necessary to keep them from utter extinction, since he had stumbled upon nothing that could take their place. He was half-asleep when they kissed one another, trailed hands over cheek and throat, came closer in the scarcely conscious linking of arms. He wanted to make love to her but a thick, warm, gray blanket was being wrapped and knotted around him, slowly, enticing him against the opposite desire, while she, more awake but with her senses also drooping, felt a disappointment too indistinct to be painful and yet . . . it was hellish . . . when you were both so tired . . . so, so tired . . . you couldn't even take . . . They fell back and slept. . . .

II

THE BEGINNING of night in late March had a subdued coolness, the reluctant compromise between winter and spring with one putting on its best front to say good-bye and the other diffidently acceptant, a meeting always robbed of its inherent gaiety and plaintiveness, in any large, American city, by a factor difficult to define in its external contacts and yet unmistakable underneath. The endless, close-packed rush and still jam of automobiles with their cough and groan, the men and women drivers never relaxing in their straight-ahead stares, their alertness to "beat the lights," if only by a fraction of a second, their effort to shoot past one another, gain a few feet by nosing into a gap, and the self-enclosed looks with which they greeted the people clogging the streets—all of these things were symptoms of an individualism vicious down to the core and yet loath to confess its identity. Men and women were sometimes caught in the middle of the streets when the lights flashed to green, and had to race for the opposite curbstones, and often the machines missed them only by inches. Some of these runners, hurrying to their own cars in garage and parking-space, turned for a moment and glared at a reckless driver—a deviation of the arrogance of "the top"—and the glare was exceptionally intense if the offender chanced to be a taxicab. The traffic-cops frowned and swore, tired of standing for hours and inhaling gasoline fumes, and aching for a chance to forget it by asserting their importance, almost always at the expense of the truck-drivers, the hackmen, the smaller cars.

The trees and bushes on the Commons were dotted with sprouts and tendrils, and strings of green were curled in and out of the tonsured lawns, but the people on the benches lining a broad, cement walk were not sharing this revival, for the most part. They were remote from any touch of a festival, of whole-hearted laughter and smiles sewing humans together, of spontaneous intermingling, of sincere curiosity concerning one another, of any of the attributes that make life and spring a keen, expectant, buoyant mating. Some of the faces were vacant, thought pounded out of them by the long day of work. Women loaded with cosmetics, in a brave, colorful show of cheap clothes and thin stockings, waited for "the pick-up"— the only chance to get a bit of recreation and avoid paying for it, if they could, and hope that it would lead to some "romance," to a meeting with some moneyed man who would fall in love with them. Other women isolated themselves, bundled in unhappy thoughts, or in fluctuations of emotions drooping to apathy.

Bands of boys and girls in their teens walked by, congregated on the benches—slyness already in their eyes, the self-assured ignorance of the "wise guy," the over-painted, gum-chewing, sulky pose of the professional flirt . . . mouldy jokes retailed as a mark of adult superiority . . . sex peddled in an endless, mean, suggestive babble. It was the tragedy of boys and girls betrayed by the swarm of lies, ignorances, and delusions, foisted on them by an economic system —the Mae West film-motive: "Come up and see me some time": the moral racketeers: the bawdy cabarets and doleful churches: the taxi-dance meanness: the endless pother about "vice" followed by endless fake-suppressions and glorifyings—all of the surface contradictions injected by a plundering, ruling class, to make these boys and girls muddled and yet prematurely hardened, and keep them harmless to the continuation of this class itself.

Ray was dressing in the locker-room of the Book Hotel. He stepped out of his blue and red-striped pants, tossed his red and gold-braid cap on a hook. Damn them, they rigged a fellow out like a general in the Peruvian army, to cater to snobs, but they wouldn't pay him a dollar more unless they were black-jacked out of it. He had noticed a tenseness throughout the day. Gallineau had hovered all over the lobby, the Purple Room, the upper floors, and whenever the employees had stopped to talk to one another, they had never been safe from his approach, his sharp order: "Come on now, get on the job." Waiting for a bellhop, Ray had heard him "lining into" a knot of the chamber-maids, who had tarried in the adjacent linen-room—telling them 'that he would get them a nice, soft bed, if they had nothing else to do.' Yet, this same Gallineau had chatted with him for the first time in weeks, told him he might be promoted soon. Even Seidendahl—a tall man with button eyes, a trick-moustache, and a skull like a stuffed egg standing on end and sliced flat at the tip—had shown an exceptional interest in the doings of the employees, had summoned Weintraub to the offices, with Ray substituting for half an hour.

Something was in the wind. Were they planning to fire some of the men for signing up with that Red union? Ray had tried to pump Alec, Wally, and Countiss, by turns, and had received nothing but distrustful looks, except that Wally had said: "Aw, ask Gally, the weasel—he's your friend, isn't he?" In the locker-room now, they were whispering with Jimmy Harrison, a sandy-capped, sullen-eyed fellow who had replaced Drossi. Drossi had quit over a month previous and it was rumored that he was hiding with his woman, "Kittens," because she had snared the wrong contact, a girl who had been shipped to a hospital, suffering from a fall and a three-day jag, and whose father, a big grocery-merchant, had informed the police.

As they were leaving the locker-room, Ray stepped beside Countiss.

"Say, what's up, Fred? Let me in on it, will you?"

Countiss squinted at Ray, drove knuckles against his own broad mouth, and hesitated. 'This guy wasn't so dumb, he thought, but he couldn't cross the last yard, couldn't quite understand that all of the bosses were lined up against the workers, every damn time, and that the patriotism of the smaller bosses had a dollar-sign on the inside, dictated by the larger ones, with a bible preaching good-will on one side and a cop with a tear-gas bomb on the other—the bastards.' He kept on talking about some kind of arrangement between the more decent bosses, and the workers, to keep the country out of anarchy or a dictatorship by the Reds—some fairy-tale like that. He blabbed about peaceful strikes and when you asked him what should be done with the scabs and the gangsters protecting them, he said that some of them could be argued out of it, if they were approached in the right way, and that fists were useless anyway when a worker was going up against guns and blackjacks: Ray repeated the question. Countiss scowled.

"What are you asking me for? You know the street and the number, if you want to go over there and find out—you're no fool. Besides, I've got to be some place in ten minutes and I'm all in, too—I feel just like a load of dishes dumped in the sink, I'm so tired."

"Yeah, Gally's certainly cracked down on us this day, the louse"—Ray was filled with a dull foreboding as he stepped through the dim basement and watched Countiss taking the basement-steps two at a time.

Undoubtedly, a strike was in the air. There was even less doubt about what side he would be on, he thought, and yet he would hate to go into it without his whole heart. If he could only believe that the men and women would not be taken advantage of by the Reds, reputed to be behind the union which they had secretly joined, would not be used simply as "the goats" to stir up trouble and then find themselves deserted by their former allies and in jail, with bruises and broken heads, or out of work, or back on the jobs with nothing to show for it. Hell, he wanted to fight and stick with his own kind, as well as they did, but he was an American, after all, and it was difficult for him to string along with leaders, most of them foreign-born, as he had been told, whose real aim was to disrupt the country and win it over to the command of the Russians. He knew what he and the other workers had to put up with, and he certainly knew that the rackets and lies were mounting everywhere and that something serious had to be done about them, but God, why couldn't men and women form their own unions and still stand by their country? Why couldn't they win fair wages and just working-conditions by walking out in one, great mass and refusing to return until their demands were granted? Why didn't some of the more honest business-men—those who tried to be as honest as they could in the dollar-grabbing whirl—why didn't these people set an example and make a willing compromise with their employees, realize that such a compromise was inevitable, if the country was not to be plunged into eventual ruin?

He understood now, indelibly, that workers had always only one interest and people with money had another one, but he still believed that the present system was the only one that could stabilize life, keep it in any semblance of order, and that the difference would have to be reconciled, improved, and yet, where were the first signs of such a swing? Every day he read in the papers, in the five-cent magazines, glowing accounts of how the country was returning to prosperity, was eating into the ranks of the unemployed, was establishing a better and more tolerant bond between the employers and their workers. Even the big, Socialist leaders, the ones that, Countiss said, were demagogues telling the worker to lie down and wait for freedom, even they were blowing their horns over the wonderful improvement brought by the N.R.A. and the inflated dollar—but where was it happening, in Timbuctoo? He couldn't see any indications of it immediately around him, in the hotels, the stores, the men flooding the employment-agencies on Scollay Square, or parking in the Commons, and a couple of days previous he had read an item in the "Post," announcing that two thousand C.W.A. workers had been laid off in Massachusetts during the past week. Funny, wasn't it—they always printed such information back on page five, or sixteen, didn't they? No headlines there. The headlines were all about the moves of Roosevelt and Congress and their success in preventing impending strikes, or some murder in a pent-house, a country-home, or some little gang-fray around the Square. Funny, wasn't it? Yes, too damn funny to suit him!

He had swung into Scollay Square now. The marquee of a movie-house spelled in close blue and yellow bulbs: "Tarzan, The Ape, and Cradle Song, with Weissmuller and Dorothea Wieck." Opposite, a burlesque theatre promised: "A Night In Paris, with Thirty Gorgeous Girls," while a clown on stilts walked to and fro, advertising the show, and the entrance held gaudy posters and stands with photographs of girls in various stages of provocative nudity. A bit further down a Religious Mission displayed its gilt signs and its window-card: "The Saviour Is Our One Refuge In All Times Of Stress And Storm. Everybody Is Welcome Here." The lunch-bars and restaurants were crowded, and some of them bore numbered permits on their glass fronts, proving that they were licensed to sell wine and liquor. Glancing into their windows, Ray said to himself: "It's no mystery how most of them manage to eat in this neighborhood—gambling, stealing, dope-selling, and men and women working one another, milking the sightseers, baiting the working-girls . . . by God, if I weren't so level-headed" . . . Curiously enough—not so curious to the people involved—the curbs of the Square were almost solidly lined with machines, while poorly dressed men, kids in slicked, cheap suits, clotted the side-walks, and sometimes, cold-eyed, hard-faced men, better clad, issued from the buildings, hopped into the machines and drove off, alone, or with beautifully shaped, furred women with eyes like sponges, faces more soulless than rubber.

Ray entered the lobby of his "hotel." Konig greeted him. Konig had a feeble face, squashy lips, and no hope in his eyes. He laughed a great deal because he had discovered that a laugher "got by" easier, nosed into private schemes, had crumbs flung to him. He worked as an automobile-washer in a nearby garage, now and then, but in between he lived on dice and cards, when he had a lucky streak, or served an employment-agency, strolling on the Square, the side streets, and striving to induce men of different trades to act as scabs, to be shipped to trouble-centers in New England. He was not innately lazy, had not been inevitably destined to be a heartless scavenger, but his environment had corrupted him, in the imperceptible way in which it operates on men of his kind. Born and raised near Scollay Square, he had worked hard at first and then found out that many of his former school-chums were "taking it easy" as the trusted lower-assistants of political and gang-leaders in the locality, and he had compared them with himself and the other workers whom he knew, pouring their strength out for miserable wages, accepting abuse as a matter of course, fired when they rebelled, paying their money to tarts, or marrying and staggering on the treadmill, day in and out, with the necessity of caring for children, also, already beginning to gnaw out the youth on their faces. Gradually, he had taken longer and longer vacations from his work, palled with "the boys," who ran the neighborhood, and returned to work only when the supply of assistants was greater than the demand, and, temporarily, the rulers 'had nothing for him.' He hung around Ray at the foot of the stairway.

"Say, Bailey, if you can scrape up the jack, you can join a little game we're having tonight, stud, up in Slattery's room. Quarter limit and a nickel out for the cards—you wouldn't need more than three or four bucks to start you rolling, if you nurse your cards and wait for a good one in the hole."

Ray was peevish.

"Yes, I used to sit for hours waiting for it to come and waiting for the other man to top it."

"Well, it's not so much to risk losing, and—"

"Oh, isn't it? You go out and sweat for it, boy, and you'll sing a different tune, you will."

"Aw, I've worked as hard as a bow-legged guy trying to skin up a grease-pole in my time" (his laugh was like a competition between a quack and a saw buzz), "yeah, and even harder too, and I still—"

"Still what did you say?"—Pete Gavin walked up.

He worked on a street-car repair-gang and he had just finished ten grueling hours of it, and had an aimless grudge "against the world" because he couldn't narrow it down to any perceptible target, except Konig and his ilk, and he felt always that more ominous skunks were lurking somewhere in the background. He had big, puffed-out lips, hungry slots of eyes, a face coated with half-washed dirt. He wore a dark cotton work-suit, out at the elbows and caked with dry mud at the bottoms of the pants, and he looked at Konig's creased brown tweed as though he would have been happy to tear it into strips.

"Looks like you had a tough day, Pete"—Konig sprinkled the oil, indifferently.

"Yeah, sure, while you was pressing your can and swigging booze at Mulrooney's, and what's more, I heard you been nosing around for the Brackett Agency and you been button-holing the boys and getting them to go and scab in different towns. Laugh that one off."

"That's a damn lie. I'd like to get face to face with the fellow who told you that"—Konig clung to an injured bluster, but his hand, extracting a cigarette from a package, trembled a little.

"You won't get his name out of me because I think you're a pretty smooth art'cle, too damn smooth, if you ask me."

"Well, what in hell did I ever do against you?"

"Nothing at all. You've never had a chance, and you're not going to get one, either."

The quarrel went on. Ray listened, looked around the lobby, with its horse-hair sofa, its brass chandeliers and small, dark blue china spittoons, rugs once red and green, with the colors practically trod out of them, and white net curtains, with occasional holes, tucked in by red ribbons, at the window. If anybody could surpass, for downright dreariness, some of the places people had to live in, he thought, then that person certainly would have to be a wizard beyond dispute. He shot a disdainful look at Konig, and mounted the stairs. Another rat, probably—he was beginning to lose count of them. But men like Gavin were far from being rats, and they outnumbered the others ten to one. They would have to become aware of their power, some day, and unite to blast out improvements in their lives, but how? What kind of unions, tactics, guidance should they have, and what could rally all of them together? The question bit into his brain; but all to no avail. Switching on the room-lights, he saw that Allene had not yet returned. This worried him because it was one of her working-days—she had secured a part-time job, for three afternoons a week, in an advertising-office—and she finished at six, and the time was nearing a quarter-to-eight now.

He took off his coat and tie, loosened the shirt-collar, rolled up the sleeves, and began to wash himself. Though he was more inured to his work, it still taxed him, sorely, and he sloshed water, rubbed soap, in a listless fashion, with his heart alert only for the sound of Allene's key. They hadn't had a quarrel since the previous Friday night when he had found her sitting and talking in the room, with Lambert, the proprietor. Of course, Lambert, calling for the rent, had plopped himself down without an invitation, just as she had claimed, but a fellow never reasoned it out that way at the time. Somehow, the long day, the drain on his strength, the bleakness of his future, brought out the pettiness in him, increased his jealousy, made him even childish, where a woman was concerned, didn't it? And Allene could probably say the same things about herself in other matters where she had sworn that he was at fault. Yes, if any personal blame existed, it was evenly divided, though the acknowledgment of this, in their saner moments, never seemed to prevent another out-burst, damn it. He heard a knocking, hastily dried himself and opened the door.

Judith confronted him. She was drunk, dropped her left hand on the door-jamb, to straighten herself. Her lumpy cheeks were clogged with rouge—a travesty on the clearer blood which life had muddied and dammed in the stream and pulse of her being. A clump of wet hair had fallen over one of the thick rims enclosing her gray eyes, eyes revealing now, the prostrate light that seeks to be devil-may-care, revealing also, undying traces of an honesty forced to revile itself, to come forth in gasps and sneaks, when the brow-beaters of her existence diverted their attention elsewhere, allowed her any moment of flimsy, imaginary repose. She was wearing high-heeled, pale blue satin slippers and a pale green and blue bathrobe in the barred and cubed pattern sold by a middle-class, which had abandoned its flowered fol-de-rols in attire and was now "going in" for futuristic effects—the endless shifts in style devised by the dress-manufacturers to swell their bank-accounts. She reeked of perfume and liquor combined to a ghastly, insinuating, unsteadying odor—one of the main narcotics of a dying system, floating, without end, from night-club, cabaret, hotel, to pretend a voluptuous confidence in itself. She dabbed at the clump of hair, twirling her fingers with the drunkard's idea of nonchalance.

"Hello swee'ness. Whatcha got on ya mind?"

"I think you're kind of pie-eyed, Jude"—Ray was embarrassed, saying anything to talk it off.

"Me? Pie-eye? Y' crazy. I nev' felt better in m' life."

She commenced to enter the room and Ray backed away, uncertain as to what he should do. She attempted a Lindy hop and almost fell, and he had to hold her up.

"Come on, cover yourself up, girl, or you'll get me nervous"—he pulled one side of the bathrobe over her breast and buttoned it.

He had to admit that he had been the least bit shaken for a second. Every normal man could be stirred by a sexual display in a woman still young, he thought—why in hell shouldn't he be honest and confess it? He had been inclined to touch Judith now, but, oh, it was hard to define—a desire not to be slinking, not to take a woman unless there was some kind of a mutual blending, a sincere notion that they were hitting it off, anyway, no matter if it lasted an hour, or . . . it was no use. He had no words for it, and what he had said to himself had a stilted impact. Judith was standing with more poise now, with the obsession that she was perfectly sober and could easily prove it.

"Say, listen, swee'ness, listen—don' stan' so far 'way fr'm me. Ya think I'm goin' ta poison ya? Why say, listen . . . I'm tellin' ya . . . I'd swear on a, ona bible, I'd swear ona stack uh bibles, I was nev' more sober in all m' li-ife. I mean it."

She lurched a step toward him. He retreated, felt a sick amusement at himself. He didn't want her but he hated to act like a shrinking school-kid. He was afraid that Allene might appear at any moment and yet, if Judith refused to leave, it would have gone against his grain to push, or carry her, roughly, out of the room—it would have smacked of a contempt which was not in him. Judith had been pushed and kicked around plenty by a life, a system, which was taking on a more and more rotten shape to him, every day—a system holding nothing but fake tears, open cruelties, cheap accusations, for girls who ended up as she had.

"What do you want of me, Jude? I'm expecting Allene back any minute now, and you know how it is, I wouldn't want her to get jealous over nothing and start imagining things. Come on, Jude, be a good kid now and go upstairs, will you?"

Judith looked vacant for a second and then brightened up.

"I'm a nitwit, d'ya know that? I f'got all 'bout what I come down here f'r. I've been tryin' an' tryin' ta open that lock an' I jus' can't do it."

"What lock are you talking about, kid?"

"It's the lock on onea m' bureau drawers. The key won' work an' I tried ta jimmy the damn thing open, an' look what I did. All bloodied up, that's what I yam."

She held up a badly torn finger-nail with a bit of cotton wedged under it. The booze made her continue to babble over the incident, to dwell on other mishaps of the previous hours, in her instinct to avoid any sight of the larger blows, past, still to arrive. Ray cut into the flow of her words.

"Can't you get Mike, the porter, to open it, or maybe one of the fellows upstairs?"

"Aw, Mike mus'n be in the buildin'. I've hollered m' lungs out f'r him an'—"

"Well how about Slattery, next door to you? Honest Jude, I'm so darn tired I hate to move."

She had always liked him because he had been moderately friendly, in snatches of talk in the hallways, the lobby, and yet had never bothered her, never given her any looks which she could have interpreted as "wrong"—the body-measuring, slanting looks dealt by some of the hangers-on in the hotel—and now, she had a drunkard's insistence on having her own way. She had no overpowering, or definite desire for him, but she was still a long distance from being thick-skinned, completely subservient. She knew that she was not particularly good-looking and, at times, she wanted to wipe out the feeling that she was accommodating men, who were buying her only because she was another woman and they could have her more cheaply—wanted to prove, to herself, that she had enough individual charm left to attract a man of his own accord, a pleasant man, who didn't have to go shopping for women because more decent girls wouldn't take him.

"Aw, Slat'try c'n stan' on his ear, f'r all I care. I hate his guts. He's always knockin' on m' door with some damn 'scuse, an' he's always tryin' ta bust inta m' room. You c'm on up an' help me, swee's, like a nice, dear boy now, won'tcha, swee's? C'm on, Ray, help a girl out. Gee whiz, y'wanna be a gen'leman now, Ray—don'tcha dear? Sure y'do. I got somepin in tha' drawer an' I jus' gotta get it out."

She leaned against him, pulled at his hands, squeezed his shoulders, as she continued the pleadings. Ray squirmed, felt nauseated and compassionate in a limp pulling-down, and asked himself, savagely, what reason he had to be disgusted with her, why he couldn't regard her as a sister—not in the sloppy, the stooping, interpretation of the word, but in the sense of two human beings, equally oppressed in different ways, with one of them simply out of his wits from too much drinking. She wasn't the ugly one, primarily, but the ugliness resided in the life hemming her in, certainly, he knew that, and yet he could tell it to himself dozens of times and still fail to down the inclination to forget it, to call her a goddamn, loose fool, laugh at her, feel on the verge of shoving her out of the room.

What was it? It shot itself into people plastered to the same level of life and strove to make them imagine that they had some pretext for considering themselves superior to one another. It scattered people, especially the workers among them, and sought in every way to fill them with sneers, and hatreds, and suspicions toward their own kind, and yet, by God, it was forever urging brotherhood and democracy, too, with the other side of its foul mouth—that was the puzzling part of it. A girl like Judith, just starting to flatten herself, needed practical assistance, had always needed it, but who in her life had ever given her anything except warnings, fried mush, leers and pocket-pickings? He decided to go to her room and see if the jammed-drawer story was a lie, and pry the drawer open, if it wasn't, since otherwise, if Allene came in and found Judith with her arms wound around him now, the situation might be even worse. To indicate that she was sober, Judith sprang up the stairs, missed one of them, stumbled and had to be half-dragged the remainder of the way. The lock was actually stuck, and he used one of her kitchen knives to pry it apart, while she kept on standing close to him, supporting herself with her hands on his back, mussing his hair, poking his ribs, to the tune of her foolish laughter. When she had finished, she backed him against the bureau, slobbered on his cheek and said: "I wantcha t' keep me comp'ny f'r a while. I got the blues, the blooies', bloosies' blue-ues, hones' I have, an' I'll give ya a drink uh the swelles' rye y' ever—"

"For Christ sake, leave me alone. I'm tired and I'm not looking for anything from you, and I'll tell you this much, if you don't stop guzzling and throwing yourself around, kid, you'll wind up lower than a doormat, that's certain."

He pushed her away and made for the door.

"Aw gee, you don' think I'm so lousy now, do yah? Do yah really think I'm a lousy somepin 'r other?"

He regretted his words, hated the sound of a woman talking like a maudlin baby, knew that the hate was not justified, in Judith's case. He thought that life was insane, induced people "to take it out" on one another, strive to ease their lot in a common jail, which they shared through no fault of their own, unless it was the fault of not tearing the damn walls down. Standing in the doorway, he turned and said: "Don't ask me, Jude. The way I feel now, the whole world's lousy, myself included."

"Tha's jus' the way I feel, but I c'n make yah feel good, too"—(she sang, out of key)—"Y' need a goo-od woman, show y' how t' do-o it right, oh rightie ri-ight"—she lurched toward him with a drooling face, mortified at his lack of response and still dimly hopeful, in the blurring of alcohol.

He fled down the hall and she followed. As he descended the stairs, she leaned over the banister and called after him, with the tremble of attempted gaiety: "G'bye, swee'ness. C'm up an' see me 'gain an' we'll kill the res' uh the bottle, swee's."

He saw that Allene was standing at the bottom of the stairs and looking up at him, with a murderous frown. He tightened himself.

"Say, Allie, you must have come back only a few minutes ago, just after I left the room."

She failed to answer. When they were inside, she took off her tan, pearl-buttoned coat and flung it into a corner of the bed. The thought that he might have "cheated on her," following the hurried afternoon-grapple with row on row of numbers, sank into her nerves and gave them a clawing sensation.

"I see you've been visiting, haven't you?"

As he looked at her, his face became, slowly, more distorted, since he was aggravated because he had to explain an incident in which he had been so utterly blameless.

"Yes, I have, but not in the way you mean. She came down here, stewed to the gills, and she wouldn't leave the room until I went up and broke a lock on one of her bureau drawers. Then she put her arms around me and she wanted me to stay and drink with her, but I scooted right out of the room and came down here, and that's the long and the short of it."

The numbers jigged in her brain, collapsed heavily, jigged again—doing a day-and-a-half of book-keeping in one afternoon, for a measly two dollars, because she knew that, if she didn't, a hundred other girls would be there fighting one another for the job, and now she couldn't even rely on the man she loved, the only refuge she had.

"Yes, it's a nice story, Ray. How long did it take you to think it up?'"

"Oh, I didn't have to think about it, kid, because I've got all of the stories arranged in advance. That's what you want to hear, so I hope you're satisfied, and suppose you tell *me* why you came back so late?"

He was sitting on the bed and punching the mattress to hold his temper.

"Oh that. That was astounding. I actually blew myself to an ice-cream sundae with pecans and whipped cream on it, and then I sat around and talked with a girl who works in the office. It's too bad I didn't follow your example, just too bad"—Allene wandered around the room, bit her finger-nails, stamped on the floor, to restrain the even harsher words crowding her mouth.

Ray jumped from the bed.

"Listen, I'm dead on my feet, and I'm not joking, either. Can the comedy. If you don't believe me, you can go upstairs and ask her yourself."

"Yes, of course, I'll humiliate myself and ask her all about it, and she'll tell me the exact truth, certainly she will, and then I'll come back and hug you, just like a little hoodwinked lamb. Honest Ray, you must think I'm an imbecile. I don't expect a man to be perfect, but I never imagined that you would live with me and then sneak up to prostitutes in between. That was beyond me."

The last fling was too much for Ray.

"God, if I had your smallness, I couldn't bear to look myself in the face."

He snatched his coat and cap from a chair.

"I work my arms and feet off, all day long, and I'm not going to tramp back here and take abuse in the bargain, when I haven't done a single thing to deserve it."

He flew out of the room, slamming the door, and she could hear him clattering down the stairs. She threw herself on the bed, and as she tossed from side to side, the glare fled from her eyes and was replaced by a bitter wonder at the love within her, so capable of flying into the pettiest of tantrums and then rejecting them with an equal, amazing swiftness. She could have chewed her tongue off now, for the words she had said, and she girded her tired mind to search for the broader reasons behind them. She had changed, tremendously, during the past few months. She had never been half as irascible and suspicious as she was now. She could remember the numerous times in which she had acted as a peace-maker between her mother and father, had walked off from a quarrelsome girl-friend, without a word, or held her temper in the face of any seeming deceit, selfishness, on the part of the men with whom she had "kept company." She hadn't been always meek, certainly not, and yet she had been infinitely more inclined to shrug matters off, to listen to explanations, even when she had felt otherwise convinced, especially . . . in the case of the two, other men, besides Ray, whom she had loved. What was behind it? The answers came, jerked their way through her head. She wasn't excusing herself, was even confessing that she was partly to blame, and yet the answers couldn't be denied. Uncertainties. Scrimpings, increasing every day. Swindles. Rooms that were eye-sores. Part-time jobs where employers loaded a girl beyond endurance, to save their filthy money. Pleasures dwindling week after week. Trudging from office to office and hearing the same old statement: "Sorry, but we haven't any vacancies just now," or "Awf'lly sorry, but the position was filled just a little while ago."

All of these realities had mounted, dug into her mind without making their inroads perceptible, and on the other side she had been absolutely lacking in any faith, to keep her chin up, to give her some kind of a weapon, anything . . . to fight the overwhelming sense that 'everything was rotten,' that those on the top of life were always robbing the others, yes, literally ripping into their stomachs, without one morsel of compunction. She heard a rapping on the door and dragged herself up to answer it. Over an hour had passed since Ray had flung himself out of the room. Judith, more sober now, stood before Allene.

"Well, Allie in the fle-esh—how are yah, kid? I jus' thought I'd stop f'r a minute an' say h'llo, 'cause I haven't been seein' ya much."

Allene looked at Judith with a weak resentment, which hovered near to friendliness but couldn't gain it, because her suspicions were not quite dead.

"Oh, I'm all right . . . I guess. Why don't you come in for a while?"

"Can't do it, kid. I'm late 's blazes. I got stewed this afternoon, ba-aby, was I, though . . . an' I almos' f'got I had a date t' meet a fellow over at Tillie's, an' I'm more 'n uh hour behind now an' they don' wait any too long f'r a girl like me, so . . . . oh well, I'll drop 'round t'morrow noon, if y' in, Allie."

She turned and walked down the hallway, and Allene watched her without answering. At the head of the stairway, Judith wheeled again, looked sharply at Allene and then—slow—retraced her steps. Surly and confused because she was aware, now, that she had drunkenly attempted to capture Ray in spite of her friendship for Allene, she had a draggy intuition that "something was wrong" and that she must try to set it right, although she hated the task, almost hated Allene in the bargain.

"Listen, Allie—I wanna tell ya somethin'. If I had a man like the one you've got, I might be willin' ta wear my feet out again, lookin' f'r a job, an' I don' wantcha ta get any crummy notions in y' head, 'cause he's a swell kid all the time."

She chucked Allene's chin and then walked quickly away.

"Hey Jude, wait a minute"—Allene was shaken now.

"Sorry kid . . . I'll see ya t'morrow"—Judith's voice rolled back from the stairway, down which she had disappeared.

Back in the room again, Allene was convinced that Ray had been faithful to her. She could have beaten herself now. She pottered around the room, dismally, and then stretched herself on the bed, worried over Ray and what he was doing, and detesting herself beyond measure, or relief. She slid into a fitful doze, with dreams of machines slicing into her head, nude women parading under banners of dollar-bills and beckoning her to join them, and men rolling themselves out into writhing, blood-mashed carpets for other men, while she and Ray, tied to boards on the side-lines, were forced to witness the proceedings. She had just awakened from the last vision, with a long groan, when Ray entered the room. She leapt from the bed, hugged him, kissed him, laughed and wept in a softened, unconscious flurry, and ended by pushing him into a chair and falling into his lap. He had expected her to be angry, or removed, and had stored up disdainful, demolishing words for her, on his way back to the room, but her sudden, abject delight and contrition melted him against his will.

A few minutes later, with realities crowding in, sandpapering their brains once more, she asked him: "Where were you all this time, hon'?"

He had a reflective scowl clamped on his face.

"I went over to the union office, over on Huntington, and I sat around, talking to the boys. We're going to pull a strike tomorrow night, and at six o'clock sharp—just when it'll hurt them most—we're all walking out, thirty-four of us, and before we're through, there'll be a lot of other hotels out, believe me."

"But Ray, how are we going to live? It's bad enough now, but starting tomorrow, gee—it'll be ten times worse. We won't even be able to keep the roof over our heads."

"That's all right. If you saw a man in a chain-gang you wouldn't tell him not to try and escape, just because there was a swamp around it. We'll have to take our chances and stick together and fight with our own kind. We'll never get anything otherwise, you can bet on that."

The echo of his defiance swelled in her heart, lifted it to a grim agreement, and yet the opposite forebodings, reduced to the barest of tremblings, would not quite leave.

"But Ray, you told me that most of the men in that union were Reds, didn't you?"

"Yeah, I did."

"Well, you haven't gone and become converted to Communism, have you?"

Ray's scowl thickened.

"I don't know about that, Allie. The boys over in the office, tonight, gave me a lot of arguments I couldn't answer to save my life. I haven't made up my mind yet about that, but I'm going to tell you one thing—this goddamn flag-waving is beginning to get under my skin. They pull it every time they're looking for an excuse to hold a worker down. There's no use blinking it in the face—about the only damn time they ever pay any real attention to a worker is when they're holding an election, or when they're asking him to pick up a gun and go and get killed in a war. I don't know whether Communism's the solution, or not, but believe me, I'm going to read up on it and find out what it's all about, before I'm through."

"Well, God knows, it's not going to hurt either of us, if we do, because we know perfectly well that everything else is rotten."

She leaned against his shoulder and they stared, through the window, at the drizzle of rain outside, the stooping, tight-faced figures hurrying down the street.

THE END

Acknowledgments

Profound thanks are extended to the following for their generous financial support which helped to defray some of production costs of this new edition of Maxwell Bodenheim's *Slow Vision*:

Alan J Abrams, Ted Adams, elif ağanoğlu, Adrian Astur Alvarez, Backer #108, Rev Justin A Baldwin-Bonney, Ross Barkan, Thomas Young Barmore Jr, Kian S. Bergstrom, BH, Andrew Bissaro, Matthew Boe, Brian R. Boisvert, Matt Bucher, Chris Call, Scott Chiddister, Wesley Chien, Chelsea Clifton, C. Colla, Jangus C. Cooper, Sheri Costa, Randy and Haley Cox, Malcolm & Parker Curtis, Robert Dallas, Victoria De Maria, Dylan & Sam Doomwar, Michael K. Ducker, Isaac Ehrlich, Curtis B. Edmundson, Richard Faught, Raymond Foye, Robert Patrick Frerich, Rowan Fulmer, Justin Gallant, Stephan Glander, GmarkC, Damian Gordon, Adam Greenfield, Richard L. Haas III, Lisa Hagerman, Ethan Hawkins, Erik Hemming, Aric Herzog, Jonathan Hope, Brian Jagodzinski, Erik T Johnson, Fred W Johnson, Haya K., Kurt Johann Klemm, Paul Kuliev, Jean-Jacques Larrea, George P. Lauber, Cari Liebenberg, Natasha A.J Liff, James Lisk, Luzius, Brian de León Macchiarelli, Elizabeth J Maxim, Jim McElroy, Donald McGowan, Justin McGuire, Jack Mearns, Sergio Mendez-Torres, Yotam Mendlinger, Dr. Melvin "Steve" Mesophagus, William Messing, Jason Miller, Spencer F Montgomery, Matt Moriarty, Jonathan Morton, Geoffrey Moses, Gregory Moses, Luke Moses, Irwing Nieto, Michael O'Shaughnessy, Andrew Pearson, Waylon M. Prince, Patrick M Regner, George Salis (www.TheCollidescope.com),

Frank V. Saltarelli, David W. Sanderson, Connor Shirley,
Bill Shute, Mindie Simmons, Yvonne Solomon,
Martin E Stein & Scott A Saxon, K. L. Stokes, Irene Turner,
Chad Michael Van Alstin, Jack Waters, William Waters,
Rachel Wells, Paulie Wenger, Christopher Wheeling,
Isaiah Whisner, Charles Wilkins, Jeff Wilson, Morgan Witkowski,
T.R. Wolfe, Stephen M. Wolterstorff, Serena Z,
The Zemenides Family, and Anonymous

Thanks also to Brian K. Skillin for the proofreading.